CRESSIDA CONNOLLY is a journalist and reviewer, and the author of two previous books: *The Happiest Days* and *The Rare and the Beautiful*. She lives in Worcestershire with her husband and three children.

From the reviews of *My Former Heart*:

'"Good" doesn't begin to do justice to the beautiful work of art she has produced ... there is a deep satisfaction to the novel, a sense of cool, calm rightness flowing through the world'
Daily Telegraph

'A writer who seems able to peer directly into the human heart, to understand its follies and strivings, and to write about them with such sparkling originality that it makes you see the world afresh. I strongly suggest readers buy two copies – one to savour, and one to throw at the Man Booker judges who unaccountably left it off this year's longlist'
Spectator

'Tortuous relationships are delineated with grace and subtlety by Connolly, who has as sharp an eye for sexual quirks and social nuance as she does for period detail'
Daily Mail

'A deceptively quiet novel, it projects the resonant inner lives of its characters without the aid of plot histrionics or high drama. Yet it packs a huge emotional punch, dramatising grief and stoicism in an utterly convincing manner'
Sunday Times

'The cool detachment and maturity of Connolly's first novel, and the absorbing nature of the story, are reminiscent of Penelope Lively's adult fiction ... deeply rewarding'
Guardian

Also by Cressida Connolly

The Happiest Days
The Rare and the Beautiful

CRESSIDA CONNOLLY

My Former Heart

FOURTH ESTATE · London

Fourth Estate
An imprint of HarperCollins*Publishers*
77–85 Fulham Palace Road
London W6 8JB
www.4thestate.co.uk

This Fourth Estate paperback edition published 2012

1

First published in Great Britain by Fourth Estate in 2011

A catalogue record for this book is
available from the British Library

Thanks to Alan Trist of Ice Nine Publishing, California for permission
to quote Grateful Dead song 'Eyes of the World' (Lyrics Robert Hunter).
'Aqualung': words and music by Ian Anderson and Jennie Anderson © copyright
1971 Ian Anderson Music Ltd/Chrysalis Music Ltd. All rights reserved.
International copyright secured. Used by permission of Music Sales Limited.
Excerpt from *The Badger* by Ernest Neal, reprinted by permission of
Harper Collins Publishers Ltd. © 1958

ISBN 978-0-00-735635-5

Set in Minion by G&M Designs Limited, Raunds Northamptonshire
Printed and bound in Great Britain by Clays Ltd, St Ives plc

MIX
Paper from
responsible sources
FSC® C007454

FSC™ is a non-profit international organisation established to promote
the responsible management of the world's forests. Products carrying the
FSC label are independently certified to assure consumers that they come
from forests that are managed to meet the social, economic and
ecological needs of present and future generations,
and other controlled sources.

Find out more about HarperCollins and the environment at
www.harpercollins.co.uk/green

To Violet, Nell and Gabriel

For thou art with me here upon the banks
Of this fair river; thou, my dearest Friend,
My dear, dear Friend; and in thy voice I catch
The language of my former heart …

From 'Lines Composed a Few Miles Above Tintern Abbey'
by William Wordsworth

Chapter 1

Ruth always remembered the day that her mother decided to go away. She didn't know the actual date, but she recalled the occasion: it was on a wet afternoon early in 1942, during a visit to the cinema. She thought she could even pinpoint the exact moment Iris had made up her mind to go, leaving her only child behind. Neither of them could have guessed then that they would never live together again.

Her mother used to give her a treat after each visit to the dentist. Because the dentist's rooms were in Devonshire Place, near Regent's Park, this was quite often a visit to the zoo. But the zoo had shut down by then. The animals had been sent to the country, partly to keep them safe, but partly to keep people safe from them. No one knew what might happen if the zoo got hit and some of the animals escaped. Ruth tried to imagine what it would be like to meet a lion ambling down Albany Street, or a rhinoceros thudding along the towpath of the canal, where she had walked with her mother and father the summer before. She thought it would be frightening, but not as frightening as the Egyptian mummies they'd been to see at the British Museum. She was glad the museum had closed and she didn't have to go there again.

Once, they had met up with an old friend of her mother's, a lady called Jocelyn who designed costumes for the theatre and who had eyes which stuck out like a pug's. Iris said that her friend was fun, but their lunch together had not been a treat; or at least not for Ruth. Jocelyn had said that she didn't want to be married, ever; and she certainly, absolutely, didn't want a family of her own.

'I dislike children intensely,' she drawled, the corners of her mouth twitching upwards at her own wit. 'They have no conversation.'

Ruth had been shocked that her mother had laughed. It had never occurred to her that anyone might choose not to have children, let alone not enjoy their company. Everyone wanted to get married and have bridesmaids and a lovely dress: that was what you did when you grew up. And when you got married you had children and a kidney-shaped dressing table all of your own, with little silver-lidded glass jars full of hairpins, and others packed with cotton wool. You had scent in a bottle with a cloth-covered rubber squisher on its side, and a swan's-down powder puff which sat separated from its powder by a disc with holes in, like the ones on soap dishes, so that the feather filaments of the powder puff did not become clogged. That was how things worked.

But this time, after Ruth's teeth had been looked at – she couldn't later remember whether she'd had to have any drilled that day – her mother took her to Oxford Street, to the cinema. The cinema was the Studio One and it had a swirly carpet, with a pattern which was meant to look like spools of film unravelling. The feature was a new cartoon from America about a baby elephant, but first there was a newsreel. Whenever Mr Churchill appeared everyone in the cinema gave a cheer. There were pictures of men getting their trousers wet as they got off landing craft, and of people waving, and of tanks, and the voice which described it all was very cheerful and urgent. Iris was hardly watching the newsreel though, because she was looking in her bag for change so she could send Ruth to get some cigarettes from the usherette, and some sweets. Before the war there would have been ices, but you couldn't get ices by then.

Iris was always rummaging in her bag, looking for a book match or a pencil, inclining her head, an escaping curl of dark hair, like a question mark, falling over one eye. Eight-year-old Ruth went and fetched the cigarettes for her mother and a small white paper bag of sweets for herself and came back to the seats with them. Now the newsreel was showing some pictures from the desert, and she could feel that her mother was concentrating on them, because there was a sort of tightness about her. When General Montgomery came onto the screen, he got an even louder cheer than the Prime Minister had had. The screen showed men in uniform marching about and then more of them, queuing with trays, outside a big tent, while others stood around a tall van in the background. Then suddenly Iris was on her feet and hissing in a loud whisper, 'Stay here, Ruth. Don't move. I'll be back in a minute.' Ruth supposed she must have needed to go to the lavatory. Lots of people all along the row had to stand up so Iris could get past. Ruth would have felt a little embarrassed about disturbing people, but Iris never minded about that sort of thing.

She seemed to be gone for a long time. The film started and Ruth was a bit frightened because the story began with a lot of thunder and lightning and she was afraid of storms. She consoled herself by trying to concentrate on not chewing her sweets, holding them against the roof of her mouth with her tongue until they dissolved and her mouth was flooded with their sugary flavour. On the screen big birds with long beaks brought baby animals down from the clouds, wrapped in what looked like towels. This troubled her. No one had ever mentioned to her the role of storks in bringing babies into the world, so she did not understand what these gawky birds had to do with the arrival of children. It was all very quick and muddling. Next there were animals going two by two, which made her think the film was going to be about Noah and the Flood. But the story turned out to be about a circus, travelling along in a little train. The train got puffed out when it went uphill. Ruth put another sweet into her mouth. Still Iris had not come back to her seat.

Now there was a baby elephant with big ears, who made friends with a mouse. The mouse was kind, but the other elephants were not. They were standoffish and then they ganged up. It wasn't fair. The baby wasn't allowed to see its mother because she'd turned fierce, but the kind mouse took the baby to where the mother was – in a sort of prison – and the mother reached her trunk between the bars and rocked her funny little baby. This was so sad that Ruth began to cry.

The one thing she could never remember was at what point her mother came back to her seat. 'There was a funny – I mean funny peculiar, not funny ha-ha – bit in the film, when suddenly the proper story stopped and there were lots of pink elephants with empty eye sockets doing dances together, and what looked like ice-skating,' she told her own daughters many years later. 'I felt scared of them because of the eyes being hollow, like a skeleton's. My mother must have been back in her seat by then, because I remember putting my hand on her arm for reassurance and it was then I noticed that she was crying. She wasn't sobbing or anything, but she had tears on her face. She hardly ever cried. She rubbed her cheek with her fist, roughly. I guessed she was crying about the poor baby elephant, as I had. "Don't worry, Mummy," I whispered, "it's only a film, it's not real." Pathetic, really, to have thought she was crying about the cartoon. And she smiled a little smile.'

The baby elephant became a tremendous success in the circus and was allowed to be with his mother again, in a special railway carriage all of their own. That was the end, and everyone got up to go, buttoning up their coats, the women pulling on their gloves, but Iris stayed in her seat. 'They're going to show the newsreel again now,' she told Ruth. 'I must just have another look, you see.' She lit a cigarette and sat back, while a new audience in different coats shuffled into their seats. Before long the same newsreel started. Landing craft, troops waving, tanks, the Prime Minister, the desert, the same men standing in the same queue outside the same tent, smiling, with the same men behind them around the truck. Suddenly Iris leant forward and tensed, as if she were a cat about to pounce on some buzzing thing.

At once Ruth guessed why. It must have been because her mother had seen Ruth's father, Edward, on the newsreel. Ruth herself had not spotted him on the screen, and over the months that followed she wondered why not; why Iris had been able to see him and she had not. She was sure she loved him quite as much as her mother did; wanted to see him just as much. She thought she must have looked away, at the precise moment, to have missed him. Perhaps she had been looking down into her dwindling sweets, licking her finger to catch the grains of sugar sprinkled in the bottom of the bag, concentrating on not spilling any onto the knobbly wool of her coat.

After that they did not stay until the end of the newsreel. They went out into the foyer and Iris spoke to the cinema manager. On their way home she told Ruth that she'd already talked to this man, when she first went out, before the cartoon had started. She'd wanted him to show the newsreel again, then, straight away. He had told her that this often happened to people: they thought they recognised a husband or a brother or a sweetheart. He always asked them to stay on and watch the newsreel again, at the end of the feature, to make sure. Sometimes – usually, he was sorry to say – it turned out not to be who they thought it was after all. But if, after a second viewing, they were quite sure, then the manager would try and obtain a still photograph from the newsreel company. So after she'd seen it for a second time, Iris was able to describe the scene in the newsreel exactly, to make sure he'd get the right picture. She gave the manager her name and address. He said he would do his best.

Ruth was used to her mother getting what she wanted; it was just another thing about Iris. Ruth supposed it was because her mother was pretty. She had long arms and legs, with the thinnest ankles and wrists, like a whippet; and wide pale-hazel eyes with gold flecks in them. Once a friend of her father's — his name was Bunny Turner — had come to lunch and stayed on for most of the afternoon. Iris had gone upstairs to the drawing room to get a second bottle from the drinks tray. As he was leaving he'd taken Ruth's shoulders in his hands and looked her intently in the face. 'You must take good care of your mother,' he'd said; 'she's a captivating woman.' Ruth didn't like that word: it sounded like captive-taking, like the poor boys Captain Hook had taken prisoner in *Peter Pan*. But she was used to people thinking that her mother was wonderful.

Before the incident in the cinema, it had never occurred to Ruth that her mother might have been worrying that Edward was dead. She had certainly never said so. Anyway, people protected children from such fears. Ruth knew from talking to her friends that grown-ups didn't tell children very much, certainly not bad things. During the worst of the bombing raids, when Ruth was six and seven, Iris had bought a pale-green silk moiré box full of rose and violet creams from Fortnum's, to take into the coal hole in front of the kitchen, where they waited out the raids. They never ate the chocolates otherwise: they were a treat reserved for the shelter. Iris had taken an eiderdown into the coal hole — it had been ruined, covered in black smudges — and a blanket for them to huddle under, and they'd eaten the chocolates together, waiting in the cramped blackness for the all-clear to be sounded. Iris had made a game of it: which was more delicious, the soapy rose or the chalky, fragrant violet? Ruth had had to concentrate, taking tiny nibbles out of first one then the other. They could never decide. Iris never said anything about being frightened in all those times, even when bombs landed nearby, which had happened more than once. She never seemed afraid of anything.

Courage came easily to Iris, but happiness was more difficult. This was something that Ruth sometimes glimpsed in her mother: a sudden plunge, as if the temperature had dropped, when Iris would sit smoking in her chair, without a book or sewing, hardly speaking. Ruth's father, Edward, had an aptitude for happiness – a gift, Iris called it – like being musical, or having a good head for numbers. For Iris happiness was something delicious but hard to keep hold of, like the almost-pins-and-needles sherberty feeling when summer air dries seawater on your skin. Ruth thought this was why Iris made decisions so abruptly, in the same way as she snapped shut her powder compact. It was as if she were trying to catch happiness in a trap.

Ruth didn't know if the cinema manager ever sent the photograph. She never saw it if he did. But she believed that Iris had made her mind up that afternoon at the cinema, when they were both, for their different reasons, crying in the flickering dark. Because three days later, Iris took her daughter to Paddington station and put her on the train. And then, even before the guard had walked the length of the platform to close all the doors, before the flag was waved or the whistle went, she was gone.

Ruth liked her grandparents' house in Malvern, except that she missed her mother and she did not like the cold, or the henhouse. She loved her grandparents, both of them; their soft voices and their routine and quiet kindness. In the evenings, before supper, her grandfather sometimes read to her, adventures by Rider Haggard and Erskine Childers, or stories by Kipling. Ruth was mousier, less emphatic, than her mother, with a sturdier frame; she felt at home with her grandparents. Even so, there were occasions when the cold was so cold as to be indistinguishable from misery: sometimes, when she cried at night, even she could not have said whether it was from missing her mother or because she could not get warm. London had been cold too, but the rooms were smaller and her mother had taken to lighting a coal fire downstairs in the kitchen grate and staying in there, where it could be made warm, even if it was not so comfortable as the first-floor sitting room.

The house at Malvern had high-ceilinged rooms with big Victorian sash windows, to make the most of the view. Before the war there had been log fires in every grate, but now there was only a one-bar electric fire in the drawing room, which would be unplugged and brought to stand in the grate of the breakfast room before they ate. But it was only ever switched on just before they came in to sit down, more a formality than an actual heating appliance. And there was never enough hot water to get really warm in the bath. Ruth developed chilblains, which made her toes tickle, then throb and burn. Until Mrs Jenkins, who came in to clean every morning, took the potty Ruth used at night and – horrifyingly – dipped a linen hand towel into the urine and dabbed Ruth's toes with it, bringing an exquisite but temporary relief, like a dock leaf on a nettle sting.

The house, like the town of which it formed a part, stood in the lee of a western slope. Even as a child Ruth was aware of the way that the whole place fell into shadow, as the sun slipped behind the hulk of the hills. But she liked the way you could still see a wide band of sunlight, sliding perceptibly across the lawn like the train of a wedding dress, away from her grandparents' house towards the distant abbey towns, with their wide rivers and gentle slopes of ancient orchards. She imagined the sun was still shining in London, long after Malvern had fallen into shade.

Her grandparents were her father's parents, although it was her mother who had sent her to stay with them. Iris's mother was alive, but she lived outside Sidmouth, a long way away, and her house was thought to be unsuitable for children; no one ever explained why. Ruth hardly ever saw this grandmother, who had been a widow for years and smelled of tobacco and face powder – dry smells, musty, like the bottom of an old handbag. But she had often stayed with her Malvern grandparents before. She and Iris had spent several weeks there together, towards the end of 1940, during the worst of the Blitz. In the winter the mottled colours of rock, dead bracken and gorse made the hills look like giant slabs of Christmas cake. Iris had played cards with her father-in-law after dinner each evening, while his wife added pieces to the jigsaw which was accumulating slowly on the writing table in the window.

Ruth had shared a room with her mother during that visit. Before bed, Iris always pinned her hair into tight coils with kirby grips, so that it would curl the next day. While she sat doing her hair she would talk to her daughter in a loud whisper; so loud, it seemed to Ruth, that it would have been better – quieter – if she had spoken in her normal voice.

'Why does your grandmother have to do those enormous puzzles?' she asked one evening. Ruth could tell it wasn't really a question.

'I don't know. Why shouldn't she?'

'Well, darling, because they take so long. I mean, an eternity.'

'She likes it, I s'pose. She likes it that they take ages.'

'Well, obviously. But if one's going to do jigsaws at all, at least do them of places further away. Why spend weeks at a time doing a yard-long picture of Bourton-on-the-Water, or the swans on the river at Stratford? Why not just go and see the real thing?'

'It's not to do with the places. It's to do with finding the pieces,' said Ruth.

'Exactly,' said Iris, dragging out the second syllable as if it were a cigarette she was drawing on. 'It's just that one might think they'd have had enough of the wretched damp countryside, looking at it from practically every window. One would think she'd want to do a puzzle of somewhere a bit more dashing. Monte Carlo. Or the Alps even.'

Ruth thought for a moment. 'I don't believe Granny wants to be dashing,' she said.

'Well,' said Iris, 'yes.'

Ruth's uncle Christopher had come back to live with her grandparents for the duration. He was teaching science at the Malvern Boys College. Or at least he said he was, and it was true that he was a teacher. It was only years later that Ruth learned that he'd actually been involved in developing signals and radar, based at the evacuated school. He hadn't been able to enlist because of his poor eyesight, although he was better at seeing things than anyone his niece knew: he could spot a buzzard from miles away, and tell it from a hawk. He knew the names of all the birds and wild flowers. Ruth liked birds, except for chickens. Soon after she arrived, Christopher began to take her for long walks on the hills at weekends. With her stumpy legs and her thick springy hair, she reminded him of a valiant little pony. He knew the secret places where you could drink the icy spring water straight from the rock, so clear that it tasted more like air – exhilarating, like sea air – than water. Christopher was an expert whistler, could whistle any tune, however elaborate. For some reason which Ruth did not understand this annoyed his mother.

It was not yet spring when Ruth arrived at Malvern. That first night she pulled her bed away from the wall and wrote 'mummy and daddy' in her neatest writing on the wallpaper, below the line of the mattress, where no one would be able to see it. It was intended as a sort of spell, to make them come back.

Gradually, over the weeks, the cold began to give way to thin sunlight. The early wallflowers in her grandparents' garden smelled of watery marzipan then, as if the summer to come was hidden inside them. There was a tall monkey puzzle tree outside her bedroom window, and Ruth used to wish that she could find a real-life monkey and open her window and put it out on a branch, to see how puzzled it would be, or whether it would be able to climb down. When she ran her hands along one of the branches, little barbs at the end of each leaf stabbed at her fingers.

Neither of her grandparents asked questions about her mother. They didn't really ask questions about anything much: they didn't interfere. They weren't strict, except about manners, table manners in particular. The table was always laid properly. Everyone had their own big white napkin, rolled up inside a silver ring; and there were special little spoons made of mother-of-pearl for the salt; and spoons made of horn, with long handles, for boiled eggs. There were fruit knives with coloured glass handles, like polished beads, and in summer there were crescent-shaped salad plates. There were two pheasants made of silver as a centrepiece; or, as the weather improved, stiff flowers in a cut-glass bowl which had a mesh made of wire, like a stiffened hairnet, to keep them in place. In London, when it was just her and Ruth, Iris had got into the habit of doing without side plates, or napkins, or butter knives: she couldn't see much point, since there wasn't enough butter in the first place. She even put the jam on the table in the jar it came from the shop in, though not if there were visitors.

Iris never wore a wristwatch, didn't even keep a clock beside the bed, as if she could outwit time by refusing to keep an eye on it. There was only one clock in their house in London, a wind-up one, in the kitchen. But in the house in Malvern there were two long-case clocks, so that if you listened hard you could always hear ticking wherever you were, except in the bathroom with the taps running. Both clocks chimed the quarter-hours, and the smaller walnut clock in the breakfast room appeared to pause momentarily, as if drawing in its breath, before chiming always very slightly ahead of the bigger mahogany clock in the hall. In this house time was ordered, it announced itself politely and was made quietly welcome. Nothing was hasty.

Ruth found the not knowing how long her mother would be away far worse than her absence itself. It was like not knowing whether you'd be staying somewhere long enough to unpack your suitcases properly and unfold all your things and put them in drawers: it made it difficult to settle. After the first two weeks her uncle Christopher made arrangements for her to attend a school further up the hill in the town. Most of the children who had come to Malvern to get away from London had gone home by then, but three evacuees were still there. Ruth was glad to hear their familiar London voices, but they were a tight-knit group, not looking to make extra friends. Out on walks, Ruth had seen the little African princesses who went to school on the other side of the hill. It was said that their father was the King of Abyssinia and that they were descended from King Solomon and the Queen of Sheba. She wondered if they were lonely, so far from home. In her class she liked a girl called Veronica, who had long plaits the colour of dust caught in sunlight. Veronica owned a pair of real tap-dancing shoes, which she sometimes allowed Ruth to try on.

Every afternoon her uncle collected Ruth from the school gate and they walked home together, looking at trees and birds along the way. Christopher liked things that other people didn't care for, as well as noticing things that other people didn't even see. He told her about crows, how clever they were, how long-lived. People generally feared them, because they were ominous and ate carrion and cawed so loudly, but he enjoyed looking at their tip-tilting jaunty way of walking. He pointed out the flash of blue under a magpie's wing and told her it was a useful lesson to remember: that even when things looked black and white, they could still surprise you. Magpies looked showy but they were thieves, they took songbirds' eggs and they made a horrid noise that sounded like mockery. Plumage wasn't everything.

At half past four tea would be waiting for them: paste sandwiches, bread and butter spread with red jam; or sometimes, as a treat, extra thinly sliced and sprinkled with demerara sugar. Then there would be a piece of the sponge cake which was baked once a fortnight; only a small piece, because it used up such a lot of fat and sugar. It was a matter of pride to Ruth's grandmother that there should be cake despite the shortages, as if she was not bowing to the Enemy by allowing standards to fall.

A few chickens were kept in an outhouse behind the shrubbery, and once the warmer weather came there was never a shortage of eggs. This was meant to be tremendously lucky, but Ruth had secretly gone off eggs, since being given the task of collecting them, most mornings. She hated the sweetly rotting smell in the henhouse, and covered her nose with her elbow when she went in. She thought she detected something almost snakelike in the furtive sideways glances of the chickens. Once, she found a hen with a dead mouse in its beak, shaking the little corpse as if to loosen its skin, like someone impatient to take a damp overcoat from a guest. After that she found it hard to swallow the runny boiled eggs she was given for breakfast once or twice a week. An egg fluffed up and hidden in a cake was not so bad.

And then two letters came from Iris. She was in Cairo, which gave Ruth a shock. One was addressed to her grandmother, who did not open it at breakfast, but went into her husband's study with it afterwards, shutting the door quietly behind her. The other was for Ruth.

Darling girl,

It is all the greatest fun here with people from all over the place, New Zealand and Australia and goodness knows where else. I think I may be able to stay on and do my bit to help out, so I hope you will settle nicely with Granny for the time being and be a good girl. I know you will.

One can find all sorts of things in the market, which they call a souk. Queer kinds of fruits like pomegranates and also great vats of powdered dyes in bright colours. Lots of odd-smelling spices in big sacks. Such a change from dreary old London! They drink a kind of tea which is made of mint leaves, rather good.

I've seen several camels! Close to they have the longest eyelashes, and when they stand up they make a complaining noise, rather like an old drawer being opened.

Darling, it will do you good, being in the country. I'm sure your uncle will teach you all about nature while you are there, so that you'll have lots to tell me when I get home. On no account let him take you to watch cricket when the summer begins! It is absolutely deadly, tell him I absolutely forbid it.

When you write, Granny will address the envelope for you to be extra sure your letter reaches me, I've sent her the poste restante.

With lots of love,
Mummy

For the time being. What did that mean? Did it mean weeks, or months? She had mentioned cricket and the summer: did that mean Ruth might be here until the summer, or throughout the summer, until autumn came? What could she possibly be doing that would help the war? Iris could type and she was quick at things, but she hadn't had a job in London. Ruth wasn't sure that her mother had ever worked at anything. And most importantly she didn't say whether she'd found Edward. The fact that she didn't, Ruth reasoned, must mean that she had not. But surely that was why her mother had gone away in the first place, to look for him? So why was she staying on? Why didn't she carry on travelling, looking for him? Or simply come home?

Ruth didn't like to ask her grandmother about these things because she thought, although her grandmother didn't show it, she must have been fearfully worried to have a son missing in the war: so worried that it was never mentioned. Instead she waited until after school, when she was alone with her uncle Christopher. But unusually for Christopher, who was so good at explaining things, he offered no clarification. 'I really couldn't say,' he told her. 'I'm sure your mother has her reasons.' Ruth felt a thin trickle of disappointment spreading down her body. It lodged in her chest, like a boiled sweet swallowed the wrong way. That night in bed, she curled the side of her mattress back, so as to reveal the words she had written on the wallpaper. She looked and looked at them, until the letters blurred.

Chapter 2

Even before she had opened her eyes, Iris could sense the brightness at the window, a weight to the light which could only come from snow. The room was cold, much colder than the nights in Cairo had been, but Iris didn't feel the cold despite her slender frame. The old hotel had been quite empty when they'd first taken it over a few months earlier, hadn't even had the benefit of electricity or running water. During the big snowstorm, before she'd arrived, they'd run out of kerosene for the lamps. But supplies had begun to arrive and the place was taking shape. They had furnished her room adequately, even if the furniture was shabby. There was a writing table in front of the window, which would do as a dressing table too; and a good comfortable chair with a footstool, set by a low table with a rather dingy lamp; and plenty of clothes hangers in a cupboard which smelled vaguely of cloves. Not that she had all that many clothes with her, certainly not enough warm things for up here in the mountains. She'd have to write to Jocelyn, the friend with whom she'd left a key to the London house, and get her to send some things out: jerseys and her tweed coat and perhaps a couple of dresses for the evenings. One of the things Jimmy was keen for her to do, once they got the place fully established, was to organise entertainments for the men, music and suchlike. It wouldn't hurt to have a frock or two.

Jimmy was a friend of Edward and Bunny's, from Cambridge days. It had been pure chance running into him in Cairo. Iris had had no idea he was out in the M.E., although one came across so many familiar faces out here – people one used to run into, for ever ago, at London parties – that she hadn't been the least bit surprised to see him. Jimmy had always been one for the most tremendous schemes, and mad on skiing of course. Terrifically good at it too. In Cairo he'd told her that he was recruiting for a mountain-training school in the Lebanon. It was just the sort of ambitious, almost foolhardy scheme one would have expected of him. When he mentioned that he was looking for someone to help with the office side of things – to go through lists of men with experience of cold-weather conditions, get in touch with them, order equipment – she at once proposed herself. 'Done,' he'd said straight away, grinning. He didn't enquire as to the particulars of why or how Iris had got to Cairo, nor what she was doing there in the first place. He didn't ask if she'd ever done this sort of work before, or any work. He wasn't that sort of person.

The Cedars was on a plateau surrounded by a horseshoe of mountains, all covered in snow. Far in the distance, six thousand feet down beyond the valley, was a glimpse of the Mediterranean. The old hotel took its name from a wood nearby, where some of the trees were said to be more than a thousand years old. There was a wall around it to protect the trees. If Iris had thought of the Lebanon at all before now, it would always have been in connection with the cedars which reached their long wide arms across familiar English lawns, shading the grass, their branches the colour of green baize. But here, in their homeland, nearly all the trees had been cut down, all but this small wood near the hotel. Great swathes of snow collected in their outstretched branches, then fell when the weight became too much for the trees to support. The sound was just like bombs, exploding in the distance. Iris had thought it was a raid the first time she'd heard it, until Jimmy put her right.

Jimmy told her that you could spend the morning skiing up here and then drive down to the coast to bathe in the sea that very afternoon. Not that his notion had much opportunity to be tested, when he and the men were out for almost eight hours a day, sometimes overnighting in tents further up in the mountains, coming back exhausted and frozen. Iris did get down to Beirut every few weeks, but she didn't bathe, although she'd have liked to. The women there didn't seem to; there were only men with fishing nets and young boys playing on the beach.

There were already signs of spring down in the city, the almond trees in blossom. It wasn't so much fun as Cairo of course, but one could dine reasonably well and buy French scent and other treats, and go dancing if one was overnighting. Generally one or other of the officers took her to lunch at the French club, where they had heavenly food: there were even prawns in that delicious pinkish sauce, and sole meunière. Jimmy told her that he'd caused the most frightful embarrassment the first time he'd been to the club. British officers hadn't been using the place then, but because he'd been doing some liaison for one of the Free French generals he didn't see why he shouldn't. He'd gone in and asked for a table, but once he was sitting down he noticed a deathly hush had descended. It turned out he was sitting in the Vichy half of the dining room. He'd been asked to move to the Free French side, and only then had conversation resumed at the other tables. Now the place was frequented by all the English officers. Some of them gave Iris to understand that they disapproved of the ski school. Why should Jimmy – and the Aussies he'd somehow managed to inveigle his way among – be allowed to create a private holiday camp in the mountains? Iris laughed. 'You should come up,' she told them. 'Anything less like a holiday could scarcely be imagined.'

True though this may have been for the men who trained there, to Iris the place did provide a kind of extended vacation, a break from thinking about what to do with her life. Not that she didn't work, and work hard. There was a great deal to get done: wood for the skis to be ordered from Turkey, supplies to be organised, the men's letters to send out, reports to be typed up. The whole building smelled as if it was constantly being polished – a familiar and comfortingly English church-hall smell of beeswax and paraffin – but the floors remained scuffed, for these ingredients were used only to make wax for the skis. The furniture was anyway too makeshift to merit polishing. One of the tasks which fell to Iris was to ensure that there were always adequate supplies to make the ski wax. Graphite was another ingredient, which it eventually became impossible to track down; in the end, she'd had to request a huge pile of gramophone records, which they'd ground down, to add to the wax mixture. To Iris this seemed a pity, a waste of music. One of the officers had a wireless, which picked up music stations from Germany and Italy, and before long Jimmy managed to obtain a gramophone from somewhere. When further boxes of gramophone records arrived, Iris kept back some of the better ones to play in the evenings.

Iris often had headaches from spending so long at her desk. But she was glad to be tired and found that she no longer felt restless or on edge. She didn't have to fret here, as she had at home, about what would happen when Edward came back, how she would explain herself. And it was better for Ruth to be with her grandmother, away from the damp foggy city, in the fresh air; and away from the danger of the city of course. Several people – including her own mother – had let it be known that they'd thought it selfish of Iris to keep the little girl in London with her during the bombing raids.

A couple of doctors had been imported to the school, since fractures and sprains were expected to be a daily occurrence, especially among men who'd never skied before. In fact hardly anyone hurt themselves: Jimmy's theory was that it helped to actually climb up a mountain before you skied down it, because that way you were strengthening the muscles first. He believed that it was because there were no ski lifts here that people didn't seem to get hurt as they did in the Alps. But they did get sunburn. Snow blindness too. The Australians in particular were averse to using protective cream or dark glasses. Sometimes at night Iris was kept awake by their horrible screams of pain from the hospital ward across the courtyard.

One of the doctors, Digby Richards, had a friend nearby, a naturalist who was stationed down by the coast, collecting things for the Natural History Museum in London. Digby was going to meet this friend in Tripoli when he next had a day off duty: would Iris like to join them, he wondered, and see the crusader castle? Digby didn't say much on the drive down, but his friend Michael turned out to be excellent company. The spring weather was a delightful contrast to the snow at the Cedars. Michael had arranged an exotic picnic for them: flat bread more like Bath Olivers than the bread at home, and salty cheese – which he said was made from goat's milk, but which Iris liked nevertheless – and some olives, with a bottle of red wine from Cyprus. After they'd eaten Michael wandered off, head bowed, while Iris and Digby sat on the coarse grass and looked at the sea, smoking in silence. Within minutes Michael returned with a posy of flowers in his hands.

'For you,' he said, pretending to produce the flowers from behind his back with an elaborate flourish.

'Well, thank you,' said Iris, smiling.

'If you care to examine the specimens, you will note that there are several types of iris among them,' Michael went on, as if he were a teacher and Iris his pupil.

'Really? I wouldn't have known. I only know the blue kind that you get in England. Oh, and those rather ugly tall brownish ones with yellow bits. I never care for them much; they look like dead leaves.'

'These are Mediterranean ones. And wild. They're quite different.'

'This looks like a cornflower.'

'Good girl! It is a close relative, yes. And this one is of course a kind of daisy.'

Iris held the flowers to her nose, inhaling their trace of scent, not floral as much as like hay and blackberries: the smell of faraway English fields in autumn.

Back in the car Michael leant forward from the back seat, telling them things. He said that one of the gorges leading down to the coast was where Adonis had lived, by the source of the river which bore his name. This was where the story of Venus and Adonis came from.

'It's terribly romantic, don't you think?' he asked Iris, his nose level with her ear so that she could feel his breath, slightly damp, tickling her neck just below her ear lobe. Iris smiled and carried on looking straight ahead.

They stopped at the crusader castle and clambered up, disturbing flicking lizards and fat black beetles as they climbed. The mossy walls were covered in honeysuckle, the honeysuckle busy with sparrows.

'What will you do when the war's over?' Digby asked her, the first question he'd put to her all day.

'I don't know. Go home, I s'pose. Carry on as before.' She was aware of how ungracious she sounded, but a sudden lurch of feeling made her monosyllabic: even as she spoke the words, she knew that she would not be able to continue with her old life. The idea of that life filled her now with panic. There was nothing terrible about it, it was pleasant enough: she had a kind husband, a comfortable house, a child. But to Iris it all felt terribly wrong, as if she'd caught the wrong train and was now speeding, unstoppably, towards a destination miles and miles away from where she was meant to be. She could feel the colour coming to her cheeks and hoped her companions would not notice her blushing. 'What about you?' she said.

'I'd like to travel. I've met some super fellows from New Zealand. Might go there for a time, see if I can help out at a hospital.'

'Nonsense!' Michael interjected. 'I know you, Digby. You'll be tucked up safe and sound up north, same as ever. It'll be a local practice: elderly ladies in narrow-brimmed hats with varicose veins, farmers with bunions. Anything for a quiet life.'

Digby grinned. 'We'll see.'

After the picnic she barely saw Digby for days. Two hundred Greeks arrived at the school, as well as a detachment from the SBS. The doctors had plenty to do, giving them all the once-over before they were sent out to train in the snow, and there was a lot of paperwork for Iris. When Digby appeared at the door of the room she used as an office, to ask whether she'd like to make up a four at bridge after dinner that night, she felt inordinately pleased to see him, as if they'd known one another for years. There was something very endearing about him, she found: his almost absurd height and the prominent bone in the bridge of his nose made him resemble a rather solemn wading bird. She liked his voice and his rather shy sidelong smile. She was fond of Jimmy, but he was always so busy and caught up with running things and anyway he was really from Edward's past life more than hers. It was nice to find a new friend. This was the first time Iris had made a friend of a man: although she knew men, and liked them, they were generally friends of her husband's or the husbands of her friends. Or else they hadn't been friends but boyfriends, which was quite a different thing. Digby was the first man she'd ever made friends with on her own account. Most evenings after that they played cards, and when they had days or afternoons off they went down to the sea somewhere or to a café in a town. Occasionally Michael joined them, reminding Iris what it was like to be flirted with.

'Has anyone ever told you what marvellous eyes you have?' Michael asked her, one afternoon.

'Now, what would you think?' she said.

'I think yes. But I bet no one's told you what colour they are.'

'No?' She smiled.

'Aventurine.' He looked very pleased with himself, as if he'd produced a winning hand at cards.

'But that's cheating!' exclaimed Iris. 'I don't know what that is. I don't know what it looks like.'

'It looks like your eyes is the thing. It's tawny-coloured glass, with flecks of gold in it.'

'Sounds lovely.'

'It is. You are.'

Iris blushed.

As the spring went on, the snow around the Cedars began to shrink back, exposing ever wider strips of bare, rocky ground. The school was to remain open for the early part of the summer at least, training men in other aspects of mountain warfare, such as rock climbing. One morning, when Iris was at her desk, Digby came in without knocking.

'Quick! You absolutely must come at once!' he told her.

She stood up, flustered.

'Where? What's happened?'

'It's nothing to worry about. Not anything like that, but you must come. Outside. Quickly.'

She followed him along the corridor, out into the courtyard and round the side of the building to a spot where they could see straight down the valley, which sloped away towards the sea. There were already a number of people standing about, looking. And then Iris saw what they were staring at: below them, suspended in the air, hung a great dark cloud which writhed and tumbled in the cool air.

'Look,' said Digby, pointing.

'Goodness!' said Iris. 'What on earth is it? Not locusts surely?'

'If it's a swarm of bees we might be well advised to get out of the line of fire,' someone said.

'They're too big to be bees.'

'You don't think they're bats, do you?'

'I hope not.'

'Are they wee birds?' someone asked.

'They must be,' someone else said.

Everyone stood still as the cloud danced closer and closer, until it was possible to discern individual shapes among its mass. Spots of colour on their wings flashed as they caught the sunlight; others were only white, fluttering upward like handkerchiefs blown from a washing line, caught in a current of air.

'Butterflies!' Iris laughed, delighted.

There must have been hundreds of thousands of them, some flying only a few inches above the ground, others as high as a three-storey house. They flew up onto the plateau and then on, up towards the pass. It was as if some invisible dam had burst, and the butterflies were flooding the sky in a swollen river of flight. Almost as remarkable as the sight of them was the silence: they moved as soundlessly as a great shoal of fish. By and by, everyone in the building came out to look. Some of the men were holding out their hats, catching the butterflies in them as easily as if they had been shrimping nets, dangled in a shallow rock pool. Iris put her arm through Digby's and they stood looking together.

The butterflies kept coming for two days. Everyone talked of little else. Teams who ventured up towards the col said the upper slopes were littered with dead butterflies, their wings darkening as they blotted the moisture from the ever-retreating snow. Iris and Digby collected several from the ground in the courtyard and put them in cigarette boxes, to take to Michael. He'd be able to identify them, they were sure.

'You don't mind, do you, the way Michael goes on?' Digby asked her, as they drove down to the coast, a week after the butterflies had stopped, with the specimens on the back seat. 'I mean, you don't find it tiresome the way he …?'

'Heavens, no,' said Iris. 'It's all quite good-natured. Anyway, he's amusing.'

'But you're not …'

'Oh no. Absolutely not.'

'Because of your husband?' asked Digby. It was the first time in their friendship that he had mentioned her marriage.

'Not actually.' Confiding didn't come readily to Iris; she preferred to live than to talk, but she felt she could trust Digby, that there was an understanding between them.

'Look, the thing is that there's been someone else. Someone since I was married, I mean. It all came to a head last year, while Edward was out of the country on service. Then things got rather complicated because he was sent away suddenly, and I didn't know where he'd been posted – this other man, not Edward. Then I saw him, I was sure it was him, on a newsreel and it was all rather frantic, and one way or another that led me to Cairo …'

Digby was silent.

'Oh dear. Do you disapprove?' asked Iris.

'No. It's not that,' said Digby.

'The thing is that I didn't find him, and now I'm not sure that it would have been a good idea anyway. I'm not sure that I want to know where he is after all. I mean as long as he's all right. I've been trying to forget about him. It was too much, you see. He isn't free either, his wife's … well, perhaps we needn't go into that. Anyway, I … I certainly wasn't thinking that Michael … I mean, it's the last thing …'

'No. I should think not.'

'You're the only one who knows. Jimmy doesn't know anything about it, and I'd rather he didn't,' she said, suddenly regretting her unaccustomed candour. 'It's all been rather a muddle. I know I'm entirely at fault, but ...'

'No, of course. I'll say nothing.'

After this she began to see rather less of Digby. Their nightly card games somehow stopped, although they still kept each other company, not talking much, when they both had a day's leave. In due course Michael went back to London. Among his luggage were several crates full of carefully wrapped insects, the shells of gastropods and of other molluscs, seed pods, snakeskins, and the butterflies his friends had brought him. Personnel changed too up at the Cedars; people came and went. By now there was a staff of some hundred ski instructors. Extra buildings had had to go up, to accommodate the two thousand students who were billeted at any one time. Jimmy offered Iris the opportunity to return to England if she wanted to, but she chose to stay on. Ruth was happily installed at her grandparents', busy with her school and a best friend whom she evidently adored, to judge by how often she was mentioned in letters. It was rather a wrench, being away from her, but it was better for Ruth to have the continuity of her life in Malvern. Iris had learned to ski herself and found it exciting. Also, somewhat to her surprise, she realised how much she liked to work, to be of use. She was in no hurry to go back, uncertain as she remained about her future with Edward. She rather imagined she might end up alone, although the thought no longer troubled her.

But in the spring of 1944, the commanding officer called Iris into his office to tell her the school would be closing down at the end of the season. Half the staff would go on to Italy, to continue their work there; the remainder would be going elsewhere. He was not able to reveal their destination, he informed her rather pompously. The thing was, there would be no post for her as of early summer. Something could be found for her in London if she liked.

Jimmy already knew of course. He was going to miss the place, his dog especially: a local Alsatian had unofficially adopted him soon after he'd arrived, joining in on training exercises, knocking people over. The dog had become a sort of mascot to them all. The commanding officers came and went, but Jimmy had been here all along; the Cedars was really his thing altogether. He and Iris sat disconsolately in his office, smoking.

'I don't know what to do with myself quite,' said Iris. 'I've grown so used to being here, so fond of everyone.'

'Mountains have a queer effect on people,' said Jimmy. 'I've noticed that in the mountains one can very easily come to love almost anybody.'

'Well, I don't know about anybody,' said Iris. 'I'm not sure if I'd have loved Dumpling, if I'd met him at home.'

They laughed. Dumpling was a thickset Italian who worked in the kitchens. He was notoriously bad-tempered. One breakfast, when someone had asked for an egg cooked for a shorter time, he'd made a fearful scene and shouted, 'If you no like-a – go lumpy!' It had become something of a catchphrase about the place.

People were leaving by degrees. Jimmy was the first to go. He was to stop in London before joining some of the others in Canada, he'd confided to Iris. Digby was due to leave the week after. On her final evening, after dinner, Digby knocked quietly on the door of her room.

'These books belong to you,' he said, handing them to her. 'And I've brought us a nightcap.' He produced a flask.

'I don't know that I've got anything we can drink out of. Will my tooth mug do? We'll have to share it, unless you prefer to drink straight from that.'

'No, let's share your glass. So long as it doesn't taste of toothpaste.'

Iris fetched it. He half filled it with clear liquid and handed her the glass.

'Heavens! It's strong. But delicious. It tastes of raspberries.'

'That's because it's made of them. Chap down at the French club gave it to me. Good, isn't it?'

She smiled. 'Very good. It's wonderful to taste raspberries again, reminds me of England. I'd quite forgotten what they were like. Here,' and she held out the glass to him.

But instead of taking the glass, he took her wrist in his hand and pulled her gently towards him. Before she had time to protest, his face was against hers. She wondered how his nose would fit, whether it would jab her eye or cheek. Then she noticed the pleasing smell of his skin, like freshly sharpened pencils. As he kissed her, his eyes surprisingly open, she realised that she did not feel indignant or even embarrassed, that in fact she felt nothing but pleasure and did not want him to stop.

'I didn't think you …' she said, as he took the glass from her hand and set it on a table and stepped across the room with her hand in his, pulling her down onto her bed next to him.

'No, but I do. That is to say, I am,' he told her, kissing her hair, her face.

They lay side by side in the dark room, their clothes forming puddles of deeper shadow on the floor. Iris could not stop grinning, and she sensed that Digby was doing the same. She felt very wide awake and very, very happy, and the happiness was not a precipice, she realised, but a veranda, somewhere she need not fall from, nor scrabble to hold on to, but a place where she might stay and make herself comfortable. It felt like a sort of homecoming, to be naked beneath the sheets with Digby.

'Well, there we are,' said Digby at last, turning towards her.

'Yes. There we are,' said Iris. And she took his hand in hers and kissed his knuckles, one by one.

Chapter 3

The air in the house seemed to be heavy with steam and the sweet, rotting smell it carried. The only escape was to stay in the sitting room and open the French windows onto the narrow terrace, even if that did mean letting in the cold Northumbrian air.

'Goodness, darling! Don't have those windows open, you'll make the whole house freeze,' said Iris, sweeping into the room where Ruth was sitting at the piano. She was pressing single keys with one finger, before singing the eight notes up and then down each scale. She had already noticed, after only three days in the house, that Iris interrupted her whenever she sang or played. The given reason was that the sound might wake the baby, although Ruth wondered if there were not some other motive, as the baby's room was surely too far for the music to carry. Iris shut the glass doors firmly and went to put a log on the dwindling fire.

'It's the smell of the nappies,' said Ruth. 'It's like boiling beetroots mixed with cabbage. It's worse than school.'

'It is rather foul,' Iris agreed, speaking as she always did, as though anything concerned with the practicalities of the baby had nothing to do with her. 'But the draught's not good for Birdle, is it, darling?' she said, addressing the corner of the room, where a pale-grey parrot was watching her from a cage on a tall wooden stand. The bird was treading from foot to foot in agitation at the sight of Iris, who usually opened the cage directly she came into the room, allowing its occupant to clamber beak first out of its confines and about the room at will.

'Do pipe down!' said Birdle. The intonation was unmistakably Iris's. She and Ruth both laughed.

Birdle had been Digby's wedding present to Iris. The parrot had become extravagantly fond of her, sitting on her shoulder in the evenings, constantly attempting to feed her pieces of seed or nut, quite possibly regurgitated ones. When she played patience Birdle often sidled down her arm to the table and picked up single cards with his beak, one after another, before distributing them at random across the thick felt, spoiling the game. If Digby came near his wife, if he tried to sit beside her on the yellow sofa, Birdle scuttled along the back, head lowered, and bit him. He shrieked whenever Iris came into the room, but only looked slyly and in silence at everyone else. The sole words he spoke were imitations of her. Ruth was secretly rather afraid of Birdle. She had held him once or twice, at arm's length in case he tried to bite, and been amazed by the lightness of him: it seemed remarkable that so forceful a personality could be contained within so light a frame. Digby found Birdle endlessly comic, despite having been given a bleeding ear lobe on more than one occasion.

Ruth had never been close to a baby before. She had caught glimpses of them, of course: pink little faces buttoned into knitted bonnets, their lower halves neatly tucked beneath ribbon-edged blankets, in their passing prams. But she had never held an infant, or even looked closely at one, until now. It was the Easter holidays of 1948, she was fourteen, and she had come to stay with her mother, to meet the new baby, a child who was, it still seemed astonishing to her to realise, her half-brother.

It was remarkable how little babies could do, except expel repellent things from every orifice, and sleep. The baby couldn't sit up, or even hold on to anything for more than a few seconds, before the object fell out of its grasp. Neither could it – he, Jamie: she had always to remind herself he would become an actual person, in future – say a word. His limbs waved about, like an upturned May bug. Yet Iris and Digby seemed untroubled by these deficiencies. Ruth did find the infant's smiles winning, and the way he wriggled his legs in delight when smiled back at, but she dreaded being asked to hold him, dreaded the feel of his squirming body, stronger than you'd think and uncoordinated. Her uncle had once taken her fishing to Lake Vyrny, and her tiny brother reminded her of a fish, flailing in a landing net, as if he were in the wrong element. She didn't know what she was meant to do with him.

It was all rather disgusting. Luckily Ruth was not expected to attend to the actual care of the child, since Mrs Lockyer came in from Hexham every day to help. But she had been asked to lend a hand here and there. She'd learned that whenever the baby's nappies were changed, its faeces had to be scraped from the muslin Harrington squares into the lavatory, before the soiled cloths were put into a special bucket with a lid, containing a solution of bluish liquid which smelled like a public swimming bath, only worse. A second bucket, with borax, came next, while the towelling outer nappies went into another, dry, bucket. Thrice a week, Mrs Lockyer boiled the muslins in a large enamel bowl on top of the stove, creating the pervasive brassica-tainted vapour from which no room was spared. It filled the house, like the steam from a suet pudding of dung. When sufficiently boiled, the muslins were reunited with the towelling squares in scalding water, to which soap flakes were added; a thin, waxy film formed on the surface of the milky water as it cooled. Once scrubbed, the squares were rinsed, then squeezed through the wooden rollers of the mangle. Before the squares were pegged out to dry, each one was firmly shaken out – snap snap – with a sound like a flock of pigeons' wings as they picked up speed in flight. And the infant went through four, sometimes five, nappies every day! It was extraordinary to Ruth that anyone would knowingly have a baby, considering the sheer work hours involved. The rewards seemed too meagre.

Ruth wondered whether Helen would have a baby, too. Despite the manifest disadvantages, she rather hoped that she might; it would give Helen something to occupy herself with. As it was, her stepmother was tremendously busy, but to no apparent purpose, like a bluebottle on a windowsill. She belonged to endless committees; she was a botherer. Ruth tried to like Helen; she wanted her father to be happy and, to judge by Digby's reaction to the infant Jamie, a child would bring him joy. But sometimes it seemed to his daughter that Edward had plumped for Helen only because she was so unlike Iris. Helen wasn't sophisticated, or beautiful, or even especially good company, but neither was she selfish or wilful or sharp. Ruth secretly thought that Helen was bossy and rather dull.

On the other hand, Ruth was surprised to find herself very fond of Digby. She knew she shouldn't be: if it had not been for him, her parents might still have been together, whereas poor Helen was blameless. But she couldn't help liking him, because he was quiet and clever and kind and he looked like some odd bird, a crane, perhaps. He reminded her of her uncle Christopher, though not to look at: Christopher had a small, straight nose and broad shoulders, like his brother. She had been touched to notice that when Digby came with Iris to take her out from school, or to meet her off a train, his face glowed with pleasure the moment he caught sight of her. He was thoughtful. It was Digby who had installed the piano, even though she was hardly ever at their house, because Ruth was good at music, and liked it. He never told her what to do, whereas Helen made her feel as though she were a small but obdurate problem, which could be solved only by a programme of constant intervention, like repeatedly dabbing at a stain.

Digby's mother lived nearby with her sister, both of them widows. They were known, collectively, as the Hillbillies. The aunt – Hilary – had been a widow for many more years than she had been a bride, her young husband having been killed during the final weeks of the First World War. There had been no children and she was devoted to Digby, and would keep arriving unannounced to coo at the new baby. She knitted moss-stitch matinée coats for him, with matching rompers. The idea was that she might look after the baby in the mornings, once he was a little bigger, so that Iris could go back to work, arranging Digby's appointments and driving him on his visits.

'Do look! Isn't he killing?' said Hilary to no one in particular, whenever the baby so much as wriggled.

Ruth was surprised and rather relieved to see that her mother was insensible to this baby worship. She seemed fond of her new son, but she didn't coo. Iris liked Digby's relations, especially her mother-in-law Billa, who was bookish and rather gruff and made no secret of the fact that she was fonder of dogs than of babies. But then Iris always liked people who felt no need to apologise for themselves.

Ruth was meant to live up here with Iris half the time and with Edward, near Tewkesbury, for the rest. But she really spent only about a third of the time with her mother. Most of her life seemed to take place at school. On weekend exeats and at half terms it was so much simpler to go to her father's, because he was less than half an hour away. And then she still stayed in Malvern with her grandparents sometimes. They kept her room for her with her childish things – her teddy and doll's house and old books – and took her out for tea at the Abbey Hotel on those Saturdays when she wasn't allowed to stay the night away from school. She didn't like to hurt their feelings by not visiting, even if she would have preferred to be with Iris.

If someone had asked Ruth where her home was, she would not have known what to answer. Was it at her father's house, or here with her mother? She liked both houses, each of which was close to a river. Edward's house had beams and windows with sills so wide you could sit on them, looking through the lattices of lead. An old orchard of plum and gnarled apple trees stood beyond the garden, between the house and the river. This river was wide and sleepy, with shallow muddy sides where swans rested among the reeds, whereas the river by Iris's house was rocky and dark and urgent, and the water there gave off a cold smell, like mountains. It took ages to get to Iris's house, down an endless rutted track, fringed in spring with carpets of violets. Iris seemed to have forgotten that she used to find the countryside dreary. Ruth loved the house, which stood quite alone, framed by three old Scots pines, a low stone wall separating it from the sheep-cropped green field which ran down to the river. It was an L-shaped house with slate floors in the older, lower part and wide wooden boards in the eighteenth-century part, which had tall ceilings and windows which went right down to the ground. It was an improbable house, neither a rectory nor a farmhouse, but with something of the character of each. Iris didn't have very much furniture, which made her rooms look elegant, and she went in for big dramatic arrangements of flowers, or just greenery: a bowl of white peonies fringed with copper-beech leaves, or masses of pussy willow in a tall jug, or in autumn great arching sprays of blackberry and rosehips. At Edward's house there were plenty of low armchairs and dark, highly polished oak furniture. There were ladder-back chairs, and place mats depicting hunting scenes, and lots of silver cruets, the saltcellars and mustard pots lined with dark-blue glass. Ruth thought that her father's made a better winter house because it was cosy, but her mother's house was lovely in the summer.

When Ruth listened to the other girls in her dormitory talking about their visits home – their ponies and Labradors, their tartan picnic rugs folded just so, their endless cousins coming and going to tennis and croquet parties, or to play mah-jong, or to take tea at shaded tables overlooking the lawn – she envied them the simplicity and order of their lives. They all went to point-to-points, or sailing in the Isle of Wight. They all seemed to do the same things and to know what those things were and when you were meant to do them. In her holidays she just shuttled between her parents' houses, and was expected to amuse herself.

She told only her two best friends at school (and they were sworn to secrecy) that Edward had won custody of her during the divorce. This was because her mother had, shockingly, deserted the marital home. Ruth preferred the rest not to know that her parents were divorced, because it made her feel slightly ashamed. The fact that her father was a respectable country solicitor, and had been decorated in the war, had endeared him to the judge, while Iris's desertion had prejudiced things against her. Edward had insisted that Ruth spend Christmas every year with him, where they were always joined by his own parents, but otherwise he was magnanimous in allowing his daughter time with her mother: they would divide her equally between them, he said. It hadn't worked out like that. Ruth did know one or two other girls at school whose parents had divorced, although not anyone in her actual form. So far as she knew, these other girls lived with their mothers. She realised that there was something not quite right about not living with hers, as if Iris were slightly shoddy.

She had to acknowledge privately that Iris was becoming rather eccentric. Her hair was longer than the other mothers' and she hardly ever wore any pins to contain it: she had given up wearing a hat. Perhaps it had been living abroad which had made her abandon such conventions. She only wore gloves in the dead of winter now, and she never put on any face powder: her face was shiny. And the awful thing was that Iris having the baby did make Ruth feel guiltily put off her mother. Iris was thirty-six, practically geriatric! It was one thing to remarry, but producing a baby was quite another. It wasn't quite respectable. It meant that Iris still did It, a thought too embarrassing to countenance. Or anyway had done It less than a year before, although not of course since: nobody could be that revolting. It probably wasn't even possible, biologically. And the worst thing was that everyone at school would know, when their mothers and fathers probably hadn't done It for years and years.

'Funny, isn't it?' Iris had said, half to herself, when she was giving Jamie his eleven o'clock bottle in the breakfast room one morning. 'First I had to get married because I was going to have a baby, and then this time I had to have a baby, because I'd got married.'

'Mummy!' said Ruth, shocked. 'You've never said that before.'

'Haven't I? Oh, sorry, darling. It doesn't mean one wasn't simply thrilled when you appeared. We both were.'

'But d'you mean to say you were actually having a baby when you and Daddy got married?' Ruth could feel herself flushing with the horror of it.

'Well, yes. But I mean it was quite early on. One wasn't monstrously fat or anything. I had such a pretty dress for the registry office: silk crepe, in a sort of oyster colour. I don't know what happened to it. Must have got lost during the war.'

'Is that why there aren't any photographs from the wedding, because you were pregnant?'

'Don't say pregnant, darling, it's so coarse.'

'But is it?'

'No, of course not,' said Iris. 'There just wasn't anyone there with a camera, that's all. But it was all tremendous fun, on the day.'

'But that means that I'm illegitimate, practically,' said Ruth, tears gathering.

'Don't be silly, darling. Someone either is illegitimate or they aren't. You can't be a bit illegitimate, I mean. And you're not. So there's nothing to get upset about.'

The thing Ruth liked best about school was the choir. Singing solo wasn't nearly as good, because it didn't give you the same sensation; a solo only came from your throat and then out of your mouth, the breath made shallow, even quavery, by nerves. But choral singing went through your whole body, reverberating in your ribcage. With choral singing it was as if you and all the other people you were singing with were one instrument, like the pipes on an organ. A choir was really an orchestra made of voices. When she sang, Ruth sometimes felt a rush of joy, like an extra lung full of happiness instead of breath inside her chest.

There was a feeling she'd sometimes had, out of doors, when she got to the top of the Malvern Hills and there were skylarks dipping above her head, or a lonely kestrel wheeling below. It was an apprehension that she was no different from the cropped grass and the rock beneath it, and the birds, and even their shadows flitting across the hillside. This feeling came sometimes at the river-bathing place across the orchard from her father's house, when dragonflies touched the surface of the water beside her, their veined, transparent wings catching the colours of light, like soap bubbles. Sometimes the cows would pause to look down from the opposite bank, munching, and she would all of a sudden feel as though she had become invisible, had simply evaporated into the silky greenish water and the cows' hot breath and the summer air. She could not predict when the feeling would come, but when it did it made her slightly giddy, this sense that she was just another living speck on the surface of the earth. Less than herself, and yet more. This sensation generally happened when she was on her own, yet what it brought was an overwhelming sense that she was not alone after all. When the whole choir was singing well it could feel the same.

Singing was the main reason Ruth decided to stay on at school after her School Certificates. If she stayed on for Higher School Cert., her teacher had told her, she might be able to get into a music school. She knew she wasn't good enough to become a soloist, either at the piano or the voice, and anyway her ambition did not extend so far. But she also knew she would have to earn her own living somehow. Perhaps she could teach music and continue to sing in a choir for pleasure. She did not know what she might do otherwise. Her father had offered to find someone – another solicitor, or the friend who owned the local auction house – to take her on as an office clerk, but she wanted to get to London if she could.

There were advantages to being in the upper school: she did not have to share a dormitory any more but had a room all to herself. She enjoyed certain privileges, such as being allowed to walk into the town when lessons finished in the afternoons; and, the greatest luxury, having two baths a week, instead of the one permitted to the younger girls. The room next to hers was occupied by an older girl called Verity Longden, who would be leaving in the summer. She was tall, with skin so pale as to be almost transparent, almost as if it might tear. Her eyelashes were very straight and fair, and thick, like the bristles on a toothbrush, and she had big, bony hands that always looked chapped. Ruth could not tell whether Verity was very plain or rather beautiful, but trying to decide one way or the other made her stare at her whenever she had the chance. Verity was a Roman Catholic, one of only a handful at the school. The Catholics walked to Mass every Sunday and when they came back to school afterwards they remained slightly set apart, at least until the lunch bell sounded, as if they were holier or more important than the rest. Verity seemed especially solemn. She was generally rather a serious girl, certainly never giggly. Something about the curve of her mouth, though, suggested a sense of humour.

One Saturday afternoon, just before autumn half term, Ruth knocked on Verity's door and asked if she'd like to come for a walk. They had barely said more than two or three sentences to each other, but they were neighbours, they might as well be cordial. And anyway, all Ruth's friends were out on exeat, or rehearsing for the school play.

'There's a hotel over in Colwall where we could get a cup of tea if you want to go that far? Otherwise we could just go up to the tearooms at the well, what d'you think?' Ruth asked her, as they began their climb. Since Verity was older – and, as it were, the guest – it seemed proper to let her decide things.

'I think Colwall,' she said, as if it were a matter of some gravity.

'It's rather a dismal place, I'm afraid, what my mother calls a brown Windsor. But I love that side of the hills. The view's even better than our side, and you get the sun for longer.'

'What's brown Windsor?' asked Verity.

'Brown Windsor? Have you never had brown Windsor? Gosh, you're lucky. It's a sort of ghastly thick soup, like liquefied meat. They have it in places like station hotels. You know, the sort of dreary places where old people don't say a word to each other the whole way through lunch, so all you can hear is scraping spoons.'

Verity did not laugh. She nodded, but said nothing. If Verity didn't like jokes after all, Ruth thought their walk was going to seem very long.

They went on up the hill in silence. Presently Verity began to speak.

'When I leave here I'm going to train to be a doctor,' she announced. 'I have a place at University College Hospital, once I've done my Highers. I want to be a surgeon.'

'Good heavens,' said Ruth. 'Are girls even allowed to be surgeons?' She didn't recall ever having heard Digby speak of a woman colleague; certainly not a senior doctor. The only women he worked with, so far as she knew, were nurses.

'Of course we are! Girls – young women – are allowed to be anything they want to be. We want to be. Nearly anything.'

'Golly,' said Ruth. 'I thought you had to be a nurse, if you wanted to go into medicine. I mean, I haven't really thought about it much.'

'That's the trouble with this place,' said Verity, 'we're never made to think about anything at all.'

'Well, I don't know,' said Ruth. 'Learning about Gladstone made me think about history quite a bit. And when we did Oliver Cromwell. What things must have been like, you know, in the past.'

'But not science?' Verity looked at her.

Ruth suddenly felt doltish. 'Not really, no. To tell you the truth, after we dissected a frog in the Lower Fifth, I was never quite up to science again.'

Verity laughed. Ruth glanced at her, just to make sure it wasn't a laugh of derision, before she joined in.

After they'd had tea at the hotel in Colwall, Verity suggested that, rather than walking back, they saved their legs and caught the train to Malvern through the long tunnel instead.

'Let's play "I went to Harrods",' Verity suggested, as they took their places on the seats, which prickled through their stockings.

'I don't know how,' said Ruth.

'Well, it's a memory game. You have to remember all the things that I say I've bought, and I have to remember all yours. And we both have to remember our own as well. And it's in alphabetical order. The first to forget is the loser. So, I went to Harrods and I bought an aardvark.'

Ruth paused. 'I went to Harrods and I bought an aardvark and a bun. Will that do?'

Verity nodded, smiling. 'I went to Harrods and I bought an aardvark, a bun and some china plates.'

'I went to Harrods and I bought an aardvark, a bun, some china plates and … and some delicious dates.'

'Are all your turns going to be food?' teased Verity.

'It rather looks like it.'

From that afternoon, they spent all their free time together. They went to teashops, or sat on walls in the sun, or talked in each other's rooms. Sometimes Verity was very serious and Ruth felt rather awed by her cleverness, but at other times she was girlish, even silly. But they never ran out of things to say. Verity's family lived at Richmond upon Thames. There were three brothers, Verity the only girl. She had told Ruth a long story about her parents' courtship, involving letters put in envelopes addressed to other people and misunderstandings and the wrong brother, but Ruth hadn't really followed it all. It was all meant to be fearfully romantic, but when she met Verity's mother and father she was disappointed: they were just ordinary, middle-aged people, who both wore glasses. Verity told her what her mother had said to her once: 'Daddy and I love you all, but we will always love each other best.' Ruth was not sure whether this statement wasn't rather unkind to the children or, as Verity evidently believed, rather magnificent.

Ruth had other friends, but she missed Verity during her final year at school. She spent the last Easter holidays in Richmond with her, and the two planned to rent rooms in London together, once Ruth started at the Royal College of Music in September. An old girlfriend of Ruth's uncle Christopher had a tall, thin house in South Kensington, where she took paying guests. The girls went to see her and liked the place, even though it smelled of cats. They would take up residence in the autumn. One of Verity's brothers was in his final year at Cambridge, and the eldest had joined the Foreign Office and been posted abroad, but the middle brother, Harry, was living in London. He was working in some sort of insurance firm in the City.

Harry laughed easily and had the same fair, oddly blunt eyelashes as his sister, as though they had been chopped in a straight line with miniature garden shears. Among the Longdens he was teased for being the least clever and for the fact that he blushed easily. It was true that he wasn't in the slightest formidable, as the rest of them were. He had ugly hands with stubby fingers, the knuckles whorled like knots of cross-graining in a piece of timber. It was his hands – or rather, the way she felt such peculiar tenderness towards his hands, a mixture of affection and pity – that made Ruth realise she liked Harry in a way that she had never liked anyone else before. His hands unsettled her. Whenever she was with him she glanced at them constantly. Harry had joined his sister and Ruth at a concert at the Wigmore Hall one evening and, sitting beside him in the dark, Ruth had spent the whole evening looking at his hands, folded loosely around the concert programme in his lap. By the time the music stopped she felt quite cross with him. The phrase: 'He can't keep his hands to himself' came into her mind. Such a condition seemed very desirable to her.

Once Ruth was established in London that autumn, Iris came down to visit, leaving Jamie with his doting great-aunt Hilary.

She was staying with her old friend Jocelyn for a few days. Ruth was to meet her for lunch at a little Italian place, by the corner of the underground at South Kensington.

'You don't mind if someone joins us, do you, darling? An old friend, I mean?' said Iris.

Ruth felt the familiar tweak of disappointment which so often occurred within minutes of seeing her mother. They hadn't met for months and she had been looking forward to their being alone together, without the distractions of little Jamie, or even the oddly menacing presence of Birdle. And she had never cared for Jocelyn. But it was a man who came into the restaurant and, smiling, approached their table. He bent to kiss Iris before holding out his hand to Ruth.

'You remember Bunny, darling? He was a friend of Daddy's, from Cambridge days.'

Ruth pretended she did.

The lunch wasn't much fun. Bunny kept ordering bottles of raisiny red wine and talking about horses, and people who lived in Newmarket, while Iris smoked continually and laughed sharply, even though nothing was particularly funny. By the time they were having their coffee, Bunny was openly flirting with Ruth, offering to take her to the opera one night, to a box. He kept insisting that he would see her home in a taxi, although it was broad daylight and her digs were only a few streets away. Iris's laughter had died away by the time the waiter had removed the plates from their main courses.

'Actually I've got a class up at the College and I'd prefer to walk,' Ruth lied. 'Thanks though,' she told him, once they were all out on the street.

'Heavens, that man has become a bore,' said Iris crossly, when Bunny had gone. 'He used to be so original. Drink of course. Fatal.'

Iris had a plan for the afternoon: they would walk across the park and up Piccadilly to Bond Street. Jocelyn had told her that Fenwick's had the smartest clothes, and she was determined to buy Ruth a coat for the winter. Iris was generous in fits. The October sunlight shone thinly through the plane trees, whose trunks bore a dappled tracery, as if they were half shadowed, half bleached with light. Iris walked fast, as always. In the store, a tired-looking assistant wearing thick, too-pale face powder brought out coats for Ruth to try on: one a dark chocolate-brown gabardine, belted; the next a pale-green swing coat with raglan sleeves which puffed at the wrists; then one in red bouclé, with big black buttons.

'Oh, I think the green, don't you?' Iris asked the assistant.

'The cut is very much of the season,' the woman said.

'It moves prettily at the back,' said Iris.

Ruth surveyed herself in the glass and was not happy with what she saw: a young woman with dark hair that wouldn't lie flat and bright eyes. Her calves were lean enough, but somehow lacked the curve necessary to make them look like the limbs of a real woman. They were a child's legs, straight down, stumpy. The green coat accentuated the flaws of her figure and concealed its attractions: her trim waist and firm bosom were utterly lost within its folds. The colour reminded her of the drabness of hospital corridors. She thought it made her look like a huge broad bean. She wished the assistant would stop hovering so she could say so.

'I'm not sure, actually,' she said.

But Iris was.

'That colour's terribly fetching on you, darling,' she said firmly.

'But I don't think I'm tall enough. I think I'd be better with a belt,' said Ruth.

'Don't be silly, darling. Belted coats are for Norland Nannies. Swing coats are all the thing, for the young, I mean. Aren't they?' she asked the assistant, who murmured in assent. Iris was already reaching into her bag for her chequebook. Before Ruth could voice any further objections the coat was being whisked towards the counter and wrapped in tissue paper, like egg whites being folded into cakes. She was handed an important-looking paper bag, with the box containing the coat inside. The bag was grass green, with black lettering swooping across its sides, and thick string handles. Iris looked expectantly at her, for thanks.

Ruth was not going to let her mother see the tears which stung her eyes, so she bent as if to tighten the lace of her left shoe. She suddenly felt much younger than her years, forlorn and childish and mutinously ungrateful.

'Well, I want to go down to Simpson's and buy some tea,' Iris announced briskly. 'I'm going to be frightfully extravagant and get all sorts of exotic things one can't find in the country, like Lapsang Souchong.'

'It's lovely being able to have as many cups as one likes now,' Ruth said. Tea had only just come off the ration. 'Last week it went to our heads rather. Verity and I drank so much tea that we felt quite sick.'

'Darling! Really! You do say the queerest things.'

They had reached Piccadilly and Ruth could feel her mother invisibly tugging away from her, like when you tried to push one magnet against another. 'Thank you for the lunch. And the coat. It's really very kind of you.'

'Well, we can't have you freezing to death,' said Iris.

Ruth was able to muster a thin smile.

Chapter 4

It was all most awkward. Iris and Digby had barely even been in the same room as Edward and Helen, let alone for a whole afternoon. They had certainly never sat down to eat at the same table before. Iris would no doubt talk too much, Digby too little. Edward's manners would prevail of course, but Helen prattled so. And all the Longden relations were Catholic and obviously disapproved. Ruth herself had received Instruction, so that it could be a Catholic service, to please Harry's parents. She had had to undertake to bring up her children within the Faith, in due course. It was rather wonderful, to think of all those saints constantly interceding on her behalf and to learn that Mary never, ever refused a prayer. She kept quiet about the aspects of her new religion in which she could not quite believe. The only difficulty occurred when Verity suggested she make no mention as to how she was related to Jamie, who was to be her page.

'But why?' asked Ruth. 'Aren't you allowed pages who are your half-brothers?'

'It's only that Father Leonard might find it difficult about him being your mother's child from her second marriage.'

'What?'

'Well, you know we don't go in for divorce. It may be – and I'm not sure, it may be that I'm erring on the side of caution – that the Church would not recognise your mother's second marriage. In which case, Jamie—'

49

'You can't mean it! That's absurd!'

'Father Leonard doesn't need to know that he's your half-brother. You can simply give his name. After all, it's different from yours.'

'But isn't that terribly hypocritical? And what about "Suffer little children to come unto me"? It's not very Christian, is it, to declare Jamie a … well, illegitimate? It's not his fault, after all.' Ruth had flushed with anger. 'He's innocent. He's a child.' It was the first time she had ever been short with Verity.

'Nobody said anything like that, Ruth. It's a question of whether or not he was born in sin. And after all, we all are. That's why we are baptised, as you will no doubt have learned. I could very well be wrong about this question. It could very well be that there is no reason why he shouldn't participate in the wedding Mass. But Father Leonard's rather a stickler. I just wouldn't want there to be any unpleasantness.'

But it was too late. The question over Jamie lodged in Ruth's upper chest painfully, like hiccups that have gone on too long. At first she was determined to bring it up with Harry, but she thought better of it. If he did not disagree with his sister, Ruth knew she would struggle to forgive him.

Ruth had other worries. She feared embarrassment: Iris was practically a pagan, went about with bare legs, seldom did her hair. 'You will wear a hat, won't you, Mummy? Only, all the Longdens are,' Ruth dared at last to ask her on the telephone.

'Of course I will! What do you take me for?' said Iris hotly.

'Of course. I didn't … it's only that—'

'Just because one isn't absolutely hidebound with formality doesn't mean that one doesn't know how to behave,' Iris interrupted. 'I am a doctor's wife, you may recall. One may live in the North, but that doesn't make one an absolute Eskimo.'

Ruth thought that Eskimos generally did wear hats, but judged it wiser to say nothing. Getting married seemed to necessitate a lot of not saying things.

At least Iris was not intending to come south in advance of the wedding. And the thought that the reception might take place at her house seemed never to have crossed her mind: there were advantages in her failure to observe convention. It was tacitly accepted that Ruth would marry from Edward's house. After the service at the Catholic church in Cheltenham (Father Leonard would officiate, by special arrangement with the diocese) they would repair there. There would be champagne in the dining room and then the guests would go into a marquee in the garden for the wedding breakfast.

Ruth could hardly wait for the day to be over. She and Harry so seldom had time on their own; that was the only snag of his being Verity's brother. Harry had been sharing a flat in Bayswater with two friends, one who worked at the Treasury and one who, like Harry, was in the City. Ruth's room in South Kensington was too small to sit about in; anyway, Verity always seemed to be at home when her brother called. Their courtship had been conducted in crowded coffee shops, concert halls and museums. It would be the greatest luxury to spend ten whole days together, just them.

Parts of the wedding day passed slowly and Ruth felt oddly disconnected at those times, as if she were a ghost, watching.

She saw smiling faces turn towards her as she processed up the aisle, a blur of goodwill like a ripple propelling her towards the altar. After the service she and Harry stood in the dining room to greet the guests; several of the women told Ruth she was radiant, which she knew was their way of saying she looked happy, if not ravishingly pretty. She hardly minded. Harry's face became pink from the exertion of shaking every guest's hand, his hair somehow tousled. To his bride he looked like an adorable little boy, come downstairs after being put to bed with a slight fever.

Every time she thought about anything, it seemed to have a bed in it. In her suitcase was a small round tin, housing a dome of thick dark rubber the colour of a flypaper. Absurdly, this would prevent her from having babies, at least for the time being – she had a final year at the Royal College to see out. Her father had suggested she quit now that she was to be a wife, with wifely things to do, but Harry saw no reason why she should not carry on and Ruth wanted to. The gynaecologist in Portland Place had instructed her to practise inserting and removing the device before the honeymoon. She must first lie down. Get the thing in. Then after use – a prescribed amount of hours later – she was to remove the thing, wash it in tepid water; never hot, for very hot water could cause the rubber to perish. At last she must dry it carefully before sprinkling the barest coating of talcum powder over the dome, like dusting icing sugar onto a fairy cake.

In her room she had blushed, alone, as she removed it from its tin. The bed felt too high, too exposed, so she lay on the narrow rug beside it. First she tried lying on her back, then on her side. The base of the dome was a sprung ring; the trick was to narrow it between two fingers, while probing with the other hand. Once in place you could let go, and the ring would resume its circular form, fitting over what the doctor had told her was called the cervix, like a tiny brimless hat. There was a knack to it apparently. Evidently it was a knack she did not possess. The device kept springing out of her hand and across the rug. On one attempt it jumped several feet, as far as the door. Ruth began to laugh. But laughing alone was ridiculous and made it harder to concentrate, which made it more difficult to get the wretched thing into place, which only made her laugh more, with the helplessness of it all. It was quite impossible. It would never fit. It would leap out at Harry, on her wedding night, startling as a frog, and she would be too ashamed ever to face him again.

For several days she made no further attempts. The tin sat undisturbed, a shameful secret in the drawer among her undergarments. Then, intrepid after a day of studying, she strode home and went straight up to her room, unlaced her shoes, unfastened her suspender belt and pulled down her woollen stockings and knickers and tried again, in broad daylight; not lying down as the doctor had told her, but standing up in her bare feet, one foot raised on the chair at the end of her bed. This was the way a Valkyrie would put in her Dutch cap, she thought, and it brought victory. Getting it out – which had worried her: what if it got stuck? – turned out to be much easier than putting it in. There was a way of hooking your finger under its rim, and yanking. It was rather like gutting a fish.

None of this augured well for the honeymoon. There was nothing pleasurable in the probing necessitated by the contraceptive device. How could actual lovemaking be any different? Ruth didn't mean to keep thinking about how it would turn out in that department, but somehow her thoughts always came back to settle on it, like a bee returning again and again to the same plant. She liked kissing – she and Harry had done plenty of that – but she did feel anxious about the next bit.

Their room at the hotel by Lake Garda had long wooden shutters and a paper of big orange-ish flowers. The candlewick bed cover was an anaemic tangerine: not the bright colour of a tangerine's skin, but the colour of the tight, pithy inside of an under-ripe fruit. At first Ruth disliked the room's decor – it embarrassed her somehow – and she gravitated towards the window, which framed a view of blue water, distant villas and air. But by the second morning she loved it all: the ugly tufted bedspread, the coyness of the spindly chairs, even the stiff bath taps. No wonder people spoke of married bliss! It turned out that what happened in bed was perfectly lovely. You could kiss all the way through, which had surprised her: she had imagined that kissing was only a preliminary, a first course. Nor did you have to keep your eyes shut. You could look, you could kiss, you could kiss any part of each other, you could take as long as you liked. It seemed there was nothing you couldn't do, there were no forbidden zones, and all of it was just the best feeling ever.

Their time in bed made her love Harry more than ever, in a slightly dotty way, at once hypnotised and ravenous. It also had the strange effect of making her fall rather in love with herself. Ruth's body was not something she had ever thought much about. She carried it around, dressed it, fed it when it was hungry. When she looked in the glass before going out for an evening she occasionally tutted at her unshapely legs, her disobliging hair. Now she found herself amazed at her own flesh while she bathed, at her heavy breasts and the freckles on her forearms. She suddenly felt for the first time that she was beautiful.

Back in London they took a first- and second-floor maisonette in Pimlico, in Alderney Street. On the lower floor was a drawing room, with a pair of graceful windows to the floor. The boudoir grand piano which had been Harry's wedding gift to her was here. There was a dining room and, at the back, a kitchen with a tiny larder off it. Upstairs was their bedroom, a dressing room for Harry and – the thing that Ruth loved best about their new home – a bathroom much bigger than any other she knew of in London. As if to do justice to their ample surrounds, the basin and bath were enormous. Ruth installed a chaise longue under the bathroom window, so that she and Harry could keep each other company while one of them was soaking.

She rode her bicycle up to the Royal College every morning, while Harry took the underground to work. A char came in three times a week, to launder Harry's work shirts and do the heavy cleaning, such as it was. Ruth arrived home well before her husband in the afternoons, in plenty of time to start preparing their dinner. Usually she practised the piano for an hour, or sang. She taught herself to cook out of a book: steak Diane, chicken à la King. Often they went to bed as soon as Harry got home, almost before he had had time to take off his coat. Afterwards they sat flushed and naked in bed, and drank sherry out of the prim cut-glass glasses they had been given as a wedding present. Sometimes they did not get up again, but one of them went down to the kitchen in a dressing gown to fetch cheese and water biscuits, which infested the sheets with huge prickly crumbs.

It was after their first Christmas as a married couple that Harry began to make noises about babies. Ruth secretly blamed his family, who – perhaps reminded of infants by the festivities attendant on the baby Jesus – kept dropping heavy hints. Even Verity, who showed no inclination of her own to reproduce, was a culprit. Ruth found this treacherous of her old friend, who had always made so much of women's careers. Harry was so genial, so dear: they never quarrelled. She never denied him anything, because he asked for so little, only her affection and interest, which came naturally. Sometimes it was rather a slog, getting up early to catch the train to Richmond every Sunday for Mass with the Longdens, followed by lunch back at their house, but it was only natural that they should see more of his family than of hers, because they lived so much nearer. And they were a proper family, she reminded herself, not like hers.

She adored Harry, she wanted to please him, but she did want, too, to finish her studies before having a baby; or at least, that was the official reason.

'They don't come overnight, you know,' said Harry. 'We could start now and you'd still be fine for your exams in June. I mean, it wouldn't arrive 'til ages afterwards.'

'I can't appear at the College bulging! It would be too … I don't know. Too odd. Conspicuous. I'd just feel funny, being the only one. I'm the only one who's married as it is. Everyone else goes back to boiled dinners in digs. I'm the only one with a home of my own, who cooks.' She frowned.

'I know, darling. Don't panic. No need to look so cross.'

'I'm not cross. I don't feel cross. I only feel torn, you see, because I don't want to disappoint you.'

'Speckle, you never disappoint me.'

'So can we have a baby later, after the summer?'

It never occurred to her that she might experience any difficulty in the getting of a baby: she assumed that all she would have to do was not use the contraceptive device. As it turned out she was right. At Easter they went to stay with Iris for a few days. Birdle, who generally reserved his worst bites for men, had taken a shine to Harry on sight. As soon as Harry came into the room, he shrieked in recognition, although he had not seen him for several months.

'Stop that racket at once, Birdle,' Iris snapped. She was not altogether pleased when Birdle liked anyone besides herself. But he continued whistling and squawking. Only when Harry went and stroked the feathers at the back of the bird's head did he fall quiet. He drooped with pleasure, bowing his head with the uncharacteristic meekness of a spaniel.

They planned to spend a night in the Lake District on their way back to London. The inn was a low building of whitewashed stone, with polished slate floors. But their room was in a flimsily built wing at the back, with narrow twin beds and thin walls. It had a mildewy smell, not altogether unpleasant, like a hymn book. They spent the afternoon walking before coming back to the place for supper. Installed in their room, they could hear a woman's voice from the next room. The words were muffled but the tone was clear – she was recounting a tale of grievance, which caused her voice to grow shriller every few moments – and every now and again a second voice, a man's, responded with a single gruff syllable. The thought that these neighbours would be able to hear them as vividly on the other side of the wall struck them as both comic and aphrodisiac. They kissed, suppressing laughter, before landing on one of the beds, clothes half on. They felt as pleased and as naughty as children enjoying a midnight feast. In the scrummage there was no time for Ruth to pad down the landing to the bathroom, with its damp-ruckled linoleum, to install the device.

Soon after she'd finished her final examinations it became evident to Ruth that changes were taking place in her body. Her nipples darkened and prickled. Sleep tugged her into its depths with the irresistible pull of a tide. She hadn't missed her periods exactly, but with hindsight she realised that they hadn't lasted as long as usual. One Sunday at her in-laws, the smell of roasting lamb suddenly caught in her throat with a cloying bloody sweetness. Brushing her teeth in the morning a few days later, she abruptly disgorged the cup of tea she had drunk minutes earlier into the toothpaste-foamed spit in the basin.

That evening she and Harry were to meet at the Albert Hall for a concert. She was early.

'There you are!' he said in greeting, as if he had been waiting for her and not the other way round. 'Hello, that's a worried little face,' he added, looking closely now, noticing her pallor.

'No, I'm not. Actually I think I might be …' Ruth found that she could not face saying the words. 'I think the thing that you've been wanting – I mean the baby thing – I think it might be happening.'

Harry beamed at her. 'Really? Have you been to the doctor? Are you sure?'

'No, I'm not. I don't really know. But I do think so.'

'Darling. Darling girl.' All the way through the concert he kept her hand in his, just a little too tightly, tucked under his arm.

She could not feel that the baby was an actual baby until it appeared, not really. For now it was just a thing, like an acorn. Even as she became larger and more cumbrous she found it hard to imagine that a new and separate life was taking shape within her. Iris sent a cobweb of a shawl, made of the finest wool, as light as candyfloss. Her mother-in-law offered to come into town and take her shopping for the baby's layette: tiny cream-coloured Viyella nightgowns, cardigans, vests which fastened on one side with ribbon, loosely knitted blankets edged with thick satin. When she got home she took these things out of their stiff cardboard boxes and tissue-paper wrapping and laid them out on the divan in Harry's dressing room, which was to become the nursery. She stood and looked down at the baby's things and tried to feel connected to them – willed herself to feel moved by the pathos of their smallness – but she could not. It was like looking at photographs of someone else's garden.

Time seemed to slacken. Whole days went by when she did nothing at all: she barely touched the piano, could hardly drag her pen across the page to write letters. Books idled unread in her hands. When she tried to sing her voice went out of tune. There was often only cold veal and ham pie for supper, ready sliced at the grocer's, with cold beetroot. She never stopped yawning, but slept only fitfully: the lump pressed uncomfortably against her bladder, her lungs, her ribs. Every day when Harry came home he talked about what was going on in the world, but she had nothing to say, because she didn't mind. She thought she would never care about anything again.

But when the nurse handed her baby girl to her, all clean and swaddled, already bathed – how had there been time? – and smelling of powder, Ruth felt something give way inside her chest, like a silent sneeze. Looking into her baby's tight little face, she felt a great welling up of emotion. It seemed utterly miraculous that a mere fourteen hours of labour could produce this entirely new being, so familiar and yet so strange. The baby hardly looked like a baby at all, but like a very small very old person, wise and well travelled, with her own secrets. The baby's pink fingers waved open and shut like the fronds of a sea anemone. Her tiny fingernails gleamed as if buffed. She snuffled adorably. Her gaze seemed both penetrating and unfocused. She was furled and quite magical.

When the linen had been changed and straightened and she had combed her hair, Harry came in to see her. Ruth hoped that he would not ask to hold his new daughter, because she could not bear to let her go, not even for a second. She could smell London streets in the gabardine of his coat as he stood beside the bed. He seemed shy and too big for the room. A nurse brought a tray, with tea and Lincoln biscuits. The biscuits were round, with little raised dots on one side which tickled the roof of her mouth as they turned mushy. These were the best biscuits Ruth had ever tasted, so crisp and sweet and biscuity. She did not think she had tasted anything as delicious in all her life. She could not imagine why anyone would ever wish to eat anything else. How had she existed, all these years, without ever considering Lincoln biscuits? To think, she had been given a baby, and now these wonderfully good biscuits! She felt so overwhelmed, so lucky, that tears gathered in her eyes.

People kept talking to her, but she could not quite make out what they wanted. Asking her things she did not know the answers to. Harry wondered if there was anything she needed him to bring, whether she would like to sleep now, whether he should bring the family to see the baby today or tomorrow. A nurse asked if she needed help to go and spend a penny. All she wanted was to be alone with her baby. She smiled wanly and kept saying thank you, in the hope they would go away.

At last they were alone in the room, she and Isobel. Isobel. As soon as everyone had gone she knew this was the baby's name. Could it really be that Iris had had such feelings for her, when she was born? That all mothers loved their babies this intensely? It barely seemed possible. Ruth began to sing quietly, her lips just touching the top of the baby's head:

> 'Row, row, row your boat
> Gently down the stream
> Merrily, merrily, merrily, merrily
> Life is but a dream.'

An image of little Isobel lying in a shallow boat among river reeds came to Ruth. It brought to mind poor baby Moses, left alone among the bulrushes; or the shadowy, grieving Lady of Shalott, only of course the Lady of Shalott was not a baby, but a grown woman. All at once the song struck Ruth as tragic, its gaiety a mask for the sorrow and transience of life. Isobel could not row a boat, gently or otherwise: she couldn't do anything for herself. Ruth would have to do it for her. She would have to be valiant on her daughter's behalf. She remembered Iris, sitting, arms around her knees, on an eiderdown in the makeshift air-raid shelter during the Blitz at the old London house. She remembered the special chocolates they'd eaten together – how the sweetness of them had obliterated the bitter smell of the coal – and how her mother had made it seem fun, an adventure. Now she had a child of her own she understood, all of a sudden, why Iris had never seemed afraid. It was because you could not – you must not – let your child see that you were frightened. Your task was to protect the child. Any chink of fear betrayed that covenant. And this seemed so daunting, so big a thing to be able to fulfil, that Ruth could hardly believe it was expected of her.

Chapter 5

Birdle, with an exaggerated side-swaying gait like a parody of a drunken sailor's, advanced across the back of the sofa. He looked around with a beady, furtive air and then hopped down once, twice, until he reached the rug where Isobel was undressing her doll in front of the fire. After pausing to make sure he was unobserved, he scuttled across its woollen fronds and bit her on the knee. The child wailed. Birdle pretended to be startled by the sudden noise and flapped up to the back of the armchair where Iris was sitting, Player's untipped cigarette in one hand, newspaper folded in the other.

'Mummy! You'll really have to put him in his cage. He's bitten Isobel again!' cried Ruth.

'Naughty Birdle,' said Iris, without conviction.

'Ghastly,' cawed Birdle, bowing up and down like an agitated waiter. 'Ghastly.'

Iris smirked behind *The Times*.

'It isn't funny,' said Ruth, bending to kiss the knee better, enjoying – despite herself, despite the child's pain – the chubby, quilted feel of the flesh on the limb her daughter proffered.

'Poor darling,' said Iris. It was not plain whether she was referring to the parrot or her granddaughter.

'Come along, Isobel, we'll go and see what's for tea.'

'See Damie,' said Isobel, longingly. She had developed a passion for her ten-year-old uncle Jamie and took every opportunity to be in his company. She did not expect to participate in his games; proximity was enough. Often she just stood, gazing at him. Ruth thought that it was his age more than his gender which so fascinated the toddler: he was like a grown-up, only smaller. He was a gentle boy, but eager, his face already bearing signs of his father's beakiness. Home for the holidays, he didn't seem to mind when Isobel inadvertently knocked over his soldiers, or pulled the croquet hoops out of the lawn in the middle of a game.

'We'll see Jamie at tea time. He's gone fishing, remember?'

Ruth took her daughter's hands and pulled her up. She hoped there would be fruit cake. She had been hungry for the whole of this pregnancy, except when she'd actually been sick. She had been feeling sick for five months now. Food brought temporary respite from the nausea, but nothing, not even vomiting, brought relief. And she was the size of a dairy cow.

Ruth was altogether disgruntled. It wasn't only the relentless nausea and the hefting of her uncompliant body about the place. There was also the fact that bed life was curtailed. During her first pregnancy, she and Harry had carried on blissfully throughout, adjusting to her increased size in increments, improvising. Until the end of the seventh month she had felt electrically sexy, as if every pore of her skin had voltage. This time the sickness meant she could not bring herself to kiss, for covering her mouth worsened the nausea, and it was joyless, making love without kissing. It was like going abroad and only seeing the sights recommended in a guidebook, without wandering about on your own, without happening on idiosyncratic pleasures: a little shop selling old-fashioned hats perhaps, or glass doll's eyes, or plaster saints. There was some sense of achievement but it was impersonal, even mechanical. She could not enjoy it, could not lose herself, which made things difficult for Harry. They had rather given up. And she couldn't really play the piano either because she was so big she could scarcely reach the keys and the pedals at the same time.

Also there was the fact that when she and Isobel went home, it would not be to the flat in Pimlico, but to their new house in Putney. Harry had wanted to move further out, nearer his parents, and it meant that they could afford a real house, with a garden for the children – there was even an old apple tree with a swing – and fresher air. And yet Ruth was sad to leave Pimlico, where they had started their married life. She loved the huge bathroom and being so close to everything, being able to walk to the Tate, and to meet her girlfriends in coffee shops. Also, she had hoped that having a second child would make theirs into a proper family of their own. Two and two: a household with its own habits and accumulating customs, with less obligation to see her in-laws every weekend. Their new proximity made such hope of separation dimmer.

She found the Longdens less and less congenial as time went on.

It worried her. She thought that her adoring of Harry should have spilled over to his relations, but instead her affection for them had receded. Their formality and routine, which had once reminded her, happily, of her grandparents – it seemed such a haven – now bored and irritated her. Could they never do anything new, or differently? And they were so smug, so convinced of their own rightness. They never forgot to be conventional, to serve stuffing with roast pork, or redcurrant jelly when it was roast lamb. Their views never deviated in even the slightest detail from those expressed in the *Daily Telegraph*. They never forgot their manners, but they weren't kind. Every time she and Harry visited, she heard his parents criticise some-one: the child of old friends, who had gone horribly wrong, or a former associate with money troubles, or some errant neigh-bour. Invariably her father-in-law would conclude, 'Well, it's not for us to judge.' And there would be a little silence during which the family drew their collective breath complacently, blithely unaware that their harsh gossip was a kind of judgement, even if it was not followed by the passing of a sentence. She was not sure if they knew that Verity was having an affair with a married man, an anaesthetist at the hospital. At Mass, Ruth sometimes glanced across at her sister-in-law, as she closed her eyes in piety ready to receive the Host, and wondered. You were not supposed to take Holy Communion unless you were in a blameless state, a state of purity; this she had been taught during her Instruction. Perhaps adultery was only a sin for the actual adulterer, the person who was married. She did not have the heart to ask Harry.

Sometimes, after Sunday lunches, Ruth would wander unob-served into her father-in-law's study and deliberately nudge the spine of a book or two deeper into the shelf, out of alignment. The order of things on his desk – the ivory letter-opener, the magnifying glass, the little papier-mâché box containing postage stamps, the cut-glass inkwell, with its polished silver lid, the blotting paper economically retained until every inch of its surface was stained – somehow offended her. Once, she had taken the torch – always kept in its appointed place on the hall table for emergencies – and dropped it into a dusty Wellington boot. The sheer childishness of her actions made giggles ferment inside her, and she had to take a turn around the garden just to stop herself from laughing stupidly.

It had been an uncomfortable pregnancy and it was an uncomfortable birth. The baby – a girl – was the wrong way round and wouldn't come out of her own accord. Ruth had had to be cut and there had been urgent tugging, forceps, and doors flapping open and then shut as nurses and then a doctor rushed in and out. It had hurt awfully. By the time the baby appeared, Ruth was exhausted. The baby wasn't like Isobel, pink and adorably round. She was skinny, with little jutting elbows and a cross face and dark hair like wet feathers. When, after being stitched, Ruth at last held her and looked down into her face, the baby averted her gaze, her eyes roving away. The thought that she was searching for another, better, mother flitted into Ruth's mind.

Ruth was worried that Harry would have liked a son, but he could not have been more delighted with his second daughter. The baby looked even scrawnier with his big hands around her little body, but he seemed to think she was perfect.

'Miranda do you think? Are you a Miranda? Or an Alice? Or a Felicity?' He beamed at the infant.

All the names she had ever liked evaporated from Ruth's memory. 'Do you think it would be too silly to call her Harriet?' she said, on a whim. A name with Harry in it had to be all right.

'Gosh,' said Harry. 'I don't know. We might get confused, rather, when people call her. Think they meant me.'

'I'd be able to tell the difference. So would you.'

They both looked at the baby, but she betrayed no sign that the name was either right or wrong.

'Emily!' said Harry emphatically. 'That's her name, don't you think, darling?'

Ruth smiled thinly. She was too tired to care.

Back in Putney the days dragged. Isobel was flushed and wilful, prone to outbursts of loud crying when thwarted in the least thing. Ruth found that she was less confident with Emily, despite having been through new motherhood before: the baby didn't cry or fret, but she seemed always to be awake, looking around her. Ruth fed her, put her over one shoulder and patted her back to rid her of wind, then changed her nappy, the pin clenched between her teeth as if she was dressmaking. Then she couldn't think what to do with her. With Isobel, she had laid her on her side in her crib, the wide satin border of the blanket tucked neatly under her chin, and the baby had simply slept. Ruth had loved the smell of warmth and baby powder and clean wool which hung in the room. But Emily didn't want to sleep.

And the child was too small to read to, or for her sister to play with.

After lunch, most days, Ruth took a rug out into the garden and installed herself upon it with a book, which she read fitfully, without concentration. She did not like this garden very much. It felt too hemmed in, too like the gardens on either side. Isobel brought her doll outside, or played in the sandbox Harry had made for her, chatting bossily to herself. Emily kicked her twig-like legs and goggled. Was she cold? Ruth always worried that she might be, being so skinny. Gradually the baby's gaze became more focused: she inspected her hands wondrously, as if they were independent, miraculously floating things. She stared at the buddleia and the butterflies which alighted on it.

Sometimes Ruth sang songs:

> 'The sun has got his hat on
> Hip-hip-hip-hooray!
> The sun has got his hat on and he's coming out today!
> Now we'll all be happy ...'

Her voice sounded thin.

'Silly Mummy!' Isobel said. 'The sun isn't wearing his hat!'

'How do you know?' said Ruth.

'Because he hasn't got a hat. It's my sunhat, remember? I've got it on, not him. If he wore a hat I wouldn't need to.' And she pointed upwards, squinting pinkly at the light.

Ruth knew she should be amused. Harry loved to hear such quaint snippets when he came home, but instead she felt wretched suddenly. Here she was, doing her best to entertain the girls, singing, bringing them outside into the dappled sunlight of her garden, just as she was supposed to, reading Kate Greenaway and interminable Beatrix Potter – had those stories always been so long? – giving them rosehip syrup and fingers of bread and butter at intervals; yet she failed to be part of the scene she was creating. She felt strangely uninvolved. It was as if she were acting. Playing mummy.

But without Harry there was no audience to appreciate her performance. Every day Ruth longed for him to get home. She got through the mornings, when her charwoman, Mrs Lane, came in (a new woman, quieter, not their old chatterbox from Pimlico), then gave the children their lunch. But from about two o'clock she felt almost frantic, restless and alone. What was funny about children was that they weren't company. She often felt lonely when she was with them, but without any of the advantages of solitude: she couldn't sit at the piano for as long as she liked, nor experience the intense pleasure she had some-times enjoyed when out of doors by herself. You couldn't talk to little children, yet they prevented you from really talking to anyone else, and whenever she had a visitor, one or other of the girls somehow made conversation impossible. Worse, you couldn't be sure that any interval in their timetable of demand would last long enough to play through a piece of music without being interrupted. Every afternoon after their time outside, while the girls had their lie-down, she practised at her piano. She progressed through scales, to scales in broken octaves, chords to broken chords, to arpeggios. She worked on her third and fourth fingers and especially on keeping her thumbs light, making her arms as free as she could without jerking her elbows. Only then was she ready to play a piece in full. Concentrating at the piano, she forgot time and was always dismayed when one or other of her girls – generally it was Emily – disturbed her. She felt as if she had only just sat down, when in reality an hour or more had passed. But if she made no attempt to practise and kept an ear out for them, the girls slept for hours, or cooed contentedly in the nursery. She would hear Isobel talking to Emily in the special instructive voice she reserved for her sister.

Harry's presence in the house made sense of things, as if Ruth and the girls were a picture that had been knocked in passing and was hanging slightly crooked: his arrival among them straightened the frame. He took the children in his arms, on his knees; he tickled and laughed. After their bath – Ruth gave it to them, while he looked at the paper or stepped into the garden with a drink – he often read to the girls, enjoying their innocent and familiar smells of soap, damp hair and hot-ironed Viyella, enjoying Isobel's questions and baby Emily's dancing limbs. Once the children were in bed, Harry poured gin and bitter lemon for himself and Ruth, while she got their supper ready, often trying new recipes. She attempted coq au vin, and, once, beef stew with olives (they agreed neither of them really cared for olives), and fish cakes made with tinned salmon. They drank water with their food, unless they were having people to dinner, when bottles of red wine would be uncorked. After eating they each had a glass of whisky, which made Ruth feel thrillingly unfeminine, as if she were a businessman in a panelled board-room and not a housewife in Putney at all. Sometimes they listened to gramophone records while they drank, or played cards; they told each other stories about their days.

Once a week or so they went up to the West End to the theatre or a concert, or sometimes to the cinema. Mrs Lane's teenage daughter, Dawn, babysat. Ruth liked the Festival Hall, but Harry thought it was hideous, like a bunker. He couldn't get on with modern architecture. Ruth loved their evenings out together, when they held hands in the prickly velvet darkness, like a court-ing couple again. But what she loved best was to be in bed. Once she had recovered from giving birth, she found a new depth of pleasure in her body, an urgency, as if her husband was a life raft and she was floundering in cold water. Sometimes she could barely wait until dinner was over to reach for him. It was only when they made love that she felt in full occupation of her body. The baby, who otherwise slept soundly through the nights in her own room, often chose the final moments of her parents' love-making to startle awake and cry loudly. Harry was able to climax, impervious to the sound of his daughter's cries, but Ruth could not, and she began to feel slightly persecuted by the child. It was as though the baby possessed a sixth sense which alerted her to sabotage her mother's pleasure, even through her sleep.

Little Isobel struggled to pronounce her sister's name, but persistently called her Lemily, which gradually got contracted to its first syllable: Lem. Iris made a great fuss of the child, rather to Ruth's irritation; she had not minded her mother being so little interested in Isobel, because she expected no more from her. Babies were not Iris's forte, as she admitted herself. But now she liked one, which only threw into sharp relief the fact that she had apparently not much cared for the one before. Ruth smarted with vicarious indignation on Isobel's part, although Isobel did not seem to notice, or care. She preferred her father's mother, whom she saw every week. Iris meant only one thing to her elder granddaughter, for where Iris was there was her uncle Jamie, her idol.

Harry's mother and brothers and their wives (all the Longden sons were now married, only Verity remained unwed) displayed no preference for one child or another, yet their even-handedness irked Ruth almost more than her own mother's favouritism. Her sisters-in-law bored Ruth, but they fitted in perfectly at the family house in Richmond: they were docile and undemanding. They talked about casseroles and the troubles they had with their charwomen ('She will forget to change the flower water, no matter how often I say. And the cushions: she puts them at the most dreadful angles, with the corners pointing up. I'm forever having to put them straight again.'). They listened when the men spoke, and laughed becomingly. Ruth longed for something to crumple the smooth surface of the collective Longden temperament. Even Verity had begun to get on her nerves. The air in the Longden household did not seem to circulate adequately; there was such a sense of stuffiness and inertia. After lunch they just sat. The evenings at home after their days with the Longdens were the only ones on which Ruth did not feel like making love with her husband. It was as if proximity to his family made their dullness and sanctimony rub off on him, clinging to him like the smell of old cooking fat.

Winter had come, Lem was almost ten months old when, one Sunday lunch at her in-laws, Ruth was overcome with sickness. She had taken a mouthful of roast chicken, scraping a little bread sauce onto her fork, when suddenly the sauce decoalesced in her mouth. It tasted not like sauce at all, but horribly like its constituents: stale, soggy bread, oniony milk, oily, pungent clove. Covering her mouth with a hand, she rushed from the table to the downstairs loo, a room she had barely entered before, since it was informally used only by the men of the house. There were old cartoons from *Punch*, along with photographs, dating from their school and university days, of Harry and his brothers in various sporting teams. There was hard loo paper folded in a little basket and a cracked piece of coal-tar soap on the basin.

Having vomited, Ruth steadied herself with one hand on the wall. She registered the smell of the soap, stale though it was: like distant creosote, as if someone a few doors down were painting their garden fence. It amazed her that she was able to formulate such thoughts at the same time as feeling such a sense of panic that she wondered if she might actually keel over. No. She couldn't be. It wasn't possible. She was still feeding the baby; she hadn't missed a period.

'I can't,' she said to herself. 'I can't.'

But why not? Another voice, oppositional, launched itself. She was happily married, a young mother already: one more wouldn't hurt. Harry wanted a big family, she knew that. It might be a boy. A brother for the girls. A son for Harry. A boy like Harry, with Harry's adorable face and pale lashes. These thoughts flitted into her head. Nevertheless she felt, overwhelmingly, that this was something she simply could not do. It was not possible. It might be possible for someone else, like translating from the Chinese, or riding in the Grand National. But it wasn't something Ruth could do. It was as if she was in mutiny.

Harry mustn't know. That was the first thing. She must regain her composure and go back to the table and finish her lunch and say nothing. She only had to get through lunch, and then the afternoon, and then the evening. The next day would be Monday and she would be able to think about it then, uninterrupted. She looked in the mirror above the basin and silently told her pale reflection: It's all right. You're all right. She splashed her face with cold water and rinsed out her mouth.

On Monday she asked Mrs Lane if she could stay on to see to the children while she went into town. Ruth could not approach the doctor she'd seen for her pregnancies with the girls: he was a colleague of Verity's and might disapprove, or worse, tell. She didn't know who she could ask, until she thought of one of the other lodgers who had lived in the same digs in South Kensington. Sasha, her name was: she'd been a student at the College of Art. She had been seeing one of the teachers there, all rather hush-hush, and then it had stopped, abruptly. Sasha had spent some days in her room. When Ruth saw her in the corridor she looked tear-stained in a too-big dressing gown, diminished. There had been drips of blood on the bathroom lino. Ruth had brought her some oranges and cigarettes and sat on her bed among the peels and the spilling ashtray, not mentioning it. Ruth had a telephone number for her, in Maida Vale.

Sasha was surprised to hear from her, but she was friendly and responded at once. They arranged to meet that afternoon for tea. Sasha wore smudged black eyeliner and big, rather African-looking jewellery, and was taller than Ruth had remembered her. She worked as a studio assistant for a rather famous sculptor three days a week, still painted herself, had had pictures in some group exhibitions. She hadn't married yet. Ruth did not dissemble and Sasha gave her the name of a Mr Burnside in

Lower Cavendish Street. Back in Putney she telephoned to make an appointment. He could see her on Wednesday.

His waiting room was awfully grand, with a white marble fireplace covered in carved grapes. Yes, she was pregnant; yes, he could help. She would need to see a psychiatrist, and there was a colleague whom he could recommend. If – at the word 'if' Mr Burnside arched his eyebrows, indicating that this 'if' was a mere formality – the psychiatrist found adequate mental grounds, he would refer her back to himself. Then they would proceed. That was how it worked. She would need to spend a night in the clinic, of course. Was there someone who could take her home and keep an eye on her for a few days afterwards? It was his experience that such things were better dealt with, with the minimum of delay. This being the case, he would suggest that she come in on the following Tuesday morning. If she would step into the waiting room he would telephone the psychiatrist and see whether he might be able to fit her in this afternoon.

Ruth walked to Marylebone High Street and realised she was hungry. She stepped into Café Sagne, where she ordered coffee and asked for the plainest pastry they had, a request which seemed to annoy the waitress. She thought over what Mr Burnside had said. In her hand was a piece of crisp writing paper, with the address of Mr Burnside's rooms in curling embossed letters at the top. He had written out the name and Devonshire Place address of the psychiatrist, as well as a time: two o'clock. Ruth had noticed that Mr Burnside handled his rather fat fountain pen with a certain flourish; when he glanced down at his own handwriting it was with a hint of unmistakable self-regard.

Ruth drank her coffee, ignoring the saliva which rose against the roof of her mouth in protest. It wasn't like making a decision. There was to be no weighing up of the pros and cons of things and certainly no discussion; no advice or reassurance to be sought. It was like getting rid of a splinter: something which had to be done as a matter of course, with no fuss. A hitch. Ruth realised that she had become something mechanical, without feeling. Once set in motion she had to go on, however stiltedly, like a clockwork figure grinding again and again against a skirting board. Had someone asked her why she must proceed, she would have had no ready answer. She did not know why really she could not face a third child, a third pregnancy, only that it was something she simply could not undertake.

She trudged through the day. The psychiatrist asked her questions which she answered automatically, as if she had already learned the answers off pat. He told her he would let Mr Burnside know that a third child would place an intolerable strain on her nervous system. Once she had put on her coat and stood up to leave he asked her, 'Is your husband well-off?'

'I suppose so. Adequately. I mean, we seem to manage,' Ruth said, taken aback. Money was not something she generally thought much about.

'I only ask because it seems to me that you would benefit from some extra help with the children. If you could find a girl to come in, even if it wasn't every day? That would give you some time to yourself. You could play your piano. I think you're overtired.'

Ruth felt a rush of gratitude and relief. Tears stung her eyes. At last someone understood. Overtired. Of course that was it. She wasn't a hopeless mother or a wicked woman or a terrible wife. She wasn't an automaton, unfamiliar to herself. She was just overtired.

In Putney she wrote a note to Iris, asking her to come and stay. The wartime habit of her childhood, which meant using the telephone only for emergencies or immediate plans, had stuck with Ruth. That night while they were undressing she asked Harry, 'Is it all right, darling, if Mummy comes next week for a day or two? Only I've got to have a little op, the doctor says, and they'll need to keep me in overnight.'

Harry stopped undoing his cuff links and came at once to her side. She could smell him, an innocent smell it was, like soap.

'Ruth, Speckle. What sort of operation? Not something serious? We can get Verity to refer you to the best—'

Ruth interrupted him, 'It's just a women's thing. It's nothing. Nothing to worry about, honestly. We don't need to concern Verity.'

'If you're sure. Of course your mother can come.'

The anaesthetic was like being dragged underwater, as if someone stronger were pushing and pushing her down below the Plimsoll line of consciousness. When she came to she could not remember where she was, nor why. A nurse offered her some sips of water. Her head was leaden. She seemed to smell gas and a sort of burnt rubbery smell. Then she went back to sleep. When she woke up Harry was there, stroking her arm. He smiled gingerly.

'What time is it?' she asked him.

'Nearly six,' he said.

'Six in the evening? It can't be.'

'It is. You've been asleep.'

'How long have you been here?'

'Not too long. Don't worry about that, darling.'

'Are the children all right?'

'Of course they are, darling. You've only been gone today.'

'Oh yes. I couldn't remember.'

Back at home Ruth felt weak. Her limbs were heavy and she kept bursting into tears. Iris was uncharacteristically gentle. She brought tinned consommé up on a tray and kept Isobel amused with colouring books and follow-the-dots, while dandling Lem. When she left on the Friday, Ruth clung to her neck.

'I wish you weren't going, Mummy,' she said plaintively.

'Darling. Well, you must come and see us soon.'

On Saturday Verity appeared.

'Poor you,' she said after lunch, while Harry was out in the garden pushing Isobel on the swing. 'You do look pale. What was it that you had done exactly?' She turned her pale gaze on her old friend.

Ruth blushed. 'Nothing. I mean, a little women's thing. D and C, I think it's called.'

'Ah, yes,' said Verity.

Verity knew, Ruth understood all of a sudden. She felt her groin and underarms prickle with fear. If she begged Verity not to tell Harry, she would incriminate herself irrevocably. Yet if she said nothing, she ran the risk that Verity might tell him, or at least voice her suspicions. The only way to prevent anything being said was to make sure that Harry and his sister were not left alone together for the rest of the day.

But there would be other days, she understood with a sinking heart. She could not keep them apart for ever. There would be family lunches in Richmond when they might find themselves alone together for a little while. There was the telephone. They could meet for lunch during the working week, as they did occasionally. Then one day Harry might come home from work with an unfamiliar expression on his dear, open face, a look of utter bewilderment and pain that his wife had so betrayed him. This was something that Ruth could hardly bear to imagine. She could not bear to think of him, travelling home towards her one rainy evening, with the knowledge of what she had done newly lodged in his heart. She could not stand the thought of coming into the hall to greet him and seeing at one glance that he knew. She understood that ending the pregnancy was not something she had done only to herself.

The day went on. Verity stayed for tea but left soon after.

Ruth put the girls to bed and came down to make a start on her and Harry's supper. As she was laying the table it came to her that she had no choice, now that Verity had guessed: she had to tell Harry herself. She must tell him before Verity had the chance, which meant today. And so, when they were sitting together on the sofa after dinner, with a record playing quietly on the gramophone, she told him the real reason that she had been in hospital.

Chapter 6

The nausea was bearable, she was used to that. It wasn't a deep or urgent sort of sickness, down in the pit of her stomach, as sometimes occurred. This was a fluttery, light nausea, struggling to gain a purchase in her chest and lower throat. If she ate dry oatcakes and drank weak tea it would go away; if she took coffee without food it would intensify. She found that gulping water, too, made it worse, even though she felt so thirsty. How could she be so thirsty when she had drunk so much the night before? She did not understand that. The thing was to take things slowly. No sudden movements. The neck was crucial: you could sit up and look around you, but you had to keep your neck rigid, as if you were wearing a surgical collar. Today the headache was worse than the nausea: insistent and metallic, like an iron brace tightening around her head. It sat behind her eyes, pulsing slightly, like a toad's throat. Any movement magnified its grasp.

When she sat up in bed she felt a lurching sensation. It wasn't just physical. Lying still, monitoring the complaints of her body, she forgot about the children, but the action of upending herself somehow triggered her memory. She reeled, like someone trying to pick up too heavy a suitcase. It was peculiar how missing them could simultaneously be experienced as a physical weight, an unmanageable load, yet also as a loss of mass, as if the whole centre of her had been scraped away. Ruth felt emptied by sadness but weighted down with it too.

Talking aloud helped a little. She coaxed herself up, like a nurse assisting a fractious patient.

'There you are. You're all right. That's it.'

She shuffled along to the bathroom. Sometimes brushing her teeth helped with the headache. Sometimes the headache spread into the roots of her teeth, tightening her jaw, clamping with pain. You could poke the toothbrush down into the pockets of your cheeks and scrub along the bone then. That helped. But it wasn't that kind of headache today. On other mornings brushing her teeth had to be undertaken gingerly. It was something she had always done automatically, with vigour: start at the front top, then front bottom, working backwards. But she had had to unlearn the process, gentle it, separate out its components. There had been mornings when the brush approaching her molars had made her sick and she had had to clutch the cool edge of the washbasin to prevent her legs from giving way.

After the headache and the nausea came missing the children. She missed the smell of their heads; the first sight of them flushed with sleep against their pillows. She remembered making Isobel's bed and straightening Lem's cot in the mornings, how the girls left residual pockets of warmth in the sheets where they had lain; how delicious those patches of heat had been to her hands, like the warmth of new bread through a paper bag. She missed holding their feet loosely in one hand when she read to them, the hinges of their knees loose, so that their calves could be jiggled up and down. She missed Isobel's questions, her certainty. She missed Lem's arms, skinny in her woollen cardigan.

Then the shame spread through her. It gripped her innards like a cramp, a shame so intense that very often it made her cry out. When she was a child she had gone to church with her father and stepmother sometimes, at the abbey in Tewkesbury. There was a tomb there, carved in stone, showing a man whose stomach was being gnawed by a rodent, presumably as a punishment for some wicked act during his lifetime; she had never known what. But this was how Ruth felt now, as if her entrails were being devoured by shame. The shame was so profound that it blocked all thoughts of Harry, obliterating his image like ink spilled on a photograph. Some nights Ruth dreamed of him and on those mornings when she awoke she wondered whether it was possible to die – literally die – from unhappiness.

Harry had not answered her letter.

After she had told him about the termination, he had not slept in their room with her again, retreating to the narrow bed in his dressing room, which had never been used for anything but laying out his work clothes. That first night she had heard sounds from his room. She had gone out onto the landing and stood there, shivering, not knowing what to do. Eventually she had opened the door quietly and gone to kneel by him without switching on the light. He had not answered when she said his name, so she had slid one arm under his neck and the other around his head and cradled his face against her chest silently. She had felt the wetness on his cheeks against the thin skin below her collarbones. He hadn't moved, that was what had been so terrible. If he had embraced her or even pushed her away she would have had hope. As it was she could not reach him: he lay completely still, immobilised with grief. He had not so much as glanced in her direction at the breakfast table the next morning, nor on the mornings that followed. His frame suddenly seemed clumsy, as if his sadness had heft. In the mornings his face was lined. Realising that he could not bear to look at her was what had made her decide to go away for the time being.

It was peculiar to be back in her grandparents' house. Waking in her old room, she wondered whether she wasn't trapped in some awful dream in which she was condemned always to be in this wintry house, always missing the people she loved most. Now that her grandmother had died her uncle Christopher had the place to himself. The haircord carpet on the upstairs landing had become threadbare in patches, whitening like an old dog's muzzle. The clock still ticked heavily in the tiled hall. Dust gathered in corners. The things Christopher collected were gradually filling the rooms, so that they could barely be used to sit or eat in. The dining-room table was covered with birds' nests, while one half of the sideboard was occupied by a game of chess which Christopher was playing by post with a friend from university, so that the pieces were only moved every few days, when a postcard came. Her grandfather's old study was piled high with papers. By the sofa and armchairs in the sitting room teetering pillars of books grew like many-coloured stalagmites. Even the little telephone table at the foot of the stairs was covered with pieces of paper, loose change, pencil stubs – and the odd slightly greying mint imperial – indicating that her uncle had absent-mindedly emptied the contents of his pockets onto it while taking a call. Only the breakfast room remained as it had been when her grandparents were alive. They now took all their meals there.

She had gone from London to her father's house, leaving the children with Harry's mother, while he was at the office. Ruth had lied to her mother-in-law, saying that her stepmother had broken her ankle and that she must go to help out for a day or two. She hadn't thought anything through. She hadn't thought how long she would stay away, nor what she would tell Harry; she hadn't dared to think how things might be when she got home. All she knew was that home was insufferable at present.

Neither her father nor his wife asked her why she had come, but on the third morning her father put a hand on her shoulder.

'It was lovely to see you, darling. But you don't look awfully as if you're enjoying it here and we thought, perhaps, you might like Helen to run you to the station when she goes up to Malvern this afternoon?'

He had reddened slightly.

'Yes, of course,' said Ruth.

'I expect they'll be needing you at home,' Helen had added, helpfully.

'Yes,' said Ruth.

So she had gone with Helen, but instead of getting on the train she had waited until her stepmother's car was out of sight and then taken a taxi to her uncle's house. She had not planned to stay on in Malvern, but she did not feel ready to go home, not yet. When she got to the house Christopher was not there. It was too cold to wait outside. She did not know what time he generally came back from work, so she pushed a note through the door:

Dear Uncle Christopher,

May I come and stay for a few days? Please don't mention this to Daddy if you speak to him before you see me. I will be at the Abbey Hotel in the meantime.

Love,

Ruth

She hid her case by the back door and walked up to the hotel to wait. A little under an hour later, after she had asked the elderly waitress for a second pot of hot water to replenish her tea, Christopher appeared.

That had been more than three weeks ago. On the first morning she had written the letter to Harry, a long letter asking his forgiveness. She had written the letter in bed, the paper propped on a tea tray on her knees. After posting it, she felt as though she were exhaling for the first time since leaving Putney, as if she had been holding her breath for weeks. She felt unencumbered, light. She decided to walk to the very top of the hill, even though she had no scarf or gloves. The steep climb warmed her a little. From the summit she could see the counties far below, stretching away to either side, the fields fading from vivid greens and browns until they blurred into a single colour, the hazy grey-blue of the distance. She leant into the wind. It occurred to Ruth that if she were to let go, to simply lift her feet, she could surely float down like dust, or like a leaf, the wind soft and cosseting, and the clumps of trees below would receive her, yield to her form, like moss.

Verity was surprised by the monotony of looking after small children. She had always enjoyed seeing her nieces, laughed at their little antics, and been suitably amused by the humorous tales Ruth and Harry told of them. But being virtually alone with them all day – Mrs Lane kept an eye on them for only an hour or two each morning – was a different thing. No one knew what to do quite: whether Harry should employ a nanny for the duration, or if his sister and sisters-in-law would be able to manage the children between them, until things were more decided. Verity was the only one who worked, of course, so it was only for this one week that she could step in.

Was it captious to observe that Isobel was really rather maddening? The child was excitable, bossy and quickly moved to tears, a temperament very different from the Longdens, although she looked so like her father. The baby was quieter, only staring around darkly like a bushbaby. Emily was the opposite of her sister and utterly unlike Harry in colouring and appearance. Verity had wondered lately if she was in fact his child. She wouldn't put anything past Ruth now.

It was obvious that Ruth had been having an affair. Why else would she have committed the terrible, immoral act which had precipitated her departure? It amounted to murder practically: it was unconscionable. Thinking back over the past few times she had seen her sister-in-law, Verity remembered Ruth as increasingly silent and edgy, almost as if she was becoming uncomfortable among the Longdens. As well she may have been!

Heaven knows, they were accommodating enough, as a family, always deferring to Ruth if questions about music came up, never criticising that peculiar mother of hers. Poor old Harry hadn't got a clue of course.

That was why she had taken the letter. It had arrived in the morning's second post, after Harry was at work, and Verity had recognised the writing at once. It was lucky that she was here when it came, to protect her brother. She had no intention of opening the letter, naturally; she wasn't the sort of person who would read private correspondence. But something about its weight – it was pages long evidently – together with a slightly frantic quality to the writing on the envelope, gave her the strongest feeling that there was a confession folded inside it. And Verity believed that learning his wife had been unfaithful would destroy Harry. He had burdens enough already.

Verity now regretted having confided in Ruth. She had told her about the affair with Peter soon after it began, three years ago. Peter's situation was a delicate one. It was important that no one at the hospital should learn that they were lovers, for the sake of his professional position and, of course, Verity's. Her discretion meant a great deal to him, she knew. There were no children from his marriage, for his wife had begun to suffer various health crises soon after they first began to live together. Mental problems. There had been hospitalisations, rest cures; he had tried everything to restore his wife to health, but even during her best times she had become too fearful to leave the house and at her worst – at her worst there had been smashed crockery, awful scenes, even attempts on her own life. It was terribly hard for Peter. Not only did the onerous duty of care fall to him, but his own manly impulses found no outlet within the marriage. Verity was able, at least, to provide him with some respite, some comfort.

She had told no one at work about the affair, but Ruth was her oldest friend and an ear at safe remove from the hospital.

Verity guessed that Ruth would tell Harry, but she knew her brother would keep the matter to himself.

'D'you not mind, that he's married?' Ruth had asked.

'Of course I do. Dreadfully. It means we can't ever be together and he's so unhappy at home. Sometimes I mind so much I think I'll have to run away.'

'And do what?'

'Oh, I don't know. Just be somewhere else, somewhere where he isn't. Seeing him most days at the hospital makes it harder somehow. You'd think it would make it easier, but it doesn't.'

Ruth felt herself reddening. 'Have you confessed? Does Father Leonard know?' She knew she shouldn't ask, but she could not help herself.

'My conscience is clear,' said Verity smartly. 'Peter's life would be unendurable if it weren't for—'

'No, quite,' said Ruth. 'It's your ... I didn't ... Quite.'

That had been a long time ago. They hadn't discussed it since, and although Ruth tended to ask after Peter, if they found themselves alone together, she did not press Verity on the subject. Harry, if he knew, had never so much as alluded to it. Anyway, she reflected, her own case was so very different from Ruth's. Ruth was a mother for one thing. Her first duty lay with her young family. And she and Harry had obviously been happy together, unlike poor wretched Peter. Why Ruth should want anyone else, why she was prepared to risk jeopardising such happiness: it was a mystery. It spoke of a horrible greed in Ruth. Rapaciousness even. Yet that was clearly what she had done. But then look at the mother, Iris: she'd gone off with someone in the war apparently, and she was the most frightful flirt. Even at Harry and Ruth's wedding she'd batted her eyelashes at someone's uncle. The bride's mother! Ruth had always seemed so demure. But the apple doesn't fall far from the tree, thought Verity.

* * *

Christmas was only eight days away and Ruth had still heard nothing from Harry. She and her uncle had settled into a kind of routine. Tea they dispensed with. Instead, an hour or so before Christopher came home, Ruth lit the fire in what had been her grandfather's study and drew the heavy curtains against the dark outside. The curtains were paler at their inside edges, where the accumulation of many summers had bleached the material and roughened it. Once her uncle came in, they installed themselves in the warm study with a bottle of sherry, the paper folded at the crossword. Christopher was teaching her how to decipher the clues.

After the crossword was done and they had had their sherry, they went together into the kitchen. Ruth had never cooked with another person before. She'd hardly even seen a man in a kitchen, except her stepfather, Digby, who liked to go and investigate what was being prepared, lifting saucepan lids and aligning his beaklike nose above the pan. Digby liked puddings even though – or perhaps because – he was so thin. At their house there was often a treacle sponge or a fruit pie and sometimes queen of puddings, his favourite. At the very least there would be rice pudding and stewed fruit of some kind and always cream, served in the dented silver jug which had come down from Digby's grandmother. But Digby didn't actually cook, he just took an interest. Harry certainly never touched anything in the kitchen. It occurred to Ruth with a pang that he wouldn't even know where things were kept.

Christopher was entirely different. It was not only the novelty of the fact that he cooked at all, he also cooked novel dishes, things with abundant sauces made from cream and dried herbs and the odd dash of brandy or wine. He went once a month by train to Oxford, where he lunched at his old college with a university friend who had become a don, before visiting the covered market to buy provisions more arcane than Malvern could offer. At home he bought olive oil at the chemist's by the post office. He squeezed tomato purée into stews and sauces. He even used garlic. Ruth wondered how a provincial schoolmaster should have come across such exotic dishes. She supposed it was in some way connected with the two evenings a week, Mondays and Thursdays, when he changed out of his work clothes at about six o'clock, bathed, then set off in his shark-blue Standard Companion, whistling throughout. He never returned until the small hours, or sometimes only after dawn. Ruth would hear him whistling quietly in the kitchen – often it would be Mozart's horn concertos at this hour, tunes she never heard from him at any other time – as he made himself a cup of tea, before coming upstairs to get into his teaching clothes.

On these evenings, Ruth cooked herself an egg or made a jam sandwich, if she remembered, food she ate standing up at the draining board, her reflection in the dark glass of the curtainless kitchen window looking back at her like a ghost. When Christopher was at home they concocted supper together and ate at the breakfast-room table, with only a fork. She thought how the Longdens would disapprove if they could see her sitting at such a bare table, without side plates or place mats or even knives. While they ate, they talked about what they were eating. This too was new for Ruth: with Harry she had asked about his day then told him about hers, detailing amusing little things that the girls had done. With her uncle she now discussed how a dish might be improved upon, or better accompanied. The two of them generally left the dirty things stacked for the charwoman to do in the morning, then repaired to the study, revived the fire and sat with their drinks, playing cards or listening to a talk, a play or concert on the Third Programme. Ruth almost felt happy then. But when Christopher announced, by standing up and stretching, that he was going to bed, Ruth was invariably jolted from her contentment. Once he had gone upstairs, she had no buffer against the shame and the loneliness; no buffer except drink. The whisky decanter sat squat on the drinks tray, implacable in its cut glass, affecting grandeur with its silver name neck-lace. Next to it was a bottle of Dubonnet, untouched for years, then a decanter of brandy and another of port.

When Ruth poured the honey-coloured liquid – with its faint scent of warm tarmac – into her glass, she held the silver name-plate against the decanter so that it would not clink. She replaced the stopper with a careful sliding action so that it, too, would make no sound. She did not know why she continued to muffle the decanter like this. Christopher was too kind and too polite ever to question her drinking, or any other personal matter. It was unlikely anyway that he would have been able to hear the sound from another storey, with his bedroom door closed. It occurred to Ruth that she was concealing the sound from herself. If she allowed the silver tag to chime against the cut glass; if the roughened glass end of the stopper grazed the smooth throat of the decanter as it was replaced; if the whole clunked against the silver-plated tray heavily as she set it down: these sounds weren't quite polite, were not quite sober. Whereas the more silently she could pour herself the whisky, the more gracious and benign she felt, almost as if she were an estimable lady from another age, pouring a drink for an honoured guest.

While she drank she sat with a book on her knee, but she did not read. It was more of a prop than a pastime. Instead she tended to stare at the fire, or what was left of it, for she seldom added new coal to the grate once she was alone. The thing was not to think about the children. That was one of the things the whisky was for, to push away thoughts of the girls. They would be asleep now, that was something. She did not have to wonder what they were doing, who was looking after them, as she did constantly during the daylight hours. She had only to try not to keep picturing them sleeping, innocent in their brushed-cotton sheets, their skin as clean and smooth as soap.

Harry had not answered her letter. That meant he could not forgive her, did not want her to come home. These truths were too terrible to face by day. Late at night, however, with a warm shield of whisky between feeling and fact, she knew that she would not be going back. Then the longing for home lurched over her, like water spilling from too heavy a bucket. Christmas. To awake on Christmas morning in a house a hundred miles – more – away from the children. What if Isobel cried, what if she asked for her mother? Worse, what if she was brave and did not? Ruth made her way untidily across the room to the drinks tray once again. Some thoughts were too dreadful to be anaesthetised with whisky. Tomorrow, she decided, tomorrow she would telephone. She must not put off the call any longer.

Her own voice sounded brittle to Ruth, harshened by the tiled floor where the small telephone table stood, by the foot of the stairs. Even as Harry spoke she was aware of not taking in what he was saying. Only a general impression remained, a sense of relief but no actual words, as after a visit to a doctor. He seemed to be saying yes, that she could come and see the children on Saturday.

On Friday night she limited herself to just one drink after dinner, so that she would feel no ill effects the following morning. She took an early train, then the underground, then walked. The just-the-same-ness of the streets leading to her own seemed peculiar, like the false familiarity of a place in a dream. The holly and privet hedges were as they had been, some trimmed low so that neat front rooms could be glanced into from the street, others high or unkempt, imbuing the houses behind with a touch of mystery. The paint was fresh on some window frames and flaking gently on others, the wood silvery beneath, exactly as it had been when she was here last. This is what it must have been like for people coming home from the war, she thought. They must have imagined, as she had, that the sight of home would be comforting, enveloping, when the reality was only blankness. The place where your heart was, where all that you thought of and longed for resided, it was just an ordinary house in an ordinary street, like all the other houses.

This impression was heightened as she opened the low gate to her own house and walked up the path. The house did not care whether she stayed or went. It was entirely indifferent. Perhaps that was the case also for the people within. She hesitated before knocking. There were footsteps, a woman's; the shape of a person coming across the hall, their outline and features smudged by the coloured bumpy glass set into the door. Then the door opened and there was Verity. Ruth felt herself colour with disappointment. 'You're early,' said Verity.

'Yes. I caught the earlier train. I hope that's all right.'

'Come in.' Verity turned and called into the depths of the house, 'Isobel! Look who's come to see you!'

Then there was scampering and there was Isobel.

'Mummy! We went to Derry and Toms' and Father Christmas was there! He lands his sleigh on the roof to come and see the children! I told him I had a doll called Florence and he asked if she—'

'Isobel, let your mother take her coat off,' said Verity. She turned to Ruth, who was waiting awkwardly. 'Well, don't let's stand here in the hall all day. Come in and sit down. I'll go and see about a tray of coffee for us.'

Isobel took her mother's hand and led her into the sitting room.

'Where's Emily?' Ruth asked.

'My sister's a baby,' said Isobel importantly, as if she were telling this to someone who knew nothing of the family. 'Nanny Harris has taken her out in her pram. She takes her out in her pram every morning after breakfast.'

'But who's Nanny Harris, darling?'

'She's the nanny. Nanny Harris. Her name is Ellen but we don't call her Ellen. We call her Nanny Harris.'

'And where's Daddy?'

'Daddy's gone.'

Ruth felt her mouth fill with panic. 'Gone where? Where's he gone?'

'Just out. He's coming back later. Aunt Verity told him to.'

'Oh. Did she tell him to go out or tell him to come back?'

Verity came into the room with a plate of biscuits before the child could answer. 'Harry's got a new woman, Mary, who comes in at weekends to help. She cooks the lunch. Usually leaves him something he can heat up later for supper. He comes to Richmond for lunch on Sundays of course, so it's only really for Saturdays. Under-seasons everything fearfully, but worse things happen at sea. She's going to bring coffee through.'

Ruth did not answer. She stared at Isobel, hungry for the feel of her child, the weight of her.

'Tell me about Father Christmas. Was he fat?'

'Very fat.' Isobel giggled.

'And did he have a beard?'

'Of course he did! He's Father Christmas. Silly.'

A woman appeared with a tray. She was younger than Ruth had imagined, with dyed hair the coppery golden colour of mint humbugs. She looked at Ruth with undisguised curiosity. Isobel leant against her mother's knees, chattering.

At length she heard voices at the back door, the nanny and Mary, the woman with the dyed hair; strangers who now occupied her house. It occurred to her that it took three women to approximate to what she, one woman, had been.

'Ah, there's Nanny,' said Verity. 'I'll go and see whether the baby's awake.'

Ruth wanted to get up and run towards Emily, to push these women aside, but she seemed to have lost the power of movement or even of independent thought. She merely did as Verity said.

'My sister can't talk,' whispered Isobel. 'She won't be able to talk 'til she's bigger.'

'You will be nice to her, won't you, though?' said Ruth, urgently.

Isobel looked at her mother. 'That's what Daddy says! I am nice to her, all the time. I promised Daddy I would be,' she said.

Verity brought Emily into the room, holding her away from her body slightly, as if the infant were a bundle of damp washing. The baby's cheeks were red from sleep and her hair stood up from her head like a young hedgehog. As soon as she saw Ruth her mouth opened wide, but there was a silence before she began to wail, a pause which seemed to go on for a long time. Almost before the sound of her crying had formed, during the interminable intake of breath required to generate the wail, Ruth stood up and took her. She clasped the baby's tight little body against her chest and patted her back gently. Ruth was not going to cry in front of Verity. She was not.

'It's all right,' she said quietly, into her daughter's hair. 'It's all right.'

Chapter 7

There was only one bicycle, so they had to take it in turns. Emily was taller than her sister, despite being younger. When it was Isobel's turn she had to stretch her leg and tilt the bike sideways for her foot to reach the ground, making her always a little nervous of falling off, whereas it was just the right height for her sister. Going up towards the town was too steep. You couldn't pedal up the hill but had to wheel the bicycle beside you, and on the way down you went too fast, the brake whining in complaint all the way. But going along St Andrew's Road to the common was just right, not too far if you were the one walking and far enough to get the wind in your hair if it was your go on the bike. Halfway along, the road rose and then fell, in a perfect undulation: you didn't have to pedal for nearly fifty yards after you'd come over the gentle summit. When it was her turn, Emily liked to freewheel with her legs stretched out in front of her, while Isobel preferred gently to back-pedal, the chain clicking quietly, like the watch she'd had for her last birthday.

On summer days the long grass on the common waved like the sea. A regatta of small bright clouds sailed across the tall sky. Then the hills resembled dark cliffs and the white-painted bungalows along the western edge of the common were like seaside houses, their ample verandas looking out across the ocean of rippling grass. The girls left the bike on its side at the edge of the common and then ran about until they were too puffed to run any more. Emily liked to pretend she was an aeroplane or a train, but Isobel secretly imagined herself as a fairy or, if that seemed too impossible, a ballerina. She imagined that one day a tall man with a sad, distinguished face would walk across the grass and tell her that she was exactly the girl he had been looking for to star in the ballet he was putting on in London, at Covent Garden. He would have searched the whole land for years on end, and his sad look was because he had thought he would never find the right girl. He would have a droopy moustache probably. Later, after she had become a prima ballerina, the man might marry Mummy, Isobel wasn't quite sure about that part. She had heard that great dancers, at their curtain calls, had flowers thrown at their feet by grateful audiences. The prima ballerina had to curtsy again and again, scooping carnations and lilies and long-stemmed roses into her pale, graceful arms. The thought seemed almost too exciting to bear.

After running, the girls would lie side by side on their backs, looking up at the sky until the blue air seemed to form revolving particles which danced before their eyes. Sitting up, Isobel would sniff her knees. The sun made her skin smell different from usual, like toasted teacake: she liked it. Emily sucked her thumb and, with her free hand, twiddled the ends of her hair.

'Bell, if you could have anything in the world, what would it be?' she asked, her voice muffled by the thumb which she had only half removed.

Isobel had been dreaming of herself encased in layers and layers of tulle, her toes bleeding a little – heroically – into the shell-pink satin of her ballet shoes, but she did not like to share such reveries, especially as her sister knew she wasn't actually very good at ballet. At her weekly lesson she couldn't stop herself from thumping undaintily and she was always forgetting to point her toes.

'I don't know,' she said. 'What would you?'

'To go on an island for an adventure, I think,' said Emily.

'What kind of adventure?' asked Isobel.

'An animal adventure. With bears and crocodiles.'

'Oh.' Isobel was not very interested in animals.

Emily resumed her thumb-sucking in silence.

It always took a day or two to get used to being in Malvern. Isobel didn't like the food. At home Mary usually made them boiled eggs with fingers of toast for tea, but here there were baked eggs cooked with cream. It was hard to tell which bit was the cream and which the egg, because it all formed a sort of horrible gloop. Most of the food had a sour, oniony taste. The grown-ups talked about what they were going to have to eat, whereas with Daddy food just appeared; it wasn't a thing you really thought about much. At home there were always puddings, but Mummy and Uncle Christopher preferred savoury things, so here they only had fruit or smelly cheese for afters. They didn't even have a biscuit barrel for tea times. At home the girls loved the smell, like a new Elastoplast, when the biscuit tin was opened after they'd had bread with Marmite or a paste sand-wich. Here Christopher sometimes gave them two shillings each, for ices. Isobel always got a strawberry Mivvi, but Emily preferred a Zoom, even though it never lasted as long and her sister would still be taking tiny complacent bites out of her Mivvi long after Emily had only the pink-stained, banana-tast-ing stick left, to suck the last traces of flavour from.

The food had got a bit better now that Ilse lived at the house. At weekends, when she wasn't working, she made biscuity things and puddings. She produced tiny crescents of shortbread sprin-kled with caster sugar, and damp heavy cakes made with apples and raisins and cinnamon. Nobody had said anything, but Ilse was Uncle Christopher's girlfriend. The girls had guessed. That was why she lived in his house. But because they were not married, she didn't sleep in his bedroom. She had her own room, which had been the spare room. When Emily and Isobel came to stay she slept in the other bed in Mummy's room, so the girls could have her room. The girls didn't understand why the biggest bedroom in the house, the one at the front that had belonged to Mummy's grandparents, was left empty. Uncle Christopher hadn't even tidied his parents' things away, although they had been dead for years and years. His mother's brushes were still on her dressing table in the window and her clothes – including her fur coat – still hung in the wardrobe. Sometimes Isobel and Emily crept into the room and opened the cupboard and held the camphor-smelling fur against their cheeks. The coat felt cold and slippery, almost slimy, not at all like the fur of a living thing.

In Ilse's room there was a wall-mounted shelf with books in German. Instead of a dressing table she had a chest of drawers with a mirror in a wooden frame, decorated with marquetry flowers. The mirror was the only pretty thing in the room, apart from a tortoiseshell writing box with silver edges, where Ilse kept special thin paper for sending letters overseas. On either side of the mirror were framed photographs of old people. Isobel imagined they must be Ilse's parents, or even grandparents. It was quite hard to discover much about Ilse from looking at her things. She was nice though. She wasn't pretty, but she had the nicest hair, the colour of corn that has been rained on, and shiny as water.

From most people's things you could tell, at least a bit, what they were like. With Granny Longden you knew she liked gardens because she had books about gardens around the place; and you knew she liked going to Mass because she kept her missal on her bedside table, her favourite passages marked with prayer cards carrying pictures of the Virgin Mary and various saints, which made the missal bulge. Emily collected china ornaments of animals. In Mummy's room there were photographs of the girls everywhere, not even in frames but propped on the mantel shelf, the chest of drawers, even the windowsill. Uncle Christopher had his things all over the place; anyone could tell that he liked nature the minute they came into the house. The girls never went into his bedroom, even though no one had told them not to. Daddy had a picture of Mummy in his dressing room still, even though he was going to get married again.

Mrs Proctor was Daddy's fiancée. He had met her at Mass. She was a widow. She didn't have children of her own because her husband had died of a heart attack before they'd had a chance to start a family, only weeks after their wedding. Nobody had known there was anything wrong with his heart at all – he was a young man, apparently healthy – but he had just fallen over, dead. Although they had not known Mr Proctor, the method of his dying made the girls uneasy for a time, until they forgot about it. To begin with, for a week or two, it frightened them to think that if this could happen to anyone, so suddenly, it could even happen to someone of theirs.

Daddy had told the girls about Mr Proctor and said it had been a tragedy for Mrs Proctor, but when they talked about it by themselves later, they agreed that it wasn't as bad as all that. They thought that if Mr and Mrs Proctor hadn't been married for very long, then Mrs Proctor had not had time to get used to her husband. It was worse if someone you'd been married to for ages died, because then you would have had more of them to miss. It would be much worse to leave your favourite old teddy on a train than a new one. They thought that their mother probably missed their father much more than Mrs Proctor missed Mr Proctor. Mrs Proctor never looked as if she had been crying. Although Mummy was happier now, because she liked giving piano lessons. Daddy had sent her piano up to Malvern, in a removal van.

Mrs Proctor wore patent-leather shoes with neat buckles, and stockings that were probably meant to be the colour of legs but were actually almost orange, like the cellophane wrapped around a bottle of Lucozade. She told the girls with some pride that she never crossed her legs when sitting down, only tucked one ankle behind the other, and that they must do the same. They didn't know why. She never went outside without wearing a silk headscarf tied under her chin in a determined little knot. She had two Pekinese dogs. The dogs made snuffly noises all the time and their eyes watered, drawing ugly dark lines on the pale fur of their faces. They always looked terribly indignant. If you threw a cotton reel or ball for them they didn't go after it but sat stubbornly, looking affronted. Isobel and Emily didn't really mind that Mrs Proctor would be coming to live with them, but they would have preferred her to have some other sort of dog.

At Malvern they did not mention Mrs Proctor. They thought it might hurt their mother's feelings terribly, to learn that Daddy was going to marry someone else. And they were embarrassed for their father. Mrs Proctor was so old! She wasn't like a bride at all. Her hair wasn't very nice, it was stiff and dull-looking. Every week she went to the hairdresser for a shampoo and set, and then she sprayed hairspray from a gold tin onto her head each night, so the curl would stay in. They preferred their mother's hair, which swung and didn't have a style. The girls hoped that they would not have to be bridesmaids at the wedding. They got the giggles when they imagined the Pekineses being bridesmaids instead, dressed up in lace and ribbons, trotting along behind their mistress, looking furious.

In fact Ruth did know about Harry's marriage plans, but she had not mentioned it to her daughters because she did not want them to discover that she was angry with him and she could not trust herself to speak of it without resentment. She had never been cross with Harry before, because she had always had utter faith in his goodness. When he had suggested that they meet for lunch – he had something he wanted to talk to her about – she had consented at once. It was probably about the girls' schools, where they should go next. Ruth was keen to have a chance to put the case for Malvern, so that they could be near her. It was, after all, the same school that his parents had chosen for Verity: she was pretty sure that Longden tradition would persuade him, even if their proximity to their mother would not.

Oxford was halfway between them and they had agreed upon the Randolph Hotel at one o'clock. Her half-brother Jamie was up at Trinity reading mathematics; she would take him out for tea later the same day. Ruth had set off looking forward to the day. Not for one minute had she thought that Harry was going to suggest a reconciliation: by now she no longer even hoped for that herself. But she was fond of him still. She looked forward to seeing him, his dear face.

It was only when their main courses had come that Harry looked very intently at her, so that she could tell he was brewing up to saying something.

'You remember Father Leonard?' he asked.

This was not what she had been expecting. 'Of course I do!' she said. 'He baptised the girls, surely you don't think I'd forget? And he was often at your parents' house.' Ruth did not add that it had been he who had officiated at their wedding: it somehow seemed improper to mention it.

'I don't know whether the children have mentioned anything, but I have been, well, I've been seeing someone. We've got to know one another pretty well and I've grown very fond of her.'

'That's nice,' said Ruth brightly.

'And the thing is, we'd like to formalise things,' Harry added.

'What do you mean "formalise things"?' asked Ruth. She tried to smile, to look gracious.

'I mean to marry.'

'Gracious!' Ruth felt her face redden. She did not want to be with Harry any more, but somehow the idea of him marrying someone else seemed very final. She struggled to keep her composure. 'Goodness, yes, if that's what you want then of course I'm glad for you,' she went on. 'I suppose this means you're asking me for a divorce, does it?'

'We will need to sort that out, yes, but it shouldn't be too difficult. The thing is, though, that Valerie is observant, as I am, and we'd like to be married within the Church. It's been very difficult, my not being able to take Communion because of the separation.'

This was a rebuke.

'Golly!' Ruth heard herself say. These exclamations kept popping out of her mouth, making her sound ridiculous to herself, like an overgrown schoolgirl, or Joyce Grenfell. 'Surely you can't get married in the Church, though, can you, while I'm about? Does that mean you'll have to bump me off?'

'Don't be silly, Ruth. It wouldn't affect you in any way. I've talked it over with Father Leonard and he is of the opinion that the annulment would be granted—'

Ruth cut him off. 'Annulment? What are you talking about? You can't get an annulment! We've got two daughters, we—'

Now Harry interrupted her. 'Essentially, Father Leonard says that the marriage could be declared null *ab initio*, on the grounds that you did not give yourself freely. That you weren't consenting, fully, at the time of the marriage.'

His shoulders drooped. He looked miserable.

'Not consenting to what?' Ruth saw an image, suddenly, of Harry and herself in the Italian hotel room where they had spent their honeymoon. She remembered him kneeling on the floor by the bed, how she'd looked down, unabashed, at her naked hips on the edge of the bed, and at his hips between her legs. It had been more than consent, with her. It had been complete abandon.

'To having a family,' he said.

'What can you mean? I did consent to have a family. This is mad! I had a family. I had two daughters. Surely you can't have forgotten.'

'But then you did the other thing.'

Ruth could not answer. For the first time in several years she wanted a glass of whisky. Ruth felt the searing indignation that only a person in the wrong can experience.

'I think I was having some sort of breakdown then. You cannot imagine how much I have suffered as a result of what I did,' she said quietly.

'Yes. Well, we've all had a difficult time of it.'

'There were times when I thought I—'

He cut her off. 'The thing is, we've come to an accommodation. Let's not go backwards now. We've managed the separation and I believe I've been more than fair about your seeing the girls, having them to Malvern and so on.'

'Yes, but you—'

'Ruth. The annulment really won't make any difference to you. You'll still have the girls during the holidays and half terms and you can still come to London and see them at weekends occasionally. It won't make any difference.'

'But they will become illegitimate! Annulment is saying that we were never married and if we were never married then that means that they must be …' She couldn't bring herself to say the word.

'Actually not,' said Harry. 'The Church has it that children of putative marriages are legitimate.'

'What does that mean: putative? What are you talking about? I was your wife! We had a wedding, we … it wasn't putative. We were married. We were.' Ruth felt tears puddling in her eyes.

Harry sighed. 'I have come to believe that the marriage was not valid. That is what Father Leonard agrees.'

'Well, I don't,' said Ruth.

'Quite honestly, Ruth, that doesn't make any difference. It's out of our hands. I didn't have to tell you, you know; I could just have let things go ahead without even informing you. But I thought it fairer to let you know. This way, you will be able to marry again, within the Church, if you should ever wish to.'

'I wouldn't ever want to marry anyone else,' said Ruth. Her voice was louder than she had meant it to be.

Harry showed no sign of having heard her.

Neither of them had finished their food. A waiter hovered, judging whether to take their plates. Then he swooped in like a jackdaw and enquired as to what desserts they would like to order.

'Just coffee for me, please,' said Harry.

'Madam?' said the waiter.

'The same, please. No pudding, thank you.'

The waiter, conveying slight disapproval, flapped away.

They did not return to the subject of the annulment. Harry clearly believed there was nothing more to say, while Ruth felt too dismayed to talk about it any more. He asked after Jamie and her uncle Christopher. They limped on through their coffee, both relieved to conclude the lunch. As they parted under the glass canopy which stretched from the steps of the hotel to the pavement outside, he made to kiss Ruth's cheek. She recoiled.

After he'd gone she considered going back into the Randolph, to the bar, and ordering a large drink for herself, to calm her nerves. During the initial period of their separation she had drunk too much. It had gone on for almost three years. Christopher had been angelic, never made even a reference to it, although he must have known. It was only when she joined the choir that the desire to drink left her, simply evaporated. Ruth had wondered if singing choral music again, as she had when she was a girl, was a cure for the emptiness, like homesickness, which had so plagued her. Out for a stroll one warm evening she had wandered into the priory grounds and heard the choir practising through the open doors of the church. She had gone in and sat at the back listening. When they had finished singing and were making ready to leave, she went to ask if she could join.

'Perhaps one spirit replaced the need for the other,' Ilse had said simply, when Ruth told her about it.

She had become a member of the choir before becoming a member of the congregation. Harry did not know that she had abandoned his church and she saw no reason to tell him. She thought Harry might perceive her return to the faith of her girl-hood as a rejection of him – another one – and, more impor-tantly, she did not want to alert him to anything in her conduct which might prevent him from letting her see the children. To the Longdens, there was only one True Church. Apostasy was probably a terrible sin in their eyes; another to add to the cata-logue of her wrongs.

There had been no drama about her return to the Church of England. She had told no one except Ilse. It had hardly been even a decision, but more as if, out walking, she had simply taken one turn instead of the other. She liked the familiar words, especially the comforting liturgy of evensong:

> Lighten our darkness, we beseech thee, O Lord;
> And by thy great mercy defend us from all
>   perils and dangers of this night

During Holy Communion services she sat still, head bowed. She did not know what the rules would be, about taking Communion in one church having converted to another, but she supposed it could not be so bad, this way round. It made more sense to her that the wafer should be just that, a wafer; it symbolised Christ's body but no one claimed that it actually was his Flesh. She had never been entirely at ease with the doctrine of transubstantia-tion, which had always struck her as amounting almost to cannibalism. Even so, she was reluctant to participate in this part of the service, in case it was wrong. She wouldn't want to get the nice vicar into trouble.

Ruth did not go back into the Randolph, but walked instead to the High Street, to the music shop. She had more than an hour before she was due to meet Jamie. Ruth needed some sheet music for two or three of her more able pupils. The familiar inky order of staves and notes calmed her: the sixteenths, each with its little flag; the gentle arc of polyrhythmic scales; the way arpeggios in broken octaves looked like London taxis, whizzing along the narrow streets of the staves.

Jamie, when she saw him standing by the railings of Trinity, looked more like his father than ever. He had Digby's beakiness and height, the same gentleness and quiet humour. She had forgotten quite how fond of him she always felt. As they walked along Broad Street everyone seemed to greet him: two girls with long striped scarves, one in a skirt well above the knees, the other's hem almost touching the pavement; an older man with a florid complexion and a tweed coat, looking too hot on this mild afternoon; a dark-haired boy with thick spectacles. Ruth felt touched by her brother, glad that people liked him. His hair was long now, well below his collar. He rolled his own cigarettes from a tin of tobacco and fumbled in his pockets for matches. They went to a café up a flight of stairs, where you queued at a counter and then carried your own food and drinks to a table. There were bare floorboards and shiny pine furniture and the pottery was a dull greyish-blue and heavy. When Ruth lifted her cup to drink her tea, its edge was rough against her lips.

Jamie spoke of home. Digby's aunt Hilary had died a few months earlier. Her sister Billa – his grandmother – who was almost ninety, had been pressed into coming to stay with them. She had brought her last remaining dog, an elderly Dachshund with bowed front legs and eyes which had lost their shine and were filmy, like the bloom on a ripe plum. Birdle pretended to be frightened of this harmless pet, which spent most of its time asleep. Whenever Billa and her dog came into the drawing room, Birdle screeched and flapped his wings theatrically, so that even Iris was fed up with him. Jamie thought Birdle was jealous of Billa, because Billa and Iris got on so well together. Even Digby, who never complained about anything, complained that he had no one to talk to since his mother had arrived. Every evening after dinner Iris had been reading Charles Dickens aloud to Billa, until they had become gripped by a sort of story fever. Now Iris read an instalment for an hour or more before lunch and another in the early evening. Often the whole of dinner was spent talking about their favourite characters, who were invariably the villains.

'But hasn't your grandmother read them before?' asked Ruth. 'I seem to remember she was a terrific bookworm, always.'

'She has. But she says it's absolutely wonderful, because now she's so old she's forgotten all the plots. She says she wants to cram in as many books as she can, before she pegs out.'

'Gracious!' exclaimed Ruth. 'Think of saying that about your own life.'

'I know,' said Jamie. 'You can see why she gets on so well with Mum.'

They wandered out into the Cornmarket. Jamie offered to walk Ruth to the railway station. She asked whether he was enjoying Oxford.

'I love it. So much so that I'd like to stay on. Teach, if I can. What about you? Do you like being in Malvern still?' he asked.

'I didn't like it to begin with. It felt so far away from the girls, you see. But I'm terribly fond of my uncle. It's odd how things work out: I seem to have lived with Christopher longer than with anyone else in my life. Even Harry. And it's familiar to me from being there so much when I was a child and the girls seem to like coming, and I enjoy teaching the piano and …' She trailed off.

Jamie noticed the gap. 'And?' He smiled.

'And, I don't know. Nothing. But I do like it there, yes.'

Ensconced on the train with its prickly seats, she thought about what she had not said to her brother. She had not said anything to her children and would surely never be able to tell Harry. She thought that there was no one she could tell. Not her mother, nor any of the friends from the Royal College with whom she still corresponded; and certainly not her newer acquaintances in Malvern, the other choristers and people she had met through mutual involvement with music; nor the staff at the schools where she taught.

To have a secret, to keep a part of yourself hidden, was a lonely thing. All her life she seemed to have had secrets which kept her apart from others. At school she had not wanted people to know about her parents' divorce. Then she hadn't wanted Harry to find out about the baby. Latterly she had tried not to let people in Malvern know how broken she was, not to be living with her daughters, or even that she was, or at any rate had been, a married woman with children. She didn't see herself as a secretive person and yet she always seemed to have had something to conceal. She thought that Isobel and Emily were lucky to have each other to confide in. They would never have to bear secrets alone, as she had. And the world was changing so fast that the sorts of things she'd felt were shameful and private were talked about in the open now.

Jamie was so much younger than herself – and a boy – that she had never felt he could be someone she could talk intimately with. Iris tended to be preoccupied with her own life and not to invite private talk. Verity had been the friend Ruth had most trusted, but she had become so peculiar, partly because of being such an ardent Catholic and partly, Ruth supposed, because of her own situation as the mistress of a married man. Verity was a forbidden secret herself.

The train stopped and started: Charlbury, Kingham, Moreton-in-Marsh. Thin strips of cloud hung in the sky like sticklebacks in a clear stream, their undersides glinting in the dying light. Her own reflection appeared in the train window. This blurred other self seemed kindly, as if she had a spectral twin travelling along through the darkening fields beside her. She wasn't alone, Ruth reminded herself. Not alone not alone not alone. The words percussed in her head, keeping time with the *tat-ta tat-tat* of the train.

Chapter 8

Ruth gave private piano lessons and also worked as a peripatetic music teacher at two of the local schools. It had been outside the smarter, larger school that she first encountered Ilse, arriving on a bicycle in a belted mackintosh the colour of wet sand. The stranger, still coasting, had begun to unbutton her coat with one hand, while the other remained on the handlebars, steering. Ruth had noticed something about the woman that she had never remarked in another person before: her collarbones. Their line was like the silhouette of a flying gull. The woman, who was about her own age, had smiled, wished her good morning in an accent Ruth could not place, then dashed ahead into the uncarpeted corridors of the school, the heels of her lace-up shoes clicking. There was a naturalness about her and she had a pretty smile, like the actress who played the second Mrs de Winter in *Rebecca*.

They had not met again for several weeks. Then, joining the other staff for tea in the common room one Friday, Ruth had found herself standing next to the same woman.

'Hello,' said Ruth. 'I think we met the other day? I'm Ruth Longden.' She extended a hand.

'Ilse Erhard. I am teaching German.'

'And I am teaching the piano,' Ruth replied, smiling.

'What is the name of this biscuit, the pink one?' asked Ilse.

'I believe they're called Party Rings,' said Ruth. 'They're for children really. They come in yellow too, look. And brown. I can't see a brown one though. Must have all been eaten. People think they'll taste of chocolate because of their colour, but they don't, not really. Just of sugar.'

'The colours are nice,' said Ilse.

'The colours are nicer than the taste,' smiled Ruth.

Ilse smiled in assent. They stood munching. Somehow during the next quarter of an hour or so they had established that they both enjoyed the cinema and had arranged to meet for Saturday's two o'clock matinée.

'At the Picture House, then? Quarter to, in the foyer?' said Ruth, gathering her music case.

It was the silliest film, a caper about doctors and nurses. Ruth felt slightly embarrassed that English humour should be so daft, so saucy, as if she, being English, were responsible. But Ilse laughed all the way through, as though Bernard Bresslaw and Joan Sims were the funniest people in the world. The spirit of the film stayed with them during tea afterwards, where they found themselves laughing at everything in the Blue Bird café: the resolute bad temper of the waitress, the paper doilies which kept sticking to the bottom of their cakes.

Saturday afternoons became their regular rendezvous, only interrupted on the occasional weekend when the children came to Malvern. They watched a film – *Born Free*, *Alfie*, several *Carry Ons* – then went out for tea and talked. *Fantastic Voyage*, with Donald Pleasance, was a favourite. Ruth said it was dotty, a word Ilse had never heard before. Thereafter it was always referred to as 'the dotty film'. When *The Sound of Music* came round again, Ruth wasn't sure what to do. She had seen the film during its first run, and been moved by the family's refusal to kowtow to the Third Reich. Now she wondered whether to propose a different outing, perhaps to Worcester or Gloucester, to see a cathedral.

She did not know how Ilse would feel about the war. It was something they had never talked about. Ruth knew only that

Ilse's parents had had her late in life and that her father had died a few years previously and that she was an only child. Ilse wanted to see *The Sound of Music*. She had heard that Julie Andrews was fantastic. Yet afterwards Ruth was hesitant. Generally they discussed what they had seen, recalled favourite scenes. Now she could not think what to say.

'I liked the dresses she made, out of those curtains,' she ventured.

'I liked the countess. She was so gracious,' said Ilse.

'Gracious in defeat,' said Ruth.

'Is that what you say? I didn't know that phrase,' smiled Ilse. 'I have never been to Salzburg. It looks beautiful, the mountains and the lake.'

'Is it far from where you grew up?' asked Ruth.

'Yes, very far. It's on the other side of Germany. Austria. I was near the coast in the north, close to Denmark. Pasture country, with cattle. It was a farm where I grew up. Meadows, flat. Here in Malvern is the highest I have ever lived. It's far from the sea here also.'

'Have you been to the coast in England?' Ruth asked.

'Only to Harwich, from the boat, at the start of each term and the end. But I never spend any time there; I just get off the boat and onto a train, or onto the ferry. Once I came to Dover because I'd been on a little tour in Belgium with my mother.'

'We should go!' said Ruth. 'We should go somewhere wild and lovely, like Wales or Cornwall. The Atlantic's much nicer than the Channel.'

'I would like that,' said Ilse.

At the end of their outings they would part straight after tea, but after a time they simply fell into step and carried on their conversation. They walked along to Malvern Wells or over the hill to West Malvern, to see the sun setting. It reminded Ruth of the walks she had taken with Verity, when they were girls. The week which elapsed between their Saturday outings began to sag, to seem too long a time. Christopher still absented himself without explanation on Monday and Thursday evenings, as he always had. One Saturday, after tea, Ruth invited Ilse to dinner the following Thursday. She made chicken with mushroom sauce and Uncle Ben's rice, copying a recipe of her uncle's, adding a dollop of cream and a dash of Worcestershire sauce. She stacked kindling and logs in the grate in the study and laid a tray ready with coffee cups and a silver jug for the milk, and mints in silver paper arranged on a blue and white saucer. It was odd to feel nervous – there was nothing, after all, to feel anxious about – but Ruth had never invited anyone to the house until now. It was not a house accustomed to visitors.

After eating they came to sit by the fire. Ruth found it difficult to sit still. Seeing Ilse here felt very different from meeting her in cafés and at the cinema. She found that she was restless, almost irritable. Nothing seemed quite right. The meal had looked pale and sludgy, and now the fire wasn't burning properly, as if the logs were damp. Ruth went to the grate and knelt to work the small leather and brass bellows. After a few minutes of ineffective squeezing Ilse put down her coffee cup and came to crouch beside her at the hearth.

'Shall I try?' she asked, making to take the bellows from Ruth's grasp.

'Do,' said Ruth, shifting a little to one side. 'My mother always says that all women believe they have exquisite taste, but all men think they're brilliant at making fires. Actually I don't think I'm very gifted in either department.'

'Well, I am good at making a fire, but I think my taste is not so good,' laughed Ilse.

It was then that the oddest thing happened. As Ilse took the bellows, Ruth turned towards her, balancing on her heels and – entirely without thinking, as if compelled by an agency not her own – reached across and put her hand on her friend's cardigan, over her right breast. As she did so she experienced a sensation of relief all through her body, as if she had been seasick before and now was able to right herself, returned to the safety of land. Neither of them said anything and neither of them moved.

Then Ilse leant forward and kissed Ruth's mouth. Kissing a woman was quite unlike kissing a man. Ruth was astonished that it could be so different, when it was doing the same thing. It wasn't just the softness of Ilse's mouth, the smoothness of her skin; it was the smell of her, the smallness of her nose and chin, the way they fitted against her own. The feel of the other woman's hair falling against her cheek. Even her breath was softer. Ruth seemed to be holding her face at an unfamiliar angle and realised that this was because she wasn't having to reach upwards, because they were the same height. Ilse's tongue against her lips was light and darting, less muscular and somehow less human than a man's tongue. It felt more urgent, like a butterfly captured between the palms of her hands, impatient to be set free. While they kissed she did not let go of Ilse's breast. She felt its surprising lightness now, and the nub of Ilse's nipple through the wool.

It all seemed entirely right and natural. Nothing they did next seemed so unlike anything that Ruth had known before as the kissing had. The kissing was the only unfamiliar part. To be naked in someone's arms, once they had undressed, to caress and taste a body and reach into its secret places: what difference did it make, whether it was a man or a woman? The desire was the same, the release from desire was the same. Ruth felt only joy and good fortune to have met someone so altogether lovely, someone she wanted to talk to and laugh with, whose body she longed to lie beside and reach for, whose curved back and legs slotted so neatly into the crescent of her own receiving stomach and arms later, through the long night when they went to her room.

On both the nights when Christopher went out, Ilse began to come over to the house. They talked, cooked, ate and made love, sometimes in Ruth's bed and sometimes in front of the fire in the study, as they had the first time. On occasion some chance touch, a hand brushing against a wrist, set off a secret signal and they found themselves on the chilly bare tiles of the hall floor, kissing wildly almost before Ilse had taken off her coat. They had even, more than once, made love on the breakfast-room table. Ruth was taken aback every time by the beauty of Ilse's body, the long curve of her hips, the voluptuous, surprising darkness of her nipples, the way they were at once firm and soft, like the leaves of a succulent. The enveloping softness of her arms. The heat and smoothness inside her. Afterwards they often bathed together in the big cast-iron bath, whose taps had dripped unchecked for decades, creating lengths of rough verdigris in the smooth white enamel. Ruth loved to wash Ilse's hair, sitting behind her, filling a tall tin jug with rinse-water, pouring so that her wet hair lay fanned across her shoulders, glistening. Ilse had peculiarly long knobbly toes, with distinct gaps in between, the second toe ever so slightly longer than its neighbours. Ruth had never seen toes like these before, and she felt great affection for them.

Ilse began to teach Ruth some German. The words felt novel in her mouth, pleasing but unfamiliar, like a food she had never tasted before. *Zwischen. Nützlich. Die Uhr ist stehengeblieben. Und so weiter. Allerlei.* The word she liked best so far was *Schlittschuhlaufen*, because it sounded so very like what it described, the swish of metal skates on ice. Some German was already familiar to her – even if she did not understand the meaning – from her musical studies, or from choral pieces: '*Entsündige mich mit Isop, dass ich rein werde; wasche mich, dass ich schneeweiss werde.*'

Ruth knew that German had been the working language of many of the composers she most loved. She was acquainted with some of the Bach cantatas and masses, and had seen most of Mozart's operas. After dinner in the evenings, she and

Christopher often listened to opera on gramophone records. She had heard – although she did not much care for – the romantic Lieder of Schubert and Schumann. But she had never considered that these were the words Mozart and Beethoven and Bach had actually spoken; that these were the sounds which came out of their mouths when they bought a loaf of bread, or scolded a dog, or made some affectionate remark to their children. When they muttered, or added up a column of figures, or called out in their sleep.

What Ruth and Ilse did not already know about one another became for each a treasury of charm and wonder. Nothing was too trifling.

'Did you have plaits when you were small?' asked Ruth one day.

'Of course! I was a little German girl. What do you think? I had two plaits and sometimes they were pinned on top of my head.'

'Really?' Ruth was never sure when Ilse was teasing.

'No, really. I did. Next time I go home I will bring a photograph.'

'Oh do! I'd love that,' said Ruth.

Ruth would usually have had Isobel and Emily for half term, but their father had announced that he wanted to take them abroad, to Brittany. The girls had never been outside England before and they were very excited. They were going to have a cabin on the boat, with beds in it and a porthole, too, probably. Ilse stayed in Malvern for half terms, only going back to Germany to visit her mother for the longer holidays. Ruth suggested that she and Ilse should go to the coast for a few days. It wasn't far, to Pembrokeshire; they could stay in a guesthouse in Tenby and make excursions.

Travelling together made Ruth feel shy. In the railway carriage they did not know how to arrange themselves quite. Ruth sat by the facing window, imagining that her friend would sit next to her, and they would enjoy the view together, but Ilse took the seat opposite, which meant her back was to the engine and she wouldn't be able to see where they were going, which wasn't nearly so nice. So Ruth suggested they swap places and then the tops of their legs touched as they moved in the confined space, making Ruth blush. Ilse looked suddenly unfamiliar, the bright sheen of her hair, the line of her jaw, the neatness of her ankles, almost formal, like a stranger's. Ruth wondered if this was how Ilse seemed to other people, whether she seemed ordinary or foreign or – as she appeared to Ruth – both. She looked so self-contained, her modest optimism evident in the pretty curve of her mouth; her lovely tawniness. To Ruth she seemed infinitely touching. More than anything she wanted never to disappoint her.

It rained for the first two days but they didn't mind. They explored the town and walked the shoreline beneath it, taking off their shoes to go barefoot on the beach at low tide. The dense wet sand was cold and hard beneath their feet. Their room had narrow twin beds; they slept in the one closer to the window, their legs entangled. The light coming through the scant floral curtains on the third morning announced sunlight. They bought a pork pie and some apples, a picnic to take to Manorbier, where they planned to spend the better part of the day.

'Are the beaches like this at home?' Ruth asked as they sat at the far end of the crescent of sand at Manorbier.

'It smells the same. I love that smell of the sea. But it's flatter, where I come from. Bigger sky. There are dunes with spiky grass and very long beaches. It can be quite windy. Very windy. Before you reach the sea you sometimes see the sails of boats, and they look as if they are gliding through fields, before you can see the water.'

'I remember dunes from when my grandfather read me *The Riddle of the Sands*,' said Ruth.

'I don't know that book,' said Ilse.

'There's no reason why you should,' said Ruth, suddenly regretting that she had mentioned it. 'It's not all that good anyway.'

'There are islands not far out, where people come for holidays. Near my house there are poplar trees and farms. Some of the old houses are like in England, you know, with wooden frames.'

'Half-timbered. My father lives in a house like that.'

'Yes. *Fachwerkbauweise*. In the town the buildings are tall, taller than here. They have little windows at the top, and orange roof tiles.'

'Did you go to town much?'

'Not so much. It was safer in the countryside and I had anyway to help on the farm. My school was in the village and there were enough shops there to get things you needed, like bread and soap, although they didn't always have those. Not soap anyway. We were lucky because we could barter: we had our own eggs and milk and some vegetables. People came to us, they brought things.' Ilse leant back on her elbows, looking out at the slate-green sea. 'Our cows were brown and white, not brown like chocolate, but brown like old brick. Sometimes a cow would have white lashes on one eye and dark lashes on the other; I always liked those ones. And we had chickens also. Once a cockerel went mad and became fierce, like a dog. He chased me when I came from school. I was quite frightened, because with a dog you know it will bite, but with a bird you don't really know what it will do.'

'I used to hate my granny's hens when I was small,' said Ruth. 'I dreaded having to go and collect the eggs.'

Ilse laughed and put her hand on Ruth's shoulder.

'I would have got the eggs for you. I used to do that every day. And feed the rabbits.'

'What happened to the mad cockerel?' asked Ruth.

'My mother killed it. I suppose we ate it, but I don't remember.'

'Did you always like girls, d'you think?' Ruth asked her. She had never asked before, but being away from where they both lived felt freeing.

'I think yes. I never was interested in a boy. A couple of girls came to help on the farm when I was about twelve years old. BDM, from Lübeck. One of them, Hannah, she was very beautiful. My mother taught her how to milk the cows and I hid behind one of the stalls, so I could watch her. She used to sit with her cheek pressed up against the side of the cow. The breath of the cows smelled also like milk. With her sleeves rolled up, you know, you could see that her arms were strong. There were little golden hairs ... I used to like to watch her.'

'Like Tess of the D'Urbervilles.'

'She stayed on our farm for the summer and the harvest and then she went back to Lübeck in October. I don't know what happened to her. Lübeck was hit, very badly, but I don't know ... I never saw her again.' Ilse stood up. 'Shall we walk now?'

Ruth stood. 'And then what happened?'

'Well, then I grew up and went to Bremen, to the university, to study. And that was my first love affair, at university. That was Ursi.'

'And did you love her?' Ruth felt jealous suddenly.

'I liked her very much. Yes.' Ilse glanced at Ruth. 'But not as much as I like you. I like you better.'

'I only like you,' said Ruth. 'I like you best of everyone.'

They stopped on the sandy path and kissed, not caring if they were seen. But there wasn't anybody there, just a lone gull, circling above the headland, and the sound of the waves.

Back in Malvern, Ruth telephoned the girls.

'Did you have a nice time?' she asked Emily.

'I tried snails!' she replied. 'I tried snails, but Isobel wouldn't.'

'And did you like them?'

'I didn't hate them. I only had one. It was like rubber with butter on it. We didn't go swimming because it was too cold. Do you want to speak to Isobel?'

Ruth said that she did. Isobel was not so easy to draw out as her younger sister.

'It was nice,' she said. 'We saw some donkeys and Mrs Proctor bought us dolls with Breton costumes on. And we had water ice.'

'Who's Mrs Proctor, darling? Your nanny, d'you mean?'

'She's … I don't know. Not a nanny.'

'Oh.' Ruth understood suddenly what she was. She felt a stab of pain, not so much because she was jealous, but because she understood, now, why Harry had wanted to take the girls abroad. To soften the introduction to his woman friend, turn it into an adventure. The fact that he had not told her in advance seemed like a betrayal: he had had the girls when it was her precious turn to see them, and she had allowed him to, because it had been for a special treat. But now the treat turned out to be something else altogether. The knowledge that there had been four of them on the holiday – not three, as she had imagined – caused a jolt to her heart. She felt a twinge of guilt now, too, that she had been so happy by the sea with Ilse. Those days had been the first when she forgot to miss the children.

'What flavour water ice did you have?'

'Blackcurrant and raspberry. I liked the raspberry best.'

'Did Mrs Proctor have water ice?'

'I think so. I can't remember.'

'Did Mrs Proctor … Did you make sand castles?'

'Daddy did, with Emily.'

'Oh. That's nice.'

The line went silent while she tried not to interrogate her daughter. It was shaming to use a child in this way, Ruth knew. What most piqued her curiosity was that the woman was a Mrs. It seemed remarkable to her that Harry would have an affair with a married woman. But of course Verity had put aside her scruples on such matters, so it was not impossible that her brother should do the same. Ruth wondered about Mr Proctor, whether he had been left at home, perhaps with little Proctors; or perhaps he had been discarded long ago, or not discarded yet, but freshly lied to. She could not imagine Harry being party to such behaviour, nor that he could grow fond of a woman who would behave in such a way. It was bitter, to recognise that she didn't know everything about him, after all. But of course he did not know about her private life, about Ilse. It occurred to Ruth that this was what it meant, to separate: the love subsided so gradually that you hardly noticed it going, but what felt like a palpable loss was that you knew less and less about each other.

One evening over dinner, Christopher announced that he was to stop working full time at the beginning of the next school year. He would teach the sixth form only.

'I've got so many other things I want to do. It'll be a relief quite honestly,' he said.

Ruth wondered if the change was entirely of his own devising, but she said nothing.

'What I thought was, we might take a lodger. Make up the difference. This house is much too big for two really.'

If her uncle had said he was to train as an astronaut, Ruth could not have been more surprised.

'Not let Granny's room?'

'Don't look so horrified! No. The spare room.'

This was the room the girls used when they came. If a lodger arrived, there would be nowhere for them. Ruth felt herself colour and tears begin to prick her eyes. The idea of a third person in the house, a stranger, filled her with dread. She felt very powerless suddenly. She was used to thinking of the house as her house, but Christopher's plan reminded her that this was not so. Houses were for men. Harry had a house, still. Her father did, and Digby too. This was Christopher's house.

There would be no more cosy evenings alone with her uncle, cooking and listening to music. There would be someone else in the kitchen, the breakfast room, the study. A stranger would occupy the children's room, leave their wristwatch on the bedside table, their dressing gown hanging limply from the hook on the door. A stranger's toothbrush would command the washbasin, a stranger's nakedness fill the bath that she and Ilse shared. Ilse. She had forgotten about Ilse. What would happen? A lodger could not be expected to go out as obligingly as Christopher did, twice a week. How would she and Ilse ever have the house to themselves again, how would they meet, be lovers?

'What I was wondering is, do you know anyone?' said Christopher.

'Me?' said Ruth.

'Yes. Aren't there any unmarried staff at either of your schools who might be on the lookout for somewhere?'

'I don't know. I could ask.'

'We'd have to have a bit of a clear-out, I s'pose, if someone else was living here,' said Christopher. 'I mean I would.'

'Yes,' said Ruth. She felt too unhappy to speak.

'I thought I might keep the dining room, put most of my stuff in there. If I wanted to do some writing, I could do it in there, you see, at the table. The lodger could have the sitting room then, and you could keep the study. So you'd still have the gramophone.'

'You've obviously thought it all out,' said Ruth. It was the only time she could remember ever having spoken sharply to her uncle.

That night Ruth barely slept. She did not know what to do.

If she were to move out and take a room somewhere, there would be nowhere for her to have the children. She didn't suppose she would be able to afford to take a whole house of her own, not on the hours she worked. Perhaps she should look for a flat. Perhaps she should look for a staff job, with a fixed salary, instead of working on such an ad hoc basis. But there was no guarantee that such a job would come up, here in Malvern. She might be obliged to move, in order to find work, and then how could she be with Ilse?

She did not see Ilse the next day and the hours passed slowly. Then it was Thursday, and Ilse was coming to spend the evening. Ruth was too anxious to prepare dinner. Even before Ilse had stepped over the threshold, Ruth was in tears, sobbing against her neck, her mouth full of Ilse's hair, tears falling onto the shoulder of Ilse's wool coat.

'Hey, stop!' said Ilse, taking her by the shoulders, stepping back, holding her now at arm's length. 'I can't help you if I don't know what you're saying.'

'It's all ruined!' said Ruth. 'It'll never work, we won't be able to—'

'Wait,' said Ilse. 'Don't talk until I've come in and we're sitting down.' Ilse took Ruth by the hand and led her into the study and sat her down, only then taking off her own coat and the scarf she had loosely knotted around her neck. Then she stood with her back to the empty grate, her arms crossed. Ruth, still sniffling, told her about Christopher's plan. Ilse only smiled.

'I don't see a problem,' she said simply, when Ruth had finished talking.

'But I've just told you! It means that we can't—'

Ilse interrupted. 'No, it doesn't. It doesn't mean that. It means we can. The lodger can be me.'

Ruth said nothing while Ilse's words alighted, then settled, in her mind. She had stopped crying, but she could still feel a tickling sensation in the bridge of her nose. A large clear drip plopped from the end of her reddened nostrils onto her hand, which lay clasped in her lap. Without thinking, she smeared the hand on her skirt, and then wiped her nose against the back of the other hand, her eyes on Ilse throughout.

'But I don't want to live with you until you know how to use a handkerchief,' said Ilse.

Chapter 9

Iris and Digby sat on the river bank, she on an old fringed tartan rug which he had spread out for her, he a couple of feet away, having made a seat for himself by taking off his mac and laying it on the long grass.

'Player's please,' he said, grinning.

We really shouldn't smile too widely, at our age, thought Iris. It gives him the most alarming appearance and I suppose I look as bad. More like a grimace really. The teeth seem too big, like a mummy's. We actually are long in the tooth. She said none of this, but rummaged silently through her pockets for the packet of cigarettes, while her chain of thought ran on. I remember the children looking rather the same, when their milk teeth had gone, before their faces were developed enough to accommodate their grown-up teeth. She wasn't sure which children she had in mind, whether it was Ruth and Jamie or the grandchildren. Their childhoods all tended to merge. She took two cigarettes out, fumbled over a book match, then lit both. She passed one to Digby.

They sat in silence, contemplating the midges rising and dipping over the clear brown water. Very often they did not speak much. Iris – who had always loved chatter and gossip – was surprised to find how much she liked the silence. It was more restful not to have to talk all the time. Mostly they each seemed to intuit what the other was feeling. If anything, they were happier in each other's company now than they had ever been.

They had both got thinner with age, like a pair of old greyhounds. Digby's hand holding the cigarette seemed almost transparent, and the skin was speckled, like the breast of a song thrush. They had a picnic with them, of sorts: a couple of hardboiled eggs and some rather stale Madeira cake. Neither of them had much of an appetite, unless there was a treat at hand: potted shrimps perhaps, or anchovy toast. Iris had become somewhat vague about cooking, sometimes producing roast chicken or pheasant if they had company, but often, when they were just two, making only scrambled egg or opening a tin of soup for supper.

They liked it here at the river. If someone had told the young Iris that her greatest joy would one day be fly-fishing, she would have barked with derision. Digby had fished as a boy, and he had had a few days away every spring during his working life, while Iris went to London to see Ruth and have lunch with friends and stock up on Floris soap. It was only when he retired from medicine that he had time to fish more often.

'Shall I come, one of the days, and have a go?' Iris asked him one evening.

'If you think you'd like to. You might get awfully bored,' said Digby doubtfully.

They had no waders in her size. The pair Digby had bought for Jamie when he'd been in his teens were much too big for her.

'I'll never be able to walk in these,' she protested.

'You won't have to. We'll put them on when we get to the bank. Once you're in the water you just have to stand still,' Digby told her.

'Not all the time?' asked Iris with mock horror.

Digby laughed.

She liked the feeling of pressure on her legs as the water tightened around her and the way you could tell the water was very cold, and yet you didn't feel cold yourself. She very much liked the smell of the river, which wasn't so much an odour as a sensation, abundant and clean and cold. The water moved more quickly than she had thought it would, surveying it from the bank, and she had to lean into the current slightly and stand askance, to keep her footing. The smooth stones on the bottom were immensely slippery, like seaweed. To begin with, her line had tangled over and over again. Digby's sailed over the water in a lovely dripping arc every time, while hers got caught on an overhanging branch or stubbornly refused to go more than a few feet. The rod felt heavy in her hands, but Digby's looked weightless in his, as if he was casting nothing but light. I haven't the patience for this, she thought. I'll never be able to do it. Frustrated, Iris had held her rod against her side with one arm while she got out a cigarette with the other hand. She stood in the river, smoking and watching her husband.

The tobacco was warm and sweet and calming. As she stood, Iris began to notice things around her. A pair of damselflies darted over the trailing leaves of a willow, their bodies impossibly slender and bright. Some were the startling colour of lapis, like sharp blue needles embroidering the pale air. She was suddenly aware that there was no human sound in this place, only the noise of the water as it moved over the smooth dark stones, and the call of birds. She looked at Digby and admired the graceful rhythm with which he cast and his quiet concentration. A feeling began to spread through her body, starting in her chest: it was very nearly bliss. It's to do with the elements, it occurred to Iris. It's because I'm in all the elements at once: earth, water, air, even fire if you count my cigarette. She smiled at her own silliness.

After that Iris often went out with Digby. She wasn't a natural fisherman. Digby had told her that some of the best fly-fishers were women, that they somehow had a knack for it. But she did not. It took weeks and weeks for Iris even to cast correctly. She didn't catch any fish at all during her first season, but she loved it. She loved being out of doors, the water, the softness of the air. Fish were the least of it, or so she imagined, that first year. Then she had caught her first trout. Digby had had to help her bring it in: it was so much stronger than a dead fish looked as if it could ever have been. She had wondered at the grey and yellow-brown and pinkness of the fish, its markings so exactly like its home of river pebbles. Its heaviness was astonishing in her hands; it had seemed so weightless while in the water. After that she couldn't wait to get to the river every day.

Birdle sulked. Since Jamie had grown up and her mother-in-law had died, Iris and Digby hardly used the drawing room any more and she had brought Birdle's cage into the kitchen, where it was warmer and he would have company. Digby had cleared the broad windowsill behind the sink for the cage, so the parrot could see out of the window. Iris generally left the cage door open, but he seldom ventured out if she was not in the room.

If she came in he would climb out slowly, using his beak to guide and balance himself, then flap over to the dresser with a terrific squawking, as if in mortal danger. This fanfare always made Iris jump and she remonstrated with him about the noise, to no effect.

'What a racket!' she'd say.

And sometimes he would answer, before she had time to complete the sentence, 'Stop that din!'

Any letters or bills left on the side he would pick up with his beak and edge forward until they flopped onto the floor. Then he would swagger along to the fruit bowl. Apples did not interest him, but he was fond of grapes, although he often seemed to yank at the fruit, turn each grape round and round in his mouth, then eject it, without actually eating any. Digby had taken to leaving a saucer of sunflower seeds out for him and these he did consume, dropping the tiny zebra-striped husks onto the floor. Only then would he hop onto the back of a chair and thence to the kitchen table, if Iris was at the cooker or sink, or onto Iris's shoulder, if she was sitting down.

When the fishing season began and she was out most of the day, Birdle's behaviour changed. He would not talk. He did not come out of his cage when she got home in the evening, but affected to be studying his own foot, like a girl with a fresh manicure. He adopted strange attitudes, hunching himself with his back half turned to her, a reproachful Quasimodo. Then Iris would have to coax him. 'It's a pity you don't want to come out, Birdle, because I've got a spray of millet here for you.'

At length he would emerge, following his usual path to the table. Once there he would tear the day's newspaper into thin strips with his beak, or stand on one of the old saucers she used as an ashtray, knocking it over. Iris was sure he was doing these things on purpose, to annoy her. Once established on her shoulder he would yank at her hair – was he grooming her, or picking a fight? – until she abandoned whatever she was doing and stroked him on the back of his head.

'Stupid bird,' said Iris, exasperated.

Isobel and Emily were coming for a few days at Easter. Much as she looked forward to seeing them, Iris rather wished they weren't staying. It was her own fault for living in the back of beyond, of course: it was much too far for anyone except local friends to visit without spending at least one night. She loved seeing her granddaughters, but it was such an effort, having people – even family – to stay. They had to have proper cooked food and the fire lit in the drawing room, and things she didn't generally notice like the tarnish on the sugar bowl suddenly showed up and she'd have to get out the Silvo, or dust the good furniture. Get groceries in. Her daily would make up the beds and do the grate, at least, but still. She got tired.

It was peculiar being old. You woke up in the morning, always earlier than you would have wished, and felt just as you'd always felt, that the day ahead was long and full of possibility. But it took such an age to do everything. Sometimes, especially in the winter, just getting dressed and having breakfast seemed the most enormous effort. The mornings seemed to go by in a flash, with barely time enough to open the post and look through the newspaper. But the afternoons lingered on and on. Had time always buckled and folded in this way? As a child she remembered interminable mornings, longing for the afternoons, to get out of doors. Now it seemed to be the other way round.

Somehow you got used to the face in the mirror. It happened so gradually, the ageing. To begin with, you just looked tired, as if a nap would restore you, iron you out, make you less jowly, less creased. That went on for several years. Then the colour seemed to fade – the lips became barely distinguishable from the skin – and your face looked almost grey, like cheap jotting paper. You couldn't call it a complexion any more. Putting on lipstick seemed to make it worse, showing up hundreds of tiny crevices on one's upper lip, making one look grotesque, like an old clown. One's hair was most peculiar, at once coarser and more sparse. And the lines! But what Iris had minded most was when a snapshot taken by Jamie showed that her eyelids had lost their depth, disappearing somehow, making her eyes seem collapsed and narrow, losing the suggestion of amusement or interest they'd always carried. That had been a shock. The mirror was kinder than a photograph, because you came at it prepared, and the fact that you could move your features when you looked in the glass did something to obscure the changes in them.

A photograph was bad, but at least it was only your own face you had to contend with, your own dismay. Iris had always prided herself on not caring what other people thought, but this, she now recognised, had been a luxury afforded by the fact that she had generally been admired. On her last London visit she'd met her old friend Jocelyn for lunch at Wiltons – it was Jocelyn's birthday – and recognised a fellow diner as he was led

across to his table by a black-clad waiter. He took his seat opposite a younger man in a pinstripe suit, who looked like a
stockbroker.

'Don't look now, but isn't that Bunny Turner?' she
whispered.

Jocelyn swivelled. 'I believe it is. Haven't seen him for years.
You know everyone thought he'd killed his last wife? She fell
down the stairs, apparently.'

'Ssh!' said Iris. 'He'll hear you!'

'I don't mind if he does,' said Jocelyn.

They talked of other things. Before they left, while Jocelyn
went to the ladies, Iris couldn't resist going over to Bunny's
table, to say hello. It must have been more than twenty years
since they'd last met. She'd said his name and he'd looked up,
surprised.

'Can I help you?' he said.

He didn't recognise her.

'It's Iris,' she said. 'Iris Richards. Iris Browning, as was.'

'Of course, of course! I thought it was you, only I wasn't
expecting you here, or I'd have known you at once. How delightful to see you again.'

But it was too late for made up pleasantries. Before he had
spoken, when she'd said her name, a look of horrified disbelief
had clouded his face. However much he attempted to conceal it
with cordial words, that look, so involuntary in its displeasure,
had been his true response to the person she had become. A
person who was no longer beautiful.

She'd known she was old before, but never with such force. It
was much worse to have been beautiful, thought Iris; then you
had looks to lose. At least if you had been plain as a young
woman no one would ever have looked twice at you. It wasn't
only that people – men – no longer desired you. She wouldn't
have minded that so much. It was that people were altogether
less nice to you: strangers, people in queues, the other passen-

gers in a railway carriage. They didn't smile or acknowledge you in any way: they didn't seem to see you at all. And the funny thing was that this made you feel obscurely guilty, as though you'd done something wrong by growing old and unlovely, as though you'd squandered a wonderful gift. Iris thought of that phrase: *She's let herself go.* As if there was any choice in the matter.

Being outside, that was the thing. The antidote. In the open air, time didn't speed or falter, like a car in the wrong gear, as it did in the house. Time didn't matter at all, working in the garden or fishing. It wasn't that it stood still, exactly. More a sense that the sky and the earth and the river and the trees were bigger than passing minutes were, more important. They operated to a different clock. Seasons counted, but days and hours did not. What Iris liked about gardening, oddly, was the very futility of it, the sense that she was hardly more than an ant, in the larger scheme of things, scratching away at the soil, planting bulbs, dividing plants.

'Have you been at your father's?' Iris asked her granddaughters, when Digby had collected them from the station.

Since the girls boarded now at their mother's old school in Malvern, it was not quite clear to Iris where they actually lived during the holidays.

'Just for a couple of days,' said Emily. 'He and Valerie are going to Portugal for Easter. They've taken to travelling. He dropped us at King's Cross. They were going on to Victoria.'

'I loathe railway stations now,' said Iris. 'One can't find a porter anywhere and all the ticket collectors are blackies.'

'Granny!' Isobel exclaimed. 'You can't say that.'

'Why on earth not? It's true. I've nothing against blackies, only it's a bore when they don't understand what one's trying to ask them.'

Emily rolled her eyes at her sister. Digby never seemed to notice when Iris said outrageous things. He carried on filling the kettle, before setting it on the gas to make them all some tea. Birdle started to whistle shrilly, pre-empting the kettle.

'One of the ticket collectors at Malvern is a communist,' said Emily. 'Every time I went through the barrier – which was quite often, really, because I used to go over to my friend's house near Worcester at the weekends – he glowered at me like anything, I suppose because of going to a snob school. So one day I went into Smith's and bought a copy of the *Morning Star* and rolled it under my arm so he'd see it, and since then he's all smiles.'

'Quite right,' said Iris emphatically.

'Of him, or Emily?' asked Isobel.

'Emily, of course. If you can't beat them, pretend to join them. That's what I always say,' said Iris.

That night Isobel appeared in Emily's room.

'Can I get in with you for a bit? Only I'm freezing,' she said.

'You can if you don't put your feet on me,' said Emily.

'The eiderdown in the other room is all heavy from damp,' said Isobel.

'That room's always the coldest. I was in there last time and it was August and I was still quite chilly,' said Emily.

'That stew was a bit strange at supper.'

'I know! I only seemed to have bones in mine,' said Isobel.

'Same here. Was it meant to be pheasant, d'you think?'

'I couldn't really tell,' said Emily. 'Some sort of bird, I think. Isn't it too late for pheasant? I don't know when they stop shooting them.'

'Digby probably ran it over, then Granny said it would be a waste and went and scraped it off the road,' said Isobel.

They began to laugh quietly.

'And the hard loo paper!' said Emily.

'What do you think Granny would do, if we brought her a proper loo roll?' said Isobel.

'Dunno. I shouldn't think she'd notice. She'd probably leave it in the kitchen, for Birdle to rip to pieces.'

They lay in silence in the darkness for a time, Isobel neatly tucked against her sister's warm back, like two forks in a drawer.

'Lem, it will be all right, won't it?' Isobel asked presently.

'What?' said Emily.

'I don't know … everything. I feel a bit scared about leaving school this summer. I don't know what I'll do. I haven't even thought about where I'm going to live or anything.'

'You'll go to London and get some sort of job and it'll be great,' said Emily. 'Think of the freedom. Think of not having to sit through assembly any more, or sign out every time you want to go and get a packet of Opal Fruits. You won't have to wear horrible uniform ever again. It'll be fantastic.'

'I know.' Isobel sounded doubtful. 'It will. It'll be great.'

It was Jamie who helped Isobel find work. Ruth had wanted her daughter to go to university, but Isobel had never been terribly academic and couldn't think of a single subject she would want to study anyway. And that would have meant another three years: an eternity. Jamie had decided against becoming an academic: his finals had not gone well and he'd become disenchanted with university life. He had gone into a small electronics firm owned by a friend from Oxford days. They made some sort of peculiar keyboard instrument. It had been the size of a van to begin with, Jamie told her, and taken up almost the whole of the shed where the four of them worked, but they were trying to make a smaller version. Despite being so unwieldy it was becoming fashionable among the more avant-garde musicians in London. Jamie seemed to know millions of people, which was funny because he was so quiet himself. He had a friend, Jasper, who was a photographer, with a studio in the New King's Road and plans to open a gallery in the empty shop premises below. Isobel could help him out.

She wasn't quite sure what she was meant to do at the studio. She answered the telephone and kept Jasper's appointments diary and produced coffee for visitors, but there were hours when she did nothing at all. Jasper didn't seem to mind. He had two long shelves covered in big art books and she began to leaf through them in turn. At least she could learn something about art while she was sitting here. Isobel wondered if she was more for show than for usefulness, to make him look successful. Which, in fact, he was. Jasper's photographs were of naked women, or portions of naked women. He'd photograph someone's knee or shoulder or breast, so close up that you could see every follicle, every tiny hair, every mole. Usually the flesh was against something hard and man-made, like a brick wall or a piece of corrugated iron.

Isobel sat at a huge glass-topped table on the far side of the studio. Jasper seemed to favour big things: her chair had a ridiculously high back and the plain white mugs in which she was required to serve coffee were more like pudding bowls with handles. One end of the studio was entirely taken up with an indoor tree which had glossy, curiously un-lifelike outsized leaves. Jasper kept several foolscap books, for appointments, client addresses, expenses.

Isobel often heard Jasper telling people that the work – he always referred to his own photographs as 'the work' – was all about juxtapositions.

'You could look at the work from a feminist perspective too. That's the paradox. It's displaying the naked female form in a way that subverts the expectations usually imposed on it by male desire,' Jasper was explaining to an American man with a pointed beard.

'So they're naked, but they're not nudes,' said the American.

'Exactly!' said Jasper excitedly. 'That's just it. The familiarity of the forms draws the gaze in, but then it's blocked; it can't complete its visual journey ...'

'Right. They entice but they resist, too.'

'Yeah,' said Jasper.

The two maintained a long silence while they studied the images. Isobel had not the faintest idea what they had been talking about.

'I'd really like to write about the pictures you've made,' the American said at last. 'You know I contribute to the *Voice*, occasionally? And I curate, also.'

'Great,' said Jasper. 'Terrific.'

'Would you be willing to ship some works over to a group show I'm putting on in January? There's a bunch of new artists I'd like to give a window to: a great guy from New Mexico who does surreal kind of landscapes; he uses actual sand and dirt, mixes them in with the paint. Then there's an interesting young woman artist, a New Yorker who's concerned with the aesthetics of protest ... provisionally I'm calling the show Intersections.'

'Terrific. Yeah,' said Jasper. 'Izzy! Can you come over and take down this gentleman's details?'

Isobel was still not used to being called Izzy, but her employer had fixed on the name and she didn't like to correct him. No one had ever called her Izzy before. She took a biro and the contact book and stood up.

She was sharing a flat with Alice, a friend from school. It was on the second floor, off the North End Road. The old house in Putney wasn't far and she often went to Saturday lunch with her father and stepmother at the weekends. Most nights she went out, either to private views of photographic or contemporary art exhibitions, or to wine and cheese dos put on by her flatmate's colleagues from the ad agency where she worked, up in the West End. Everybody seemed to know everybody, wherever she went.

'You work for Jasper Sanderson, I hear.' The speaker was an older redhead with deep burgundy lipstick and a shirt with extravagantly medieval-looking puffed sleeves.

'Yes. I answer the phone, that sort of thing,' said Isobel.

'Oh. I'm Jenny, assistant creative manager.' The stranger did not seem to think it necessary to tell Isobel what organisation she was assistant creative manager of.

'We might be interested in getting Jasper on board for an upcoming project. It's a new account. The client is quite keen to go arty, campaign-wise. Is Jasper still doing ad work, or just editorial?'

'I don't know,' said Isobel, baffled. 'I only started last month. He's never said.'

'Oh. Right. Well, give me the studio number, can you, and I'll call next week?'

The following weekend Isobel met Jamie for tea at his favourite café, a long dark room by South Kensington tube station where hostile Polish waitresses served hot chocolate in tall glasses with metal holders. There were unfamiliar cakes displayed on glass shelves. They looked delectable, but they tasted dry and sandy. Isobel had never had a hot drink out of a glass before.

'How's it going?' asked Jamie.

'Fine, I think,' said Isobel. 'They all talk such gobbledegook, though, it takes a bit of getting used to. I thought a transparency meant something see-through. Well, I s'pose it does, in a way. I had no idea what Jasper was talking about at first, when he kept going on about them.'

'That's what working is. Learning the lingo.' Jamie smiled.

'It makes everyone seem important, I suppose, if it has its own language,' said Isobel.

'I suppose it does,' said Jamie. 'It's a bit like being in a club. You should hear some of the technical language that gets bandied about, with us. A normal person wouldn't understand half the stuff we're saying.'

Isobel's only real ambition was to lose her virginity. It felt like a burden to her, a badge of her provincialism. She was nearly nineteen and it was shameful, embarrassing. She worried that people could tell, just to look at her. Her flatmate, Alice, had done it with two guys already. She sounded very practised, when Isobel heard her and her current boyfriend at it, through the wall. Isobel met plenty of men, but she didn't seem to be very good at small talk or flirting. It was another kind of language she needed to learn.

The only guy who had persisted beyond a fumble was Andrew. The trouble was, she didn't really fancy him. He had thick hair in a centre parting, which had the effect not so much of framing his face as of carpeting it. In all weathers he wore an unbuttoned army greatcoat which made him sweat rather. Isobel supposed it was a Soviet army coat, or some such; it didn't look English. He'd got her telephone number when they'd met at some do and had rung her three times in a week, until she had agreed to meet. They'd gone to a Spaghetti House. Andrew announced that garlic bread was his favourite thing, then looked expectantly at Isobel, as if waiting to be congratulated for his culinary sophistication. When he kissed her, afterwards, his breath was heavy with the metallic tang of it.

Intercourse was an anticlimax. It was a sharp feeling, jagged, unpleasant in its insistence. She'd expected bloodied sheets, febrile declarations, a sense of deliverance.

'I'm not on the pill,' Isobel had whispered, as they were kissing.

'It's all right. I won't come inside you,' said Andrew.

Instead he had deposited a puddle of sticky hotness across her pubic hair and belly. As it cooled against her skin, she wondered about the polite way of dealing with such things. Presumably you had to pretend to be pleased. She imagined it was bad form to wipe it off straight away; anyway, she had nothing to wipe it with, except the sheet, and she didn't want this alien substance on her bed linen any more than she wanted it on herself. While Andrew reached out of the bed into the pocket of his jeans for a cigarette, she glanced down. It looked like the kind of glue used for putting up wallpaper.

'Just going for a pee,' she said.

'Righto, babe,' said Andrew, leaning back against the head-board with his cigarette, looking pleased with himself.

Andrew was a graphic designer. He was working in commercial publishing at the moment, but he really wanted to get into the music business. Album covers: that was the aim. After the first night at Isobel's, they spent most of their time at his place. He lived on his own so they had the flat to themselves, unlike at Isobel's. It was more convenient, too, because he lived so close to the tube station. Isobel had never spent time in a basement before and it seemed intriguingly grubby and bohemian. Andrew had an extensive record collection, housed in brown cuboid shelving. As soon as they came into the flat, before making a cup of tea, before opening his post or, if it was dark, drawing the ochre-coloured Indian bedspread he used as a curtain, he would go to the shelves and select an album. He had a particular way of getting the records out. First he slid the record onto its side, so that the inner sleeve with its waxed paper lining was dislodged from its cardboard casing. Some came more readily than others, tipping obligingly into his waiting palm. Then he slid his hand inside the white vest, lodging his middle finger across the hole in the middle, allowing neither his palm nor his other fingers to graze the glossy black surface. Now, with the rim of the disc tucked between his thumb and first finger, he eased it out. Sometimes he flipped the LP over between his flattened palms – he took a quiet pride in his comprehensive knowledge of the commonly less-played second sides and often, perversely, played them first – before blowing across it. After blowing each record he always studied the tiny concentric circles which marked the tracks, tipping it back and forth like a panning gold prospector, to catch the light. Only then, satisfied, did he place the LP on the altar of the turntable and lift the stylus onto its revolving surface.

None of his records were scratched, because he never let anyone else touch them. Isobel didn't know why he bothered to check each one so meticulously, unless the whole performance was a silent ritual of self-congratulation. At her flat she and Alice barely bothered to put LPs back in their sleeves, simply dumping them on shelves or even leaving them strewn across the floor. They kept their record player on automatic, so that each disc clunked down onto the turntable and the stylus jerked across to meet it, like a mechanical bird at a mechanical feeder. Andrew, though, seemed to believe that putting the stylus onto the record by hand was a mark of connoisseurship. He kept a special little duster by the record player, impregnated with some chemical. At the weekends he liked nothing more than to spend an afternoon circling the surface of each record with this cloth. Isobel couldn't believe how much time he spent over the care of his LPs. It was a hobby in itself, just to own records, before you'd even listened to a song. He never called them records, of course, or even LPs: he always referred to them as albums.

Most of the music was actually pretty dire, she thought. Yes and Jethro Tull she especially dreaded. Some of the American stuff at least had melody and words that sometimes made sense. As seriously as he took the records as physical objects, their content was almost sacred to Andrew. To talk during certain passages of music amounted to blasphemy. He himself sang along, at times, although Isobel was not encouraged to do the same. He sang not carelessly but with great deliberation. He would look intently at Isobel while he mouthed the words, as if the lyrics he was parroting contained a meaning more urgent, more esoteric, more uniquely intended for her hearing, than any words of his own devising.

'You ain't got time to call your soul a critic, no …'

He fixed her with a serious, slightly triumphant gaze, a look which struck her as wildly at odds with the song that was issuing from the record player, a song which could surely only be described as very silly. He was a troubadour in Barons Court. The song plinked and clonked along.

> '... sometimes we visit your country and live in your home
> Sometimes we ride on your horses, sometimes we walk alone
> Sometimes the songs that we hear are just songs of our own.'

When he sang at her like this, Isobel didn't know where to look. It was almost enough to make you pretend you wanted to hear *Tubular Bells*, merciful in its absence of lyrics. It was difficult to gauge how she was meant to respond: should she nod encouragingly, smile or look solemn? She felt almost queasy with embarrassment, not only on his behalf, but her own. What would anyone think if they could see her sitting there, receiving this gibberish? Was this what all the young couples in London were up to, behind closed doors? Were all the guys in London looking deep into their girlfriends' eyes, mouthing the words 'Aqualung my friend!' as if the world depended on it?

Sometimes she felt she didn't really have anything in common with Andrew. Most of the time she was pretty bored in his company.

'Have you noticed,' she asked him one evening, 'that the best track on almost every album is track two of side one?'

'You just can't say that,' Andrew said. 'No way.'

'Why not?' said Isobel.

'Well, on a concept album there's no merit in one track over another. We've gone beyond tracks. Sure, it might have been track-based, in the early years. But where we're at now – where we've been, basically, since *Pet Sounds* – it's bigger than that. It's not songs that bands are really into. None of that commercial stuff. It's to do with a sound, a vibe. Building a soundscape.'

Isobel sighed.

The one thing she enjoyed was when he told her about the artwork which went into album-cover design. This was something she had taken entirely for granted before. Most of her own records just had pictures of the singer or group on the cover, looking sunny or sultry, depending on how cool they were: smiling was uncool, basically. The idea that it might be someone's job to design the covers, to select lettering, pose photographs, create an ambience, was new to her. Andrew showed her record covers which often made no reference to the musicians at all. One had naked, impossibly pale children clambering over flat rocks beneath an orange sky; another, a slice of cake with a huge eye, sitting on a red swing. A Rolling Stones LP had a photograph of the flies of a man's jeans with an actual zip covering – Isobel couldn't help noticing – a palpable bulge. Andrew's own favourite was *Brain Salad Surgery*, a gatefold album which opened out to show a strange skull, half stone, half bone, its lips and chin encircled in a paler beige and still, sinisterly, bearing their flesh.

'It's an amazing image,' he said, inhaling deeply from a Rothmans Special.

Isobel didn't like this one so much, partly because it was frightening, but also because the music on the LP was, she thought, so peculiar and awful. She and Alice always watched *Top of the Pops* on a Thursday evening: she would never have confessed as much to Andrew, but she liked pop. She liked music you could dance to, whereas Andrew didn't dance but preferred to do what he called 'freak out', which meant flipping his head up and down and around with his eyes closed, while seated. Andrew disapproved of singles because they were too commercial and too brief a form to allow the development of concepts. Most of his LPs didn't even include any tracks which had been released as singles. They didn't get played on the radio, at least not at any time of day when a normal person might have had the radio on. He just bought records, without even listening to them first.

There was one other thing Isobel did like about Andrew. After their first, disappointing experience in the bedroom, Isobel had steeled herself. At least he was interested in her, or meant to be; in fact he seldom asked her a question. But he was a boyfriend. Subsequent bouts of intercourse were little improvement on the first, but they were the price you paid for being able to tell people you were going out with someone. It didn't actually hurt again, but it wasn't much fun either. It seemed to go on and on. Sometimes it went on for the entire side of a Yes album.

Then, on their fourth or fifth night together, Andrew did something miraculous. Instead of rolling over on top of her after a few minutes of preamble, he lifted her nightie up to her chin and began to very slowly descend her torso, navigating by kisses. It was as if a snail was inching across her skin, depositing a silvery trail. By the time he reached her groin, pleasure and wonderment had overtaken reserve: when he parted her legs and pressed his face against her, Isobel entirely forgot how irritating Andrew could be. It was as if he was a different person, some sort of delivering angel.

'I love you,' she heard herself say.

There was a solo album by Graham Nash on the record player. The voice – plaintive, half lisping – was suddenly beautiful, the slide guitars delicious and slithery. Eventually Andrew's face appeared above hers. He wore the same expression – half smug, half priestly – as when he mouthed along to the words of his albums and, for a moment, she fancied that he might be about to break into song. But now she wouldn't have minded if he had.

Chapter 10

Emily had to learn a list of the presenting symptoms for the most common ailments in dogs. Some were straightforward. Ear mites, say, or roundworm were easy to spot. Cheyletiella (which sounded like the name of an Italian opera, thought Emily), the mite known as 'walking dandruff', wasn't hard to diagnose, once you'd seen a case. Roger, who ran the surgery where she was learning the ropes after she'd finished at college, filled her in. When a dog dragged its backside along the floor, tail lifted, owners always thought it was a sign of worms, and while it could indeed indicate infestation, it was more likely to suggest that the anal glands required draining. Some breeds were more susceptible than others. Cavalier King Charles were the worst. If people knew what they were in for, before they acquired a King Charles ... They had trouble with their ears, too. And breathing. Overbred, that was the trouble. Mongrels were always more robust. Owners tended to kill with kindness: overfeeding, over-coddling. Hip dysplasia was aggravated by carrying too much weight, but try telling the owners that. Some dogs you had in were so fat they could hardly walk.

There were things to find out about owners, too. Women were braver than men. Cat owners tended to be worse than dog owners. More neurotic. And cats could get nasty, on the table. They could give you a ferocious bite, as well as scratching, and they were harder to keep under control during examination:

you couldn't really hold their muzzles. The trick was to get the owner to man the top end. Unless some parent had the bright idea of making their child deal with the pet. You could hear them, talking in harsh whispers in the waiting room: you asked for it, you said you'd look after it, you were meant to feed/walk the wretched thing every day. So now you can hold it while it gets wormed. Children often took fright if the animal struggled and just let go, which could make things tricky if you were in the middle of a procedure. Emily learned that the owners everyone dreaded most were the old age pensioners, especially if they were on their own; especially if there was something really wrong with their pet. You dreaded having to give them bad news. They'd come in with some ancient and adored pet, its eyes glassy with age, its hind legs rigid with arthritis, and all the time it would be looking at the owner with an imploring expression. It broke your heart, if you had to destroy the animal, knowing you were sending the owner home to an empty house.

When she got to the larger herbivores, Emily would be surprised, Roger cautioned. You could turn up at a farm and be greeted by a great big bloke, red face, calloused hands, boots covered in mud and shit: the lot. Salt-of-the-earth types. But tell them an animal wasn't going to make it and you had to look away, pretend to rummage in your bag, while they composed themselves. 'Important rule,' said Roger: 'people don't like it if you see them cry. They never really forgive you for it. You can guarantee a farmer will shed a tear over an animal. Funny, really. If it's a bullock, it'll be off to the abattoir or the local slaughterman before it's two years old, but that farmer will still come over all red-eyed if it has to go any sooner. Same with a dairy cow, and a heifer. It's not just the money they're going to lose on them, although that can be considerable; it's that they get to know their cattle as individuals. With a sheep a farmer won't be so bothered. You get the odd one.

'The people who don't show emotion are the serious horsy types,' Roger went on. 'The women, that is. Not the little stable girls who go in and help out on a Saturday morning: they're still starry-eyed. They'd cry about a run-over rabbit. The men tend to choke up too. But women who work around horses all the time, they'll call you out to come and shoot an animal, if it's broken a leg, say, and they'll greet you as if you've come for sherry, as if they haven't got a care in the world. It's all a front of course. Those people love their horses, but it's a funny thing: riding a lot makes people brave. In the First World War you've got our cavalry facing German guns. Cannon fire. You or I would bloody – 'scuse my French – run for it. But they did it. They stayed and fought.' One of Roger's friends worked as an ambulance driver and this friend said those seasoned horsy type of women were the bravest people he ever had to deal with. Didn't matter if they'd got a really painful injury, a nasty break: they never asked for anything stronger than a cup of tea.

Roger and his wife Pat invited Emily for lunch one Sunday, soon after she'd arrived. Their house was detached, red-brick, with mothy evergreens screening it from the road. At the back was a pond with pampas grass to one side and a few plum trees, where Pat's bantams were standing about. A lone bird with a long neck stood by the side of the pond.

'What's that?' asked Emily.

'Indian Runner,' said Pat. 'Used to have four of them, but they're daft, even by ducks' standards. Fox got the other three and I'd put money on him nabbing her too.' Pat seemed unperturbed, even complacent. 'You can't afford to get too attached, not to ducks.'

This was a phrase Emily had hardly heard, until her training. Now it was repeated like a sort of litany: you can't get too attached. That's what everyone who worked with animals said, all the time. Rule Number One: Don't go getting too attached.

Emily found that this suited her. She loved animals, admired their beauty and movement; liked nothing better, out walking in the woods, than to glimpse the bright eye of a deer through the trees, in the moments of enhanced stillness before the animal sensed that it was being watched, before it leapt away in one movement of a tawny flank. Walking across a field of sheep, she liked to stop and listen to them, grazing. The way they quietly tore at the grass sounded like a bristle hairbrush, brushing hair. Geese descending on an autumn river meadow at dusk, all honking madly, like furious drivers; or a hare, so surprisingly tall, racing through a field of bright, young wheat: these were the sights which Emily loved. But she felt no need to own an animal herself, to bring one indoors.

Emily enjoyed her own company. She chose to live by herself, even though it was more expensive than sharing, renting a little first-floor flat in an old building – it was Number 2, Butter Lane, chosen partly because she so liked the sound of the address – which looked out at the oversized town church to one side and, to the other, onto a row of old houses like crooked teeth, some half-timbered, some brick. On the far side of the church was a monkey puzzle tree, which she walked past every day, on her way to and from work. The tree reminded her of her mother's home in Malvern.

'Where on earth is Alcester?' asked Isobel, when Emily rang her sister to say she'd found a place to live.

'You sound like Granny! That's just how she'd say it,' Emily laughed.

'Yes, but where is it? Seriously. Surely you don't want to live somewhere where you don't know anybody.'

'It's near Stratford-upon-Avon. It's nice. I can walk to work.'

'But you haven't got any friends there!'

'Well, I came here for work, not just to make friends. You didn't really know anybody, much, when you went to London,

146

and now look at you: out every night. I can make friends. I will make friends, later. I like being on my own anyway.'

'But what will you do? For fun, I mean?' said Isobel. 'London's full of, I don't know, people and parties and things. And men. There can't be much going on in Alcester.'

Emily just laughed. Sometimes she didn't tell her sister things. Sometimes, even as a little girl, she fibbed: Isobel always wanted to know everything and she didn't always want to tell her.

In her third week, a man had brought in a strangely lethargic ferret. It was the first time she had seen a ferret up close. Its body was much longer than she would have imagined and its fur had a yellow-brown tinge, like a smoker's fingers.

'How long has he been floppy like this?' she asked the man.

'Since yesterday dinner time. He'd normally try and have half your arm off. He's not right.'

'I can see,' she said. 'What I think is the problem is that he's got heatstroke. Where do you keep him?'

'Out the back. He's got a run and a little hutch and that,' said the man.

'And are his living quarters in direct sunlight?' asked Emily.

'Well, yeah. The hutch is, and he's got the run. Part of that's in the shade,' said the man. 'Is that wrong then?'

'Well, it's not normally as hot as it's been this week,' said Emily. 'But ferrets don't sweat and they don't pant, which are the ways most of us keep cool. So they can overheat pretty easily. You need to be aware that, when you feel hot, your ferret feels very hot. Uncomfortably hot. I'm going to pop him in a bath of room-temperature water and introduce some fluids. Maybe be a good idea to leave him with us overnight, so we can keep an eye on him. OK?'

'If that's what you think he wants,' said the man. 'What time shall I come back for him?' He looked worried.

'Late morning, early afternoon. You could leave him 'til later, if you're at work?'

The man grinned, rather sheepishly she thought. 'I'm unemployed, just at the minute.'

'You might want to move his hutch into the shade then, if you have time,' she said.

He came back for the ferret at half past one the next day. His name was Gary James. He didn't thank Emily, but she was getting used to that. People tended to express gratitude in inverse ratio to what she might have expected. The worse the prognosis for their pet, the more precarious its future, the more they seemed to thank you. The ferret was fine, now.

'You busy later?' he asked.

'Sorry?'

'After. You doing anything?'

'Well … no, not really.'

He asked her if she'd come for a drink.

Before yesterday, before she had dealt with an actual real-life ferret, she might have described Gary James as a ferret-like man, by which she would have meant that he had bright, mischievous eyes and a pointy nose. But now that she had handled a ferret, she saw that he was really nothing like one: his eyes were not so far apart, nor his nose tucked so close below the eyes. A ferret's mouth was just a little line, like the imprint of a thumbnail, beneath its snout, whereas Gary had a fairly wide mouth, especially when he smiled. He had a long, prominent nose. There was a gloss to his dark hair. If she was honest, he looked much more like a rat. A nice rat. If you were being kind, you could say he had a look of James Taylor. But really he was more like a rat. She quite liked rats.

At the pub he drank a half, then another. He offered her an Embassy from a red and white pack which he pulled out of the pocket of his denim jacket. Emily, who didn't much care for drink, had a lemonade shandy followed by a ginger ale.

'Ginger ale? With nothing in it? That's the last drink I'm buying you. I've got my reputation to think of, you know,' he said.

'Oh dear. Am I letting the side down?'

'I'll get over it.' He grinned. His nose was not only long, but bony. You could see the shape of the bone at the bridge of his nose: two little knobs, with a flat bit in the middle, as if a hazelnut had lodged there.

He told her stories. How his mum had put ten No. 6 in with his sandwiches for school every day, from when he was twelve years old. How he and his mate had gone round to scrounge sherry off a married woman in a big house on the Evesham Road, when they were lads, until one time her husband came back and caught the three of them, plastered, and chased the boys out of the house with an umbrella.

'Did you ever go back there, afterwards?' she asked.

'Nah. He was angry enough just to see us in there. But not half as angry as he was going to be, when he found out his silver lighter had gone, off the table in the lounge.'

'You didn't!'

He grinned again.

He told her how he had been apprehended by a keeper over the other side of Stratford, but still got away with two and a half brace of pheasant, because the bloke had caught him after he'd already gone back to put the birds in the car. The only reason he'd found him empty-handed was that he was on his way to get more.

'There seems to be a bit of a theme emerging,' said Emily.

'What's that then?'

'You, nicking things.'

'I'd only take from someone who could afford it. I'd never have anything off a friend. I'm Robin Hood, me.'

'I needn't hang on to my handbag then,' said Emily.

'No, you're all right.'

'Right then,' said Emily, replacing her empty glass on the table. 'I'd best be off.'

He stood up. 'Tell you what. I'm going fishing, Saturday. You could come along. It's nice down by the river. I know a good spot.'

She laughed. 'I'll see,' she said.

They had had the drink on a Tuesday and he had not been in touch on any of the days afterwards. By the time she left work that Friday, she'd given up on him. Probably just as well, she told herself. He's obviously a dodgy character. But she couldn't help feeling a little disappointed.

On Saturday morning Emily was woken by a long, insistent ring on her doorbell at home. She looked at the clock: it was a quarter to six. No one called at Butter Lane. She assumed someone had rung the wrong bell, that the caller, whoever they were, wanted someone in the lower flat. It rang again. Whoever it was had pressed the bell for so long that it was almost rude. Annoyed now and wide awake, she got out of bed and went to open the window in the living room at the front. She looked down at a mop of straight dark hair.

'Hello! Yes? Up here!'

It was Gary James. He tilted his head back and smiled up at her. She could see his throat, paler than the skin on his face.

'You coming then?'

'What? Are you bonkers or something? I'm not dressed. Do you know what time it is?' She felt quite cross. Disturbing her so early on her day off. She hadn't even said she'd go with him!

'Best part of the day.'

'I'm not ready. I'm not even dressed.'

'Sounds nice.'

'I might not even come. I've got things to do today.'

'What, and let me spend the whole day by myself? Show some mercy, girl.'

She didn't answer.

'Aren't you going to invite me in, for a cup of tea?' he asked. 'I can't stand here all day, you know.'

'Oh, all right then,' she said. 'I'll have to come down to let you in.'

She put on her dressing gown – it was faded, an old candlewick one that her grandmother had given her, years ago – and filled the kettle, before she went barefoot down the stairs and let him in.

'Tell you what, I'll make your breakfast, while you get ready,' he said, once they had climbed the stairs and he had followed her into the kitchen, where she got out mugs and teabags.

'But you don't know where anything is,' said Emily.

'I think I'll be able to work it out,' he said. 'This kitchen's all of six by eight.'

'Just a piece of toast then.'

No one had been to her flat before, not since the landlord had first shown her the place. Gary seemed to take up too much room. She felt awkward, passing him in the kitchen doorway. She could smell him, as she squeezed past, tobacco and a cleanness, too, like the smell when you fold a newly washed towel. But there was something else, too, a smell that she recognised but couldn't, for a moment, place, something flammable.

Emily took her jeans from the back of the chair and looked for a T-shirt and jumper, then took off her dressing gown and nightdress. It occurred to her that she was standing naked, only a few feet away from Gary James, that if the wall wasn't there they would be near enough to touch each other, almost. She could hear him, opening cupboards in the kitchen. She felt annoyed that he'd woken her, that he was rummaging in her cupboards. She dressed.

'Have you been down to the river before?' Gary asked her.

'No, I haven't. I knew there was a river here, but I hadn't really taken in where, or how to get at it.'

'In actual fact, there are two rivers. You could more or less throw a stone into one of them from your place,' he said.

'Really? Is it that near?'

'We're not going that way just now. It's not so good for fishing, bit shallow. But I'll show you next time.'

She was aware of feeling pleased that he was thinking there would be a next time. They walked along the street. Emily could see two men working in the back of the baker's shop already, lifting and stacking great trays of what looked like doughnuts or rolls. There were signs of life, too, at the newsagent – the grille was up – but Fine Fare was still shut up and in the dark. It was much too early for shoppers and there were no cars. Empty like this, the place looked picturesque, like a place on a postcard. They turned right at the end of the street. Emily found it difficult to keep up with Gary. He had a loping kind of gait, leaning forward slightly into a long stride. It was a tall person's walk, although he wasn't especially tall. She followed as he went left past a pub. There were some old half-timbered buildings and then the lane came to an end at allotments, with open fields beyond. At the far side of the allotments they climbed over a gate.

'You all right?' he asked.

'Yes,' she said.

'Not too far for you?'

'No, I like walking. I like being outside.'

'And I do,' he said.

They came to the river and carried on, along the water's edge. Looking back, she could follow the river's course by the willows which lined its banks, although the water itself was not visible below the level of the fields. After a bit they came to a place where the river curved.

'This'll do,' he said. 'You get fish on a bend, where there's an undercut.'

Gary stopped and took out a cigarette. He had a Zippo lighter: the source, she now understood, of the smell she had noticed earlier. He seemed to have a lot of gear. There was a hooped net which stretched open like an accordion, and a rod, and a big metal box like a tool box – or perhaps it was an actual tool box, she wasn't sure – and a fraying canvas bag from which he produced a tin full of bait. It was an old tobacco tin, with a green and yellow lid. The lid had rough holes gouged through it. After a few draws on his cigarette, he opened the tin.

'Crikey! That stinks,' she said. 'What on earth is it?'

'Sweet corn and maggots. Bit of meal. Works a treat.'

'It smells horrible.'

'Yeah, but you're not a fish, are you? You've not got to like it.'

'Why are the worms that funny colour?'

'Iodine. Fish are attracted to a bit of colour. Brightness they like.'

'My granny goes fishing.'

'Where's that then?'

'Up north. It's nearly Scotland, where she lives. She catches trout. Salmon, sometimes. She loves it.'

He grinned. 'We won't be seeing any salmon today. Might get a perch.'

'I don't know much about fish. We don't get fish, really, at work. Only the odd goldfish. They're prone to fungal infection. By the time people notice there's anything wrong with them, it's too late anyway.'

'You cold?' he asked her.

'A bit.'

'It's still early, it'll warm up. I normally have my coffee mid-morning, but we could have a cup now, if you like?'

She nodded. From a pocket he produced a slightly flattened Marathon bar.

'Tell you what, you break that in half for us, and I'll sort the coffee.'

She tore the wrapper and bent the chocolate. The toffee formed strings as she divided the pieces, giving the bigger of the two to Gary. She wouldn't have chosen a Marathon – too salty, too sticky – but in the cool early-morning air it seemed delicious. From the canvas bag Gary produced a tartan-patterned thermos. He poured coffee into the cup which formed its lid, and handed it to her. The cup had a dent in it. She wondered if he'd had the flask for a long time, but she didn't ask him. The coffee tasted thin and oversweet. After she'd taken a few sips, she handed it back, for him to finish.

They sat side by side. Some of the time they chatted, quietly, but mostly they were silent. Emily didn't mind or feel awkward at all. She had never thought she was very good at talking anyway. She enjoyed watching the sunlight flicker on the surface of the river. The water was the colour of caramel and in places it dimpled and eddied, like syrup coming to the boil. A coot busied itself among the bramble branches which overhung the opposite bank. Its call sounded like coins clinking against each other in a pocket. There were ducks, and songbirds announced themselves to one another from the trees. She kept glancing at the side of Gary's face.

She didn't know how long they had been there when Gary got a fish. He jumped to his feet and reeled in the taut line, a few inches at a time. She could see the line tugging against him, as if a terrier was playing a game with a stick. The water broke and seemed to froth as the fish emerged into the strange element of the air.

'What is it?' she asked.

'Looks like a tench. Quite a good fish, this one.'

With a final lift of the line the fish was in his hands. He held it at waist height, one hand under its head, the other at its tail, the fish facing outwards. Its underside was ever so slightly pink. Once Gary had it in his grip the fish stopped writhing and stayed still, only pulsing, its mouth open.

'Have a feel of his skin, go on,' said Gary.

Emily hesitated, then put out a hand and ran just the tips of her fingers along the fish's back. It felt viscid, almost oily.

'That's really weird,' she said.

'Doctor fish, they call them. That slime is meant to have medicinal qualities, see. He can go back now.'

'Aren't we going to eat it?'

Gary knelt, balancing the fish in the declivity of his thighs. He gently removed the hook from the fish's cheek – it seemed to be panting now – before leaning forward to slip it back into the river, his arms submerged for a few moments in the shallows of the water, as the fish came free of his grasp.

'Nah. They're no good to eat,' he said, standing up. There was a dark patch of moisture on his jeans, where the fish had been.

The day grew warmer. Gary caught another fish, a chub, and then a second tench, smaller than the first. The silveriness of the chub was as bright as a new ten-pence piece.

'He'd make decent eating,' he said.

'Do you put them all back?' asked Emily.

'Not all. Sometimes I keep one, if it's a good fish, for dinner. It's more about just being out here, spending time, you know? Speaking of which, what time is it? I've got to be back for half two. The fish don't tend to feed, not once the sun's this high anyway.'

It was almost one o'clock. The morning seemed to have gone by in minutes. He packed up his things and they walked back the way they had come, the sun warming their backs. When they rounded the corner and the monkey puzzle tree in front of the church came into view, she asked if he'd like a quick something to eat, a sandwich. He followed her up the narrow stairs. His fishing rod made a *tack-tack-tack* sound as it caught on the banisters.

There was a piece of Cheddar in the fridge, and a couple of tomatoes on the side. Emily cut them into slices, while Gary went to use the bathroom.

'Just wash my hands; the bread'll taste of bait, else,' he said.

Emily took their plates through to the room at the front, which doubled as a place to sit and to eat, with a small table in front of one window and a television with its back to the other. Gary perched on the windowsill nearest the table, while Emily sat on the sofa. She found it distracting, his presence in the room. Instead of having her plate on her lap, she left it on the arm of the sofa, dropping crumbs of bread and cheese onto her jeans. After he'd eaten his sandwich, he pushed the plate a little further away from him, towards the middle of the table. His outline was dark against the brightness from the window.

'Come over here,' he said, holding out a hand towards Emily. She stood up, crumbs falling onto the carpet as she stepped towards him.

After that he called for her every Saturday and often met her after work on a Tuesday or Wednesday as well. Almost opposite her flat was a tiny street Gary showed her, called Meeting Lane.

'I rang the council roads people, asked them to rename it that, so I could meet you there,' he told her.

'Oh yes? What was it called before, then?'

'Nothing Lane. Lonely Lane. Who'd-bother-to-come-down-here Lane.'

On weekdays he waited there for her, and they walked down the lane, past leaning cottages and a grand but now abandoned-looking walled garden, until they came to what must once have been an orchard, where rough grass and weeds and patches of bramble grew under old apple trees, to the river's edge. On fine evenings they lay in the grass here together, where no one could see them. Gary laid his denim jacket underneath her. On Saturdays he took her fishing with him, always on foot, but to different places: one week it was downriver, to the Arrow Mill; another, they'd go in the opposite direction, to the Alne, up by the weir. In the deeper, slower-running stretches of water closer to Evesham there were bream and sometimes, when he'd caught a decent-sized fish, Gary would kill it with one sharp blow to the side of its head and give it to her, to cook. Emily noticed but didn't much mind that he never offered her a go with the rod. She did not want more than she had, with him. She liked it when he told her things: how maggots were sold by the pint, like ale; how barbel, of all coarse fish, put up the hardest fight, pound for pound; how he varied his bait, because most things were worth a try and he'd had good luck with weird combinations sometimes, like mixing luncheon meat with curry powder. He told her that the metal implement which he used to kill a fish once he'd got it landed was called a priest.

'And that's as near a churchman as you'll get me,' he said.

She took to bringing a book along, although often she simply sat, or leant on her elbows, idling. Often there were water birds to look at, ducks usually, or swans. She liked listening to the sound of a swan, drinking. Their delicate lapping seemed at odds with the appetite suggested by the power of their great necks and muscular wings. They sipped at the water daintily, like a prospective bride taking tea with the vicar. Emily liked looking at Gary when he didn't know her eyes were on him, just watching him baiting his hooks, or getting a knot out of his line. She wondered if he was thinking, as she was, of what they would do with each other later on. How he'd lift her arms above her head, one by one, and kiss her underarms and breasts. She could picture his body, pale and insistent and wiry, underneath his clothes.

In the autumn, when Emily found out she was pregnant, the first thing that came into her mind was to wonder whether the child had been conceived outside, in the old orchard. She found herself hoping that it had. As soon as that sliver of a wish lodged within her she understood that she would keep the baby. She knew she ought to consider what to do, whether she should have an abortion, what to say to Gary. She had no idea how to break the news to her family, or the people at work. Roger and Pat had been so kind to her, she didn't want to let them down. She didn't know how she would support herself, with a child. Animals had no need to reckon such things, she thought, they just got on with it. Perhaps she could simply do the same.

Chapter 11

Ruth worried about Christopher. Always the first of the household to get up, he had begun coming down long after she and
Ilse had breakfasted. Sometimes, on those mornings when she
was teaching, Ruth did not see him at all before she left the
house.

Then she would go up to the landing and call out, 'I'm just off
now. See you later!' and wait, one hand on the top of the banisters, feeling a little flutter of apprehension, for a response from
him. Sometimes there would be a long pause before he answered,
'Cheerio, Ruthie!'

She did not know what she would do if, one morning, her
farewell was met with silence. She would have to go in and see
that he was all right, and to enter his bedroom would feel like
trespassing. They had navigated each other's privacy so adroitly
during their many years of living under the same roof. Ruth
almost never entered his room nor he hers, and Ilse also was
physically reticent. The three of them managed, somehow, to
share the bathroom without inconveniencing each other: no
one ever tried the door when someone was in the bath, or on the
loo.

In the early years, Christopher had sometimes come down in
his dressing gown to make tea. The dressing gown was very
familiar to his niece, the same one he'd had ever since Ruth
could remember, thick wool the colour of teddy bears, with a

rough texture not unlike a toy bear either. It had maroon piping and a shiny maroon and fawn cord, like a bell pull. But after Ilse came to live with them he only appeared downstairs dressed, and the dressing gown was seldom seen. Christopher still wore a tie every day, usually a single-coloured wool one, even on days when he did not leave the house. He was untidy, but fastidious: piles of old newspapers folded at articles he meant to read and copies of the *Listener* and letters from the RSPB accumulated, but he himself was always shaved and neat. Ruth and her uncle very seldom touched, unless she had been away, in which case she kissed his cheek on her return. She did the same on special occasions, like birthdays. Ilse had more contact with him, often putting a hand on his sleeve when she wanted to emphasise a point, or when he made her laugh. Sometimes they spoke in German together, which Christopher enjoyed, having learned the language in his schooldays. It was Ilse too who played chess with Christopher. None of them had ever exchanged a word in temper.

But now something wasn't right, Ruth could feel it. The colour had drained out of his face and he seemed listless, as if his limbs had become heavier. More than once, while she moved about the downstairs rooms, switching off the lights before bed, after having bade him goodnight, she had discerned his form on the unlit half-landing, slightly bent over, pausing as if to gather his strength to complete the climb upstairs. She had given no sign that she'd seen.

Alone with Ilse, she fretted.

'Why don't you take him to the doctor, if you are worried?' Ilse asked.

'I don't think I could. It would be too interfering. We've never done anything like that.'

'For sure. But if you are really concerned ...'

'Perhaps I'll leave it for another week or so. See if there's any change,' Ruth decided.

There didn't seem to be much change, for good or otherwise. Sometimes he appeared a little breathless, or was she imagining it? And was he less talkative over dinner? For some time now he had not gone out on a Monday night as he used to, but only on Thursdays, returning, as he always had, early the next morning. Then one Thursday, about a month after Ruth had begun to notice a change in him, he had not gone to open the garage to get the car out as usual. Instead the doorbell had rung at half past four.

'Car for Mr Browning?' the man asked.

Ruth, who had gone to the door, looked doubtfully at the driver.

'Can you just wait a minute? I'll go and see,' she said, turning to go into the house and find out.

'Oh, there you are,' she said, taken aback to find her uncle just behind her in the hall, his coat ready buttoned. Christopher shot a brief, apologetic smile in her direction.

'See you tomorrow then.'

When Ilse got home, just after five, Ruth was still puzzling over the taxi.

'Why wouldn't he take the car? There's nothing wrong with that car. He hardly drives it; it's always been serviced and looked after. Why would he take a taxi?'

'I don't know,' said Ilse. 'Perhaps the garage doors are becoming too heavy for him. Perhaps he can't see so well. You should ask him.'

But Ruth knew she couldn't.

It was a busy time. Several students were preparing for examinations, requiring extra lessons, and Ruth's choir was rehearsing for an especially ambitious concert, in aid of the church hall, which was chronically damp. One of the music teachers at the girls' school had developed shingles and wouldn't be back at work for a month at least, so she had to cover her colleague's lessons as best she could. Ruth was out of the house a great deal.

It was normal that Christopher should seem older, she reassured herself. He was bound to slow down a little, seem rather less spry. And anyway, he seemed better now. More colour in his cheeks.

Weeks passed. During a fifth former's piano lesson – a girl with red hair called Hettie Gilbert – there was a knock at the door and the school secretary came in.

'Hettie, can you go back to your form room and see if you've got any prep to finish off? There's a good girl,' she said. She waited until the girl had gone. 'There's been a call for you, about your uncle. He's been taken into the infirmary at Worcester.'

'Is he all right?' asked Ruth. It sounded such a stupid question, even as she was saying it.

'Apparently his friend told the nurse your whereabouts and she got the school's number from directories. So I assume he's conscious. But we don't know any more, I'm afraid.'

'What friend? Was it my ... was it a woman with a foreign accent?'

'I don't know any more, I'm afraid. It was a nurse who telephoned the school.'

Ruth went at once to the station. There was a Worcester train in seven minutes: she would be there in less than half an hour. She ran from Foregate Street station to the infirmary, without stopping for breath. She could hardly speak, once she got there, to ask what ward her uncle was on. She walked along what felt like miles of hospital corridors, her shoes squeaking faintly on the linoleum.

Sitting in an orange plastic chair beside her uncle's bed was a man in a brown tweed suit, his hand resting on top of Christopher's. His clothes seemed too formal, or old-fashioned, she wasn't sure which. Christopher smiled at Ruth. His face was the colour of putty. The stranger at once stood up to proffer the chair.

'Here's Ruth,' said her uncle. 'Ruthie, this is Peregrine.'

The man shook her hand. 'How very nice to see you,' he said quietly. She didn't know how to respond. She hadn't expected someone else to be with her uncle. The chair stood empty.

'Are you all right? What happened?' she asked Christopher.

'They think it was a heart attack,' he said. 'It felt awfully peculiar. Thank God I was in the hall, so I was able to get to the telephone for an ambulance. I think I may have lost consciousness on the way, because I can't remember the actual journey.'

'When was this?'

'This morning sometime. I lost track of time, I'm afraid.'

'It doesn't matter,' said Ruth. 'I don't know why I asked actually. It's just the shock.'

'Would you like to sit down?' Peregrine asked her.

'Thank you, yes, I will,' she said.

'I'll go and see if one of the nurses could find you a cup of tea,' he said.

Ruth said thank you. 'Do you need anything from home?' she asked, once she was seated. 'I mean, how long are they going to keep you in for?'

'I'm all right. Perry brought some pyjamas, as you can see.' He was wearing unfamiliar pale-blue cotton pyjamas with white piping. 'Actually, you could bring me something to read. There's a W. H. Hudson by my bed at home. They haven't said how long I'll be here.'

'Oh, OK,' said Ruth. She paused. 'But how did he, you know, know you were here?'

'Perry? Well, he didn't. I rang him to begin with. It was he who insisted I get the ambulance. Arrived at exactly the same moment as a matter of fact, so he must have driven at an awful lick. He came with me from the house.'

'Oh,' said Ruth.

Peregrine came back. 'She's going to bring some tea in a minute.'

'Thank you,' said Ruth, again.

The tea was brought and Ruth sat, sipping. It tasted of metal, as if the tea leaves had been exchanged for iron filings, but she didn't mind. She felt only relief that Christopher was here, alive, beside her. After a further quarter of an hour she stood up.

'Well, I mustn't tire you. Will you be all right? I'll come back tomorrow after school, shall I, bring your book? Then we might know more. About how long you need to stay here.'

'That's it,' said Christopher.

'Let me see you out,' said Peregrine.

He walked beside her along the corridors, not speaking. When they got to the entrance he said, 'The thing is, we were lucky this time. He was near the telephone and he didn't take a fall. But it could happen again.'

'Oh Lord,' said Ruth. 'I hadn't thought of that.'

'I don't believe you have my telephone number,' Peregrine went on. 'So I wonder if I might trouble you to take it? Then perhaps you would be kind enough to let me know, if Christopher were ever unable to get me himself.'

'No, of course. Yes. Do,' said Ruth.

From an inner coat pocket he produced a slender silver pencil, of the sort that took a tiny independent shard of lead. The lead could be extended by clicking the top and then retracted after use, so it didn't break, by twisting the narrow writing end of the pencil. Ruth remembered having had such a pencil, as a girl. Spare leads were stored in a little barrel – like tiny bullets in the chamber of a gun – which was revealed when the top was unscrewed. The silver of this pencil was dented in one or two places, suggesting long use.

'I've only got a used envelope, I'm afraid,' he said. He pronounced the word 'omvelope'.

He took a letter from the envelope and put the folded paper back into a pocket. He wrote a number, then handed the envelope to Ruth. She put it in her bag without looking at it.

'Thank you,' he said. 'I hope we meet again.'

On the train home, Ruth took the envelope out and turned it over. It was addressed to Mr Peregrine and Lady Celia Darby, Brensham Court, Severn End, Upton upon Severn.

'What does he look like?' Ilse asked her later, when Ruth recounted the scene at the hospital.

'Nice. Twinkly. A bit like Wilfrid Hyde-White,' said Ruth.

'I don't know who that is,' said Ilse.

'Of course,' said Ruth, 'there's no reason on earth why you should. He's an actor … he's an actor who plays nice, old-fashioned, rather grand minor characters, like the solicitor who has to read out the will in an Ealing comedy. He's one of those people whom you can't imagine as a child, or even a young man. But likeable, always. You couldn't not like him. Peregrine's the same. The sort of man you'd trust.'

'And you never heard your uncle talk about him?'

'Never.'

They sat in silence for a time.

Christopher returned home after two days in hospital. The doctors said he had had what they called a coronary episode. He was to rest – which made him laugh, since he said he could hardly do less than he already did – and start taking a number of pills. Edward and Helen came to the house to visit him the day after he came home.

'Dear girl. Aren't you good?' said Helen, kissing her stepdaughter on one cheek.

'Oh no, it's nothing, I …'

'Fearful smell of damp in the breakfast room,' announced Edward, who had undertaken a tour of the downstairs rooms as soon as they arrived. 'Are you remembering to leave the Dimplex on in there, occasionally?'

It was a source of irritation to her father that the Malvern house was still without central heating, to which he was a late but ardent convert.

Christopher appeared in the hall.

'You're dressed!' said his brother, almost indignant.

'Yes. Well, you know, life goes on.' He smiled.

The autumn deepened. The air smelled clean, like apple peel. Christopher didn't cook any longer: Ilse made soups with pearl barley or dumplings, to tempt his dwindling appetite. He seemed vigorous, apart from eating less. In the evenings they listened to concerts on the Third Programme, or read by the fire in the study. They ate pieces of Bournville dark chocolate, passing round the bar in its gold foil and red outer paper. If there were any clues unsolved from the day's crossword, Christopher would read them out. To Ruth's shame, Ilse got more answers than she did.

Ruth's shortest working day was a Wednesday. She taught only three lessons, two in the morning, the third during the first period after lunch. She was generally home by half past two.

She and Christopher usually went for a walk together once she got back and sometimes they went to a tearoom afterwards. On the first Wednesday that November, she came in through the back kitchen door as she always did, putting her music case down on one of the chairs. As soon as she'd taken off her coat she became aware of a great stillness in the house, an empty quiet.

She felt very calm and unhurried. She moved slowly, up the stairs and along the landing. Some reticence made her knock quietly at Christopher's door, even though she half knew he could not hear her. She opened the door and saw that he was not in his bed, but lying across the rug in front of the window, his back facing the door. He didn't look quite tall enough; it was this small diminution, even more than the stillness of him, that made her sure he had died. She stepped just across the threshold into the room, but she did not want to have to see his face and came no further. There was a funny smell in the room. A solitary late wasp buzzed at the glass. Perhaps, she thought, Christopher had been going to let it out when he fell. Ruth moved like a swimmer underwater, as if her limbs were meeting great resistance. She retraced her steps and, at the foot of the stairs, looked in the frayed address book on the telephone table for the doctor's number.

When the doctor arrived she showed him up the stairs and into her uncle's room.

'He hasn't been there long, lunch time or thereabouts, I'd guess,' he told her.

Ruth had the odd thought that he somehow wished to be congratulated for this intelligence.

He handed her a piece of paper. 'You need to take this along to the registrar. He'll give you the green slip for the funeral directors. Have you considered arrangements?'

Ruth looked at him blankly. 'What sort of arrangements?' she asked.

'Rung the undertakers, that sort of thing,' he said.

She had not thought of that, and said so. The doctor offered to telephone for her.

'They're very good. Local people,' he said. 'I play squash with the son occasionally.'

It had never occurred to her that undertakers could be either good or bad, nor that they played games in their spare time. She'd never thought of undertakers doing anything but under-taking or possibly sitting sombrely between undertakings. After making the call, the doctor hovered, evidently wanting to take his leave.

'Please, don't feel you have to wait,' said Ruth. 'I'm all right.'

'If you're sure,' he said, advancing towards the front door.

After he'd gone she went to the telephone and rang the number Peregrine had written on the envelope. Then she went into the kitchen to make a pot of tea. She didn't ring the school to summon Ilse, there seemed no point. It wouldn't make any difference, her coming back early, Christopher would still be dead when she got home. She made the tea and stood drinking at the kitchen table.

After a time there was a subdued knock at the front door. Two men in dark suits stood before her. It was clear, she wasn't quite sure how, that the taller and younger man was senior to his partner. Almost as soon as she had shown them into the house, Peregrine too appeared.

'Might I …?' he said, as he took off his hat.

'Yes, of course. Go up,' Ruth said.

While Peregrine was upstairs, she offered the undertakers a seat and a cup of tea. They murmured a polite refusal.

'We suggest that you come in to discuss arrangements in a day or two. Give you time to talk over any preferences with other family members, if need be. And you will be required to bring the form, from the registrar. If you wish to pay your respects at that time, that will be possible, in our chapel of rest. All right?'

'Yes,' said Ruth. 'Shall I ring you tomorrow to fix a time?'

'At your convenience,' said the undertaker. 'If you have any queries, day or night, you can reach us by telephone.'

Ruth thanked them. The men stood at the foot of the stairs, heads slightly bowed. They didn't seem to mind being kept waiting. Ruth felt awkward standing with them, so she went into the study and stood looking out of the window at the trunk of the monkey puzzle tree. At last Peregrine emerged. His eyes were dry, but rimmed with pink.

'Would you like a drink?' Ruth asked.

'Do you know, I think I will,' said Peregrine.

'Brandy?'

'Please.'

Ruth poured the drink and then stepped out into the hall.

'I'll take you up now,' she told the taller of the two undertakers.

'Thank you, madam,' he said. Madam sounded like a lovely word, so tender, so consoling. It was as if it was a word she'd never heard before, reserved for just this occasion.

She led them up the stairs and along the landing.

'We would advise that you attend downstairs,' said the younger man.

'Of course,' said Ruth, relieved. She didn't want to watch them take her uncle's body away. She felt a rush of gratitude, almost like love, that they were sparing her this sight, that they would take care of everything. There seemed to her to be infinite gentleness just beneath the surface of their solemnity.

'I'll just be in the study, second door on the left, if you need me,' she said. She went back downstairs and into the study, closing the door behind her.

Peregrine stood with his back to the fireplace.

'It's been over thirty years, you see,' he said.

'That is a long time,' Ruth agreed. She felt very tired.

'My wife inherited a small family estate, more of a farm really, over in Northamptonshire,' Peregrine went on. 'She goes every week to meet the tenants, talk over repairs and so on, that sort of thing. Then she has a night in London, a theatre usually. Occasional ballet or concert. Her sister lives near the park. There's a nephew she's very fond of. She dines with one of them.'

'The Mondays and Thursdays,' said Ruth. It was not a question.

'Yes,' said Peregrine. 'The cook gets those evenings off, because Chris likes to make dinner. Liked to. As I'm sure you know.'

'I'd better ring my father, I suppose,' said Ruth.

'Yes, of course. Don't let me keep you,' said Peregrine. 'It suits Celia, you see, to have the cook on Saturdays and Sundays, when she's at home.'

'No, of course,' said Ruth, not knowing how else to reply. 'Please don't feel you must rush off. Do stay for a bit.'

They stood, not speaking.

Then he said, 'When I let the dog out, last thing at night, I generally step out into the garden too, have a sniff of air. From our lawn one can see the electric lights up here. The shape of the hills gets lost, sometimes, in the darkness, so that one can't say where the hills end and the sky begins. It's only from the twinkling that one can tell where the town is. Every night I look up in the direction of Malvern and I think: One of those lights is Chris's.' He bowed his head. 'Well.'

A few days after the funeral it came to Ruth that there was nothing more she could do for Christopher. The days between his death and the service had been so full: choosing hymns, checking the order of service, taking calls from old friends who'd seen the notice in the paper, making sandwiches and cakes for people to have back at the house afterwards. All of this felt as if it was in service of Christopher. Now Ruth found herself wandering about the rooms, picking up things of her uncle's, then putting them down. By his bed was the book he had been reading: *The Badger* by Ernest Neal. She opened the book at the page which was marked with an unwritten-on picture postcard of Gloucester Cathedral, and read: 'It is probably true to say that a badger in the course of its rootings will eat most insects it finds which are of reasonable size … Caterpillars are not despised, and I once found the perfect skin of a hawk-moth larva in some droppings in September.'

It made Ruth happy to imagine her uncle reading these words. She held the pages up to her nose. The book had a faintly musty smell, like a damp church porch. It was comforting.

There was the question of Christopher's things. Ruth understood, now, why he had never had the heart to clear his mother's dressing table or wardrobe, or anyway had never finished the job. The sight of his spectacles, or his dressing gown, engendered a physical ache just below her ribs. Ruth remembered this sensation from the days when her daughters were small and they had gone back to their father's house, leaving some little belonging behind – a crumpled nightdress, a cardigan – in the new quietness of the house. There was such a sadness to these things, at once so full of the personality of their wearer – even carrying a trace of their smell, or the imprint of their body – and yet, at the same time, so empty. The maleness of her uncle's belongings, though, seemed designed to resist sentiment. His shaving brush, the brown leather stud box on his chest of drawers, his small collection of rather mothy ties, seemed almost taunting in their modest utility.

In the drawer of his bedside table she found four photographs. All but one were in black and white. There was a picture of herself as a child, around the first year she'd come to stay in Malvern, during the war. She was holding what looked like a cabbage and smiling crookedly, as though the sun was directly in her eyes. It surprised her that she had no recollection of the picture being taken. There must have been some shared joke about the cabbage: had it been grown in the garden or won perhaps at some fête? She couldn't remember. Ruth looked next at a picture of Christopher, leaning back on his elbows, legs outstretched on a picnic rug, apparently laughing. Beside him, but sitting upright, was a slender man in pale clothes, a straw hat shading his eyes so that it was difficult to read his expression, although from his mouth it looked as if he, too, was laughing. Ruth turned the picture over and saw that Christopher had written on the back, in pencil: 'Self with P, August '48'. Ruth wondered who the invisible third person, the one taking the picture, had been.

The only colour photograph among the pictures she recognised at once as Peregrine, standing beneath a lintel of carved stone, perhaps the door of a cathedral, a pale mackintosh folded over one arm. There was nothing written on the back, so she could not tell the place or date. The last picture was tiny, perhaps two inches square, with serrated edges. It was a picture of a dog. Ruth turned it over and at once recognised her grandmother's handwriting. 'Meggie in Cornwall'. This photograph made Ruth feel overwhelmed with sadness for her uncle, for the lost world of his and her father's boyhood, with its childish adventures and pets and days at the seaside. He had never mentioned a boyhood dog. But then there were so many things he had not told her. And many things she had never thought to ask until now.

Peregrine had come to the funeral, sitting by himself near the back of the church. Ruth, seeing how the church was filling up, left her place in the front pew to make sure the vergers had enough orders of service to hand out. Catching sight of Peregrine, she had gone over to him.

'Would you like to come and sit with us?' she whispered.

'Thank you, but I think I'm better off back here,' he said.

After the service he had slipped away, not coming back to the house. Ruth was sorry not to have had the chance to see him again. She handed plates of sandwiches round, while Ilse filled empty glasses with more sherry. There were quite a few people she had never met, former colleagues of her uncle's, she supposed. The old people seemed to be enjoying themselves, as Iris had predicted. Funerals are the cocktail parties of the over seventies, she had told Ruth that morning.

'You'll never get rid of them. Once they get a glass of Madeira in them they'll be here all night.'

'Mummy, honestly. It'll be sherry anyway.'

'Same difference. Don't give them too much to eat, for God's sake, or we'll never see the back of them. Provincial types never know when to go.'

An animated lady in tweed was talking to the vicar. She wore a brooch made out of what looked like a pheasant's foot, and the kind of stockings, like uncooked pastry, that Ruth had not seen for years. Were they called lisle stockings? She would have to ask Iris later. The woman engaged Ruth in conversation.

'You'll remember, dear, the King of Abyssinia's daughters? I was just telling the vicar here about them,' she said.

Ruth laughed. 'It's true, they were here, during the war. I wonder what happened to them.'

'How odd,' said the vicar. 'When you first mentioned them, I thought you must have been referring to some kind of butterfly.'

'Heavens, no! They were girls. African girls.'

172

'What on earth were they doing here? Did you ever discover?' Ruth asked the woman.

'I've simply no idea! I believe their father, Highly Mutassi or whatever he was called, left them here. Can't think where he went. Back to Abyssinia presumably. They must have found it fearfully cold.'

'Selassie,' the vicar interjected. 'The Emperor Haile Selassie. Of Ethiopia.'

'That's the one!' The woman beamed. 'Very good-looking fellow as a matter of fact.'

'I wish I'd known them. I could have made friends with them.' Ruth smiled apologetically as she moved away.

Iris stayed on for the night, after the others had gone. Ruth generally saw her mother in London, during one of Iris's visits to the city, or else she went to stay at her house. It was novel, waking up here at home, to know that Iris was under this roof. Ilse went to bed early, having washed up all the glasses and plates and put the remnants of fruit cake into a tin.

'Did you know, I mean, did it ever occur to you, that Uncle Christopher … well, you know. That he wasn't terribly interested in women?' Ruth asked Iris, when the two were installed by the fire in the study.

'Lord, yes! Of course,' her mother retorted.

'But how? He wasn't flamboyant, or anything. I mean, he loved cricket.'

'Well, darling, anyone can love cricket, even a bugger. Though God knows why. Deadly game.'

'Mummy, honestly!'

'What?'

'That's not a very nice thing to call him.'

'All right. Queer then. I think he knew I knew. We never actually talked about it. But I always got on with Chris. Better than with Edward, in a way. I think being queer meant that he wasn't so tied down to convention as your father always was.'

Neither of them spoke for a time.

'Did Daddy know?'

'He never said, in my day. Shouldn't think so. I rather doubt any of the Brownings took it in. You have to remember, it was illegal. He could have gone to prison.'

'I don't think I ever knew that. I knew people disapproved, but ...' said Ruth.

'Oh yes. Right up until Wolfenden. 'Sixty-six, I think it was. Or '67. People were sent to jail,' Iris said.

'Gosh. That's awful.'

'Ghastly. It was all right in London, I mean, where no one could have cared less who people slept with. But somewhere like here, where everyone pries ... The most marked characteristic of the provincial English is that they disapprove of everything.' Iris gave a little shudder, as if Malvern were distasteful to her.

'You live in the country though,' said Ruth.

'The North is different,' said Iris. 'What are those lines, from Tennyson?

> 'Bright and fierce and fickle is the South,
> And dark and true and tender is the North,
> In the North long since my nest is made.

'I may not have got that quite right. Anyway, that's how I feel.'

Ruth wished her mother could stay on, but Iris said she had to go the next day: she had plans to lunch with Jamie in London before going back. After seeing her onto the platform, Ruth glanced back at Iris. Her mother stood looking straight ahead, her handbag balanced on her case beside her. At this little distance Ruth saw, suddenly, that her mother was old. Iris's hair was fine and dull and her bouclé wool coat, though evidently well made, sagged slightly at the hem from years of use. Her thick sand-coloured tights wrinkled at her ankles. To the other passengers waiting at the station, to people who didn't know her, she would just look like any other old lady, spindly and unremarkable. This apprehension made Ruth dither by the taxis outside. She half wanted to go back and embrace her mother, as if to shield her. But they had already said their goodbyes and Iris didn't go in for lingering embraces. It would be awkward to go back. Iris might think something was wrong.

Ruth walked up the hill to the post office. In her bag was a little brown-paper parcel containing Christopher's leather stud box, worn pale at the hinge. His initials, C.B., were only barely discernible on the lid. She had taken out all the bits and pieces: a safety pin, some collar studs, a foreign coin, two small mother-of-pearl buttons. Her uncle's gold cuff links she had wrapped in a clean tissue and tucked back into the box. After some hesitation, she put the foreign coin in, too. This she had done the night before, once Iris had gone up to bed. She had taken a sheet of writing paper and written 'Dear Peregrine' at the top. Her pen hovered over the blank page for minute after minute, but no words came. In the end she had scrunched the paper into a ball and thrown it into the embers of the fire in the study grate. She had not enclosed a note, only addressed it to him, without giving a return address. He would know.

A few days later, Edward telephoned and invited her to lunch. 'Come early, can you, darling? We need to have a bit of a talk. To do with the house and so on. About twelve?'

Ruth had already decided that she was going to ask her father to let her stay on in the house until next spring. She knew that Edward had never been entirely happy that she had settled in Malvern with his brother. To him, it had always seemed a funny sort of a life for a young person. Although of course she was no longer young. Now she needed time to go through all the things she and Ilse and Christopher had accumulated – old toys and bikes and books of Emily and Isobel's, too – and to decide what they should do, where they might go. Ilse's mother had talked of selling the small farm where her daughter grew up. Her sister –

Ilse's aunt – was living in a new apartment block in Bad Segeberg. Germany was a possibility.

Her stepmother came to the door and took her coat.

'It's only cauliflower cheese. Will you mind?' Helen looked flustered. 'Come through, Daddy's in the morning room.'

Ruth could feel herself tremble, slightly, with resolve. She felt as she had when, as a little girl, she had asked her father for an increase in her pocket money. It was odd to think how many decades had gone by since, without her ever asking him for anything. Six months, she thought. Surely he'll give me six months.

Chapter 12

The man was not a handsome man; as for the dog, it was probably the ugliest dog Isobel had ever seen. Hardly anyone – in fact, no one – had ever brought a dog into the gallery, at least not since she had worked here. Down towards Park Lane she sometimes saw slightly continental-looking elderly people in smart old-fashioned overcoats, buttoned to their chins, with rickety dogs. These dogs did not pull eagerly as the expanse of the park came into view, nor strain to sniff where other dogs had been. They were polite and greying and their leads hung slack at their owners' side, like ribbons. But at this Piccadilly end of Mayfair dogs of any kind were a rarity.

Isobel wondered what combination of breeds in this dog's ancestry could have created the animal in the gallery. She knew about breeds, because she and Emily had made a detailed study of *The Observer's Book of Dogs* throughout their childhood. Sometimes they had just flicked through the little book, silently; at other times they had played a game of matching breeds with the people they knew. Daddy was the Otterhound with the kind, rather sad face, and Mummy was the Egyptian Sheepdog, bright-eyed and eager-looking, but always slightly worried, like the dog in the picture, in case she wasn't doing things right. Ilse was the Wheaten Terrier and Granny Iris, of course, was the Saluki, and so was Digby. All Daddy's side of the family were spaniels or setters, of one sort or another, except their stepmother, Valerie, who was a bit pinched and disapproving, like the Sealyham. They couldn't match the funniest-looking dogs with anyone, so they called each other their names.

'You're the Affenpinscher!' Isobel teased Emily.

'Well, you're the Griffon! No, the Dandie Dinmont!'

Their favourite dog in the whole book was the Puli because it looked exactly like a string mop and you never, ever, saw one in real life. The fact that its name began with a P added to their enthusiasm, because the dogs were described in alphabetical order, so it took dedication to reach the Puli. They always studied every entry, for every breed, Isobel often reading aloud while her sister sucked her thumb in mute concentration; to gloss over a page never occurred to either of them and to have turned straight to their favourite, skipping the rest, would have been heresy. When they grew up, the girls agreed, they would have two Puli dogs each. They even had names for them.

Isobel guessed that the dog in the gallery was descended from some sort of bull terrier, probably a Staffordshire, to judge by the implacable broadness of the shoulders and the closeness and colouring of the coat, with perhaps some border terrier to explain the otter-like shape of its jaw and the suggestion of tufted dark brows above its eyes. Its coat was the colour of ginger nuts, flecked with black then overlaid with irregular white splodges, as if someone had been decorating a ceiling while this dog reclined below, and the brush had dripped paint onto its back. Its tail had been docked, but badly, so that a long stump remained, clumsily wagging whenever it looked in the direction of its master. It had warty lumps on either cheek and above each eye, from which grew irregular clumps of coarse whiskers. The eyes had the bulge as well as the mystery of a seal's. The dog's expression spoke of boredom, reproach and patience, sorely tried but bravely borne. The surprisingly dainty little nails – some dark, some pink – clicked on the gallery's glossy stone floor.

It was love at first sight.

'If there's anything I can help you with, a price list, artist information …' said Isobel. The man glanced at her as if mildly surprised to be spoken to at all.

'I like your dog,' she added. Now the man peered at her as through fog, narrowing his eyes, but still made no reply.

Grumpy sod, thought Isobel. She turned back to her electric typewriter: '… since the early 1950s, the artist has lived for most of the year in Crete, where the vivid light has continued to exert its influence on his …' Grumpy fat bastard, she thought, glancing in the man's direction as she typed. The man had thin lips and thin, straight hair which grew a couple of inches over his collar, but everything else about him was plump, even his hands. He moved very slowly among the pictures, standing with his arms limp at his sides. He appeared to be sighing heavily: he did not seem to be enjoying himself much. She guessed that he had come into the gallery simply to kill a little time. Perhaps he was on his way to meet someone and found he was early. Or perhaps he was just walking his dog. She supposed that he didn't like the pictures; maybe he didn't like art at all, but it was probably easier to take a dog into a gallery than into any other kind of shop, at least around here. She carried on copying out the notes for the gallery's next exhibition: '… palette and the rugged shapes of rock and mountain on his forms. Water, and especially the movement and course of water, has become a presence in the more recent work, whether the white-fringed cascade of a waterfall or the slower trajectory of a stream, running through …'

'The Roger Hilton isn't dated. Do you have a note of when it was made?' She hadn't heard the man approach the highly polished elm table where she worked. He had a funny accent, like an American accent and yet not. The sound of the dog's nails on the hard floor must have been drowned out by the matching clack of her typewriter. If he recognised a Roger Hilton, she had been wrong to think he had no interest in

179

painting. When people described a picture as having been 'made', it usually meant they were involved in the art world; ordinary people said 'painted'. Maybe he was an important collector.

''Sixty-seven, I think. I can find out, if you'd hang on for a minute?'

Again the man made no answer.

'Would you like to wait, while I look out the details?' asked Isobel.

'Why not?' said the man, brusquely.

Isobel got up and went to the back of the gallery, where an office was concealed behind a plasterboard wall which formed the focal point of the gallery and where their best work was generally displayed: in this case, a large Ivon Hitchens, of sage green, moss green, and rust-coloured paint, with a startling bright-blue form – perhaps depicting a stretch of water – on its right-hand side. Isobel went to the file where information about the pictures was kept and re-emerged with a sheet of paper in her hand.

''Sixty-six, it turns out.'

'Do you like it?' the man asked her.

Isobel cocked her head to one side and looked. The canvas showed a tip of black paint emerging from a large blob of black paint, pointing towards a red line and an orange square in the top right-hand corner.

'I don't know if I like it, exactly,' she said. 'But there's something quite satisfying about it. I like the way the black looks like a witch's hat.'

For the first time the man smiled.

'What's your dog's name?' she asked.

'She's called Rita,' he said.

The man continued to stand at Isobel's desk.

'Will your next show be a group exhibit also?' he asked.

'No. It's a one-man show. John Craxton. From the fifteenth.'

'Good,' said the man, and he left the gallery, without speaking further. As the door fell to, a faint cologne-like smell, half citrus, half spirit, reached Isobel's nose.

She thought no more about him until, three weeks later, her boss, Jonathon, handed her an envelope.

'Fellow left this for you,' he said.

Isobel opened the envelope. Inside were two tickets for a production of *King Lear*. The theatre was one she had never heard of, near King's Cross. The tickets were folded into a piece of lined paper with zigzag tears along the top, where it had evidently been torn from a spring-bound pad.

'Bring a friend and we'll have a drink afterwards. Jacob.'

'I've no idea who these are from. Did he say anything else? What did he look like?'

Jonathon, always dapper, noticed what people looked like. Today he himself wore a bespoke suit in brown wool, complete with a many-buttoned waistcoat. The point of a bright-orange silk handkerchief emerged from a breast pocket.

'Well-covered. Well, fat, if you really want to know. Had a dog with him. My sort of age.'

Isobel couldn't think who she could ask to come with her to the play. She had done *King Lear* at school and remembered it as interminably long. She supposed the man – Jacob – was an actor and she wondered what part he would be taking. Perhaps he would be playing the King himself, although she didn't think he was old enough. It was an odd sort of evening to subject a friend to, not exactly fun. In the end she decided to go by herself.

Jacob didn't seem to be in the play at all, unless he was so disguised that she did not recognise him. The cast all wore modern clothes, but grotty ones. The King, a belching slob of a man in slippers, had evidently won the football pools and his wicked daughters were tarty, shrill young women in skimpy halterneck tops with flamingo-coloured manicures; they kept filing and repainting their nails on stage. Lear's loyal followers wore nylon football shirts and drank beer out of tins, while the Fool seemed to be a match referee, with a whistle on a string around his neck. The play had been compressed into an hour and a half, with no interval.

As the lights came up, Isobel saw that Jacob was waiting for her in the aisle at the end of her row of seats.

'Food or drink?' he asked. He did not seem either surprised or curious that she had come alone.

'Could we have both, do you think?' she answered. She had not eaten before the play.

Out in the dark street Jacob found a taxi, which despatched them to a Greek restaurant, somewhere behind Tottenham Court Road.

'Where's Rita?' asked Isobel.

'At home.' The word home sounded like whom, the way he said it.

'Where are you from, originally I mean?'

'Toronto. But I've been in Europe for over ten years now. Hamburg to begin with, then Amsterdam. I've been in London six years, almost.' Canadian: that explained the accent. His 'O's sounded like double 'O's.

Isobel was not familiar with the things on the menu. She asked Jacob to order for her. A succession of little dishes kept appearing: rings of squid in salty batter, a drab-looking paste which tasted of bonfire smoke, slices of sausage with fennel seeds embedded in the spicy meat. Jacob ate quickly, but not coarsely, scooping the food onto little edible shovels of flat bread.

'What did you think?' asked Jacob, after eating in silence for what felt to Isobel like many, many minutes.

'Of the play?' asked Isobel.

He nodded.

'Well, I thought it was a clever idea to make Poor Tom be a drunk. Otherwise he's so annoying and boring. I liked Goneril and Regan, doing their nails all the time. It was a good idea, having it set in the present, and Lear a pools winner.'

'And what didn't you like?'

'I thought the Fool was too silly, even for a fool. Blowing his whistle all the time. And giving him that accent – Liverpool, was it? – was too gimmicky. But then the whole thing was a gimmick, really. It's a bit long, even cut down like that, but that's the play, isn't it? It does drag on. Are you involved in the production somehow?'

'Yes.' He did not elucidate.

'Oh. Should I have been more tactful?'

He smiled. The rarity of his smiles seemed to imbue them, when they came, with an almost magisterial quality, as if he were bestowing a precious gift.

'I like it, that you say what you think.'

Isobel felt disproportionately thrilled.

'But I don't really know what I'm talking about,' she admitted. 'What did you do, then?'

'I directed.'

'Oh. Goodness. Well, well done! What a thing. What a lot of work that must be, all those people ...'

He took no notice.

'If you'd like to see Rita, we could have coffee at my place?'

Isobel had never seen a flat like it. It was more like the galleries where she had worked than someone's home. Jacob seemed to own almost nothing, but the things he did have were all strange and rather beautiful. In the sitting room was a long wooden settle with a rush seat and beside it an old round oak table with a carved stone lamp set on it. There was a rug on the wall – Jacob told her it came from Isfahan and was late eighteenth century – but the floor was bare. There was nothing else in the room. The entrance hall gave onto a square kitchen and seemed to be where Jacob ate his meals, since it housed the only table a person could sit at. In the hall were a pair of dark ladder-back chairs and bookshelves from floor to ceiling on two walls; French windows opened onto a narrow balcony. Nothing was soft. The dark floorboards were bare; there were no cushions and no curtains. The windows all had wooden shutters.

She followed Jacob into the small kitchen, where he made coffee in a pot which looked as if it was made of antique pewter. From a shelf he took a round wooden box with exotic writing on its lid. Inside were rough squares of Turkish delight, their jewel colours barely visible beneath a drift of icing sugar. He set this and the coffee things on a bamboo tray, which he carried into the room with the rug on the wall. Rita lodged herself on top of his feet, grunting quietly. After a moment's hesitation, Isobel sat next to him on the hard settle. There was nowhere else to sit.

'Where does she sleep?' asked Isobel. She hadn't seen anywhere where a dog might get comfortable. There didn't seem to be a television, to lie in front of, nor even a stereo.

'With me. Luckily I have an enormous bed to push her off onto, because she's like a stone.'

He pronounced the word stone like a Scottish person would say town.

When she asked where the bathroom was, Jacob told her it was through the bedroom: the room was furnished only with a vast bed, the biggest Isobel had ever seen. On one wall was a black and white close-up photograph of an oyster, its folds suggestively fleshy and viscous, framed above the pillows. By one side of the bed, on the floor, was a mound of books and papers. The bathroom beyond contained the flat's only mirror, a sliver of dark antique glass above the basin. On the side of the basin was a shelf with toothpaste and two brushes in a glass. The sight of a second brush made Isobel's tummy flip. There was a glass bottle with an old-fashioned label, gold lettering on dark blue. She undid the lid and inhaled a scent of freshly cut limes.

Back in the room with the settle, Isobel felt peculiar, almost giddy, sitting in this flat with this man. This was only the second time they had met, and he had barely said a hundred words to her. He didn't even seem particularly interested in her. He was fat, not good-looking, and he wasn't easy company; he was too old for her and probably too clever; and – not that she set much store by these things – being Canadian just wasn't cool. Even coming from some unheard-of part of rural America was cool, but being Canadian was almost an embarrassment, like coming from Lincolnshire or mid-Wales or somewhere. They hadn't kissed. There was an unexplained toothbrush in his bathroom. But as she sat sipping her too strong coffee, Isobel felt a great certainty that this flat would become her home, that she would come to live here, with him. Rita would be her constant companion and that would be lovely, but Isobel found herself wondering what on earth she would do with all her stuff, her clothes and records and paperback books. Her things would seem awfully tatty, in the austerity of Jacob's rooms. She had never felt this certain about anything before. Until now, things had simply happened: you met someone, you spent a night or more together; one job followed on from another.

They were married five months later, on a Tuesday, at Old Marylebone Town Hall. Isobel took the afternoon off work, but went into the gallery for the morning. She could not concentrate on the catalogue she was meant to be editing, but catching the tube down into central London made her feel marvellously strong and exciting, as if she were a girl in a glamorous film, living a double life. Everything seemed to take on more intensity with Jacob, and more speed. She soon realised that he was not fat because he was lazy, but because he was a man of huge, impulsive appetites. Suddenly he might want to eat lobster, or make love, or find the best whisky sours in London, or go to an all-night cinema screening, and she would be swept up in his enthusiasms, carried along. She had always thought of herself as rather a cautious person, but Jacob made her feel otherwise, as if she were daring and capricious.

It had come as no surprise that he had been married before, to a Turkish German who had insisted that she was a performer, an artist – an important artist, as the world would surely discover – in her own right, and not merely an actress. She had wanted Jacob to take her name when they married, as a gesture of feminist solidarity, although, Jacob remarked wryly, she had felt no such qualms about obtaining a Canadian passport. A touring production had brought her experimental theatre company to Canada. When they returned to Europe Jacob had gone with them. The marriage had lasted less than two years.

It never occurred to Isobel that a man who had shown such little resolve to stay with his first wife might be anything less than fully committed to her, his second. Instead, she relished the flurry of her wedding, the spontaneity. Not waiting set their marriage apart from other people's plodding, careful romances; it made her feel special. Isobel's wedding guests were her two best girlfriends, Jonathon from the gallery, her mother and her sister Emily and her uncle Jamie, with his wife Shura. Emily had left the baby with Ilse for the day, which disappointed Jacob who, when Isobel had brought him to Malvern to meet her mother, had taken a shine to Ilse, talking to her in German, flirting slightly, so that she went a bit pink and laughed immoderately. This had pleased Ruth, who sometimes felt that Ilse did not get enough attention from the family. It made her favourably disposed towards the man who was about to become her son-in-law, despite knowing so little of him.

Isobel's father Harry and stepmother Valerie were away, a cruise to Madeira. Which was just as well, since Harry could barely disguise his consternation. Isobel was sad that her father would not be present to give her away, but in a registry office there wasn't an aisle to process down, just a short length of royal-blue carpet; there wouldn't have been much for him to do.

She was relieved too: it always felt awkward to their children when Ruth and Harry were brought together, and Valerie didn't help by always referring to Ilse as 'your mother's friend', never by her name and never without a heavy intonation, thick with ridicule. And who was this Jacob, anyhow? That was what Harry wanted to know. Not English (though Canadians were nice enough people, he had to concede), not especially young. Didn't have a proper job. Worse, not a Roman Catholic – and a divorcé! It was really too bad.

'But, Daddy,' Isobel had teased, 'if they were married outside the Church and the Church doesn't count non-religious weddings as proper marriages, that means you don't have to believe Jacob even is a divorced man, surely?'

Harry couldn't remember when Isobel had become so difficult. She had been a chattery, biddable little girl, with her lovely hair like Devon cream, and always smiling. If anything, it had been her sister, quiet, watchful Emily, whom he would have expected to become the wilful one. Not that Emily was any easier, now. One simply didn't know what to say, when people asked about her. To begin with, he had only mentioned the child to his closest relatives. Poor Verity had been all for simply cutting Emily and the baby off altogether. But he had to acknowledge that his sister had become somewhat embittered, never having had a child of her own; and that frightful man keeping her hanging on all those years, until his invalid wife died at last. Then, instead of doing the right thing by Verity, he had married the nurse within weeks, and she nearly thirty years younger. Small wonder then that his sister was a little testy about Emily. But it wasn't the child's fault, after all, to have been born to an unmarried mother. Isobel had pointed out, naughtily, that Our Lord himself had been born to an unmarried woman and in a way, as long as she didn't repeat it to Valerie, he had to admit she had a point.

As soon as he'd held the child he was smitten, utterly. It wouldn't be human, he felt, or at all decent, to disapprove of such a miraculous, perfect thing as a baby. And the surprise was that Valerie was just as taken with the child. She could hardly leave the house without coming back with some knick-knack for the new arrival: a knitted hat or a row of rattling ducks that fitted across the pram, or a spoon with a bunny on it. Being a step-grandmother was much nicer than being a stepmother. She was not the interloper who had come, uninvited, into Ruth's place, not so far as this child was concerned; she was a fait accompli, someone to be accepted, even loved. And the child had all the more need for grandparents, with no father. Having seen her father soften so towards the baby, Isobel was confident that he would come round to Jacob once he knew him better.

As his wedding guests Jacob brought only the young man who worked as his assistant, and Rita, with a big daisy-like flower tied to her collar in a flourish of dark-green satin ribbon. Rita hadn't been allowed inside the registry office, even though Jacob had told his assistant to wear dark glasses and pretend to be blind, so as to pass her off as a guide dog, the only kind of canines permitted; but neither man nor dog had given a convincing display and Rita had had to wait outside, tethered to a handrail. She didn't like being left alone in an unfamiliar setting and her mouth gaped with worry, displaying a jagged expanse of mottled gum, half pink, half dark. By the time they emerged into the sunlit street, Rita had managed to work her collar round in order to chew off the flower. The ribbon was shredded, blackened with spit, and what remained of the petals stuck damply to the pavement, becoming transparent, like rain-soaked blossom. This was the closest the bridal pair came to confetti. There had been no bridesmaids, no hats. They'd kissed on the pavement before heading off, in a loose convoy of black taxis, for lunch at a fashionable fish restaurant that was a favour-ite of Jacob's. Jonathon deposited Rita at the gallery on the way. The dog was becoming rather a fixture, since Isobel had moved in with Jacob: she even had her own water bowl at the gallery.

Jonathon thought it gave the place character: an ugly dog had edge.

'*Fruits de mer* and Sancerre,' said Jacob into his new bride's ear. 'Then I think we should go back to bed for the rest of the day.'

They were to take their honeymoon later, once the production Jacob was working on was up and running. Soon after they met, Jacob had been approached by a senior arts officer from a south London borough who had been impressed with his *Lear*. The idea was to stage a *Romeo and Juliet* in which ordinary members of the public, people with no experience of acting, would take the lead roles. Jacob had taken the notion a step further: the Capulets were to be played by white Londoners; the Montagues, by residents of West Indian descent. The idea was to see whether this piece – Jacob always called a play a piece, Isobel had noticed – about conflict could actually bring a community together. It had taken some months to get the funding together and find a rehearsal space. The guy he'd found to play Tybalt – he was perfect: charismatic, shaven-headed, with more than a hint of menace – had close affiliations with the National Front, if he wasn't an actual member. Tempers had run high, had threatened at times to escalate into violence. Jacob had brought in a yoga teacher to work with the cast, calm them down, before each rehearsal. Theatre people were always going on about the breath, using it as an excuse for fluffing their lines, or emphasising in the wrong places, or mumbling. With an untrained cast, Jacob told Isobel, the breath was a real problem. You couldn't make a play if the cast couldn't control the breath adequately. The yoga was intended to help with the breath, as well as subduing hostilities.

It was only natural that Jacob should keep irregular hours during the rehearsal process. Isobel was busy at work too, preparing a show: paintings and works on paper by an artist who'd been a fellow student with Lucian Freud at the Dedham

189

art school. Isobel was learning that some – in fact most – artists whose reputations had fallen into obscurity were neglected for a reason: they weren't much good. But this work she liked: strange, intricate pen drawings of shells and leaves and small landscape paintings, redolent of Samuel Palmer, but executed in fierce colours. There were some ceramics too. Isobel was enjoying putting the pieces together. Instead of commissioning an essay from some worthy at the Slade or the Royal College, she had asked a young poet, whose evocation of a vanished rural England was drawing favourable comparisons with John Clare, to write something about the painter's relationship with landscape. And she had interviewed the artist herself for the catalogue.

Afterwards she wondered whether she could have read the signs more quickly. The one art form Jacob had never shown any interest in was music, yet he now professed to find the interminable dingle dingle of the santoor deeply moving. He had always washed in the mornings, but now began to take his bath every night, however late he came home from rehearsals. When she bagged up their clothes for the launderette – there was no washing machine in the flat, because Jacob didn't like the look of machinery, nor the sound – his pockets were already empty, where before they had yielded ticket stubs, scraps of paper, receipts. Words he had never said before, words like alignment and meridians, issued from his lips, pronounced without irony.

But as soon as she saw them, side by side at the private view party in the gallery, Isobel knew. Jacob had brought three or four people he was working with on *Romeo and Juliet*: the assistant stage manager, Tom, who painted in his spare time; a nice girl called Amanda who did costumes; a younger man with shaven hair like Fuzzy-Felt and a dazzling gold-toothed smile, presumably the one who was to play Tybalt. The other woman with them had thick curls which dangled over her shoulders and she was slender, with a back which curved like a dancer's. Her silver bangles slid up and down her long arms as she gesticulated. There was something provocative about this woman. The spirals of her hair looked heavy, like jewellery, as if she had been adorned. She was sinewy, hard. Jacob was standing next to her, listening, his head inclined, nodding as if in agreement.

Isobel felt two things almost at once. The first was a sense of wrenching, as when she was a little girl, when she and Emily had been in Malvern for weeks on end during the summer and then the morning came of the day when it was time for them to go back and not see their mother again for ages and ages, for what felt like an eternity; away from the hills and the long afternoons and the grass tickling your bare legs, and the creaking landing and the bath tap which dripped year after year; and the warm familiar smell of your mother's neck as you buried your head against it, your nose in the hollow of her collarbone, and whispered, 'Please don't make me go. Don't make me go.'

And she felt tired.

There was the rest of the party to get through, and then a dinner in honour of the artist in the private room of a nearby restaurant. As the party thinned at the gallery, Jacob came over.

'We're going to walk up to Old Compton Street, get some spaghetti. I'll see you later.'

She stared at him. He still looked the same, which was odd, because everything had changed now. He sounded the same and the faint smell of limes still came to her as he leant in to kiss her on the cheek. Over dinner, Isobel tried to decide what she would say when she got home. Whether she should confront him outright, or try to trick him into revelation. She wondered whether he would stall, lie, try to pretend nothing had happened. Whether he would weep and beg her to forgive him.

By the time she returned to the flat, she felt too weary and too disappointed for guile.

'I know you're having sex with that woman you brought to the gallery. Is she the yoga teacher?'

Jacob did not blench, nor colour. He merely looked straight at her.

'Yes.'

Isobel began to cry.

'But we've only been married for five minutes! I thought you liked me. You're meant to like me.'

'Of course I like you. I love you. This doesn't mean I don't.'

'What does it mean then? Is it that you don't want me in bed?'

'No! I love you in bed, in my bed. There's no one else I want to wake up next to. It doesn't mean anything.'

'Then why? Why risk making me so unhappy for something that doesn't even mean anything to you?'

'It just kind of happened. It's been really good for my back. You know I've had a lot of trouble with my lumbar vertebrae.'

Isobel could scarcely believe her ears. She stopped crying and wiped her nose on her sleeve.

Women, he explained – sex – they were one of life's greatest pleasures. Enjoying them was like enjoying food, or wine, or art.

'You wouldn't expect me never to see Brecht because I like Chekhov as well, would you?' he asked. 'Or never to eat tuna again, just because I said I liked salmon.'

'But dead fish don't have feelings, and I do,' Isobel wailed.

'I just don't see why marriage should mean that you don't want the person you love to enjoy life,' said Jacob. 'Think of all the things that life has to offer. Where does it say that being married means being so ungenerous? Don't you desire the happiness of the person you love? Why should a wedding band mean that you deliberately restrict that person's pleasure? Anyway, you're the one I want to spend my life with. You're the one I want to talk to. We should celebrate how special we are together. This stuff is superfluous.'

'So is this your way of telling me that you're not going to stop, just because I've found out? Is that it?'

'OK, OK, I'll never do it again.' Jacob smiled and raised his hands as if in surrender. 'I'll come over to your view that loving someone should be all about sacrifice. You can make me a coat out of stinging nettles, like the girl in the fairy tale. Or a hair shirt.'

Isobel sighed. 'What is a hair shirt, do you think?' she asked. She lacked the energy to argue.

'A shirt made of hair, I suppose. It would have to be pretty long hair, wouldn't it? To be woven.'

'You'd think that would be nice and smooth, though, if it was made of long hair. Not a punishment,' said Isobel.

'Suits me,' said Jacob.

They'd got through it. But the yoga teacher turned out to be only the first. The next had seemed worse, horribly glamorous and threatening, a blonde in faded jeans and cowboy boots who produced cultural programmes for radio. Fiona. Isobel had come home from work one day to find this woman in the flat, drinking coffee with Jacob on the long wooden settle. She wore a chunky belt buckle and bracelet, Navajo-style pieces made of silver, inset with bold slabs of turquoise. Next to her, Isobel felt mousy and somehow uncourageous. Fiona hadn't been Jacob's favourite – that had been later, the Spanish actress with the annoying little-girly voice. Each time, Jacob managed to persuade her that it was shamefully bourgeois to get upset, that she was welcome to take lovers of her own. Their marriage was strong enough to withstand these things, because they were unique. Special.

The girlfriends left traces on him. There was something he did to her with his hands, when they were in bed, that he had not done before, a way of flexing his fingers which made her gasp. The pleasure of it was shameful to her, that he should have learned some trick in the bed of another woman, then brought it back to perform on his wife. He started buying a different newspaper, another brand of coffee. Unfamiliar paperbacks, new tapes of music, appeared in the flat. When it was the Spanish girl, volumes of Lorca turned up on the bedside table. It was a disappointment to both of them that Isobel couldn't prevent herself from minding. During the time she spent with Jacob she came to believe, at his insistence, that the blame for her unhappiness lay with her own childishly conventional belief in exclusive love. It was so ordinary of her to be jealous, and Jacob prized the sense of not being like other people. It was as if she, with her common or garden emotion and not he with his unfaithfulness, were letting them both down.

'Another adult can't make you miserable. You can only do that to yourself,' Jacob told her gently. 'It's a choice. You can choose. You can choose whether to be generous in love, or to be selfish.'

She came to believe that he was right. And then, while Jacob was assembling French bread and olives and cheese for a Saturday lunch, Isobel, looking for something to read on the shelves in the hall, had taken out a book with a dark-green spine. It was called *A View of the Harbour*: on the cover was a painting of what looked like a little Cornish town, St Ives perhaps; painted cottages, their gardens gay with flowers, giving way to a glimpse of Atlantic blue water. A scene of innocence. She opened it at random and read a couple of pages, liked them, turned to the front to find out more about the author, and there it was, an inscription: 'For Jacob, a souvenir of our perfect day by the sea, with my love, Sarah.'

Nice handwriting. They always had nice handwriting. They were a type, women with long fringes and hoop earrings and arty aspirations, who wrote with calligraphy pens. Below the inscription was a date, not distant. Isobel's heart lurched, then began to thump, as though a fugitive was tapping an impatient steel-capped toe within her chest. Her mouth tasted bitter, as if she had drunk too much coffee. A tangled knot of disappointment began a spin cycle in her stomach. She felt herself unravelling.

If he had been able to keep them out of the flat, had he confined them to anonymous rooms, then she might have been able to go on. Instead they invaded every crevice of her life, her bookshelf, her bedroom, even her body. Just when she supposed herself to be alone with Jacob, they ambushed her, announcing themselves without pity or care.

Isobel went into the other room and pulled a suitcase from under the bed.

Rita followed, her brow furrowed. The dog's shoulders had become bulkier with time, her neck thicker. From the protuberant moles on her cheeks sprang ever wirier hairs, now flecked with grey. Departures always made Rita anxious. She had a habit of sticking close to whichever of them looked set to be going somewhere, as if her vigilance would ensure she did not get left behind. Isobel generally did take Rita, since the dog had become an accepted fixture at the gallery. The thought that she would have to leave the dog behind – she was Jacob's dog really – was even worse than leaving her husband. Isobel loved the dog. It wasn't the dog's fault.

When she had filled the case and snapped the buckles shut, Isobel sat down on the edge of the bed, like a traveller in a distant hotel room, pausing to gain a moment's composure before stepping out, a stranger, into the bright street. The dog came and put her heavy face into Isobel's lap. She looked up balefully. Together they stayed still for a few minutes, regarding each other, until Rita seemed to become embarrassed by the unguardedness of her own emotion and licked her chops self-consciously and looked away.

Chapter 13

Everyone had been amazed that Emily's baby was a boy, except Iris, who claimed she'd always known because she'd had a dream in which he had appeared.

'Granny's turned into such an old witch,' Isobel told her sister. 'She's always on about signs and stuff. She told me that the morning Digby died, she went down to the river and a heron came and circled, just above her head. Herons are shy of humans, apparently. She said they never fly close. But this one did, for ages.'

'And?' asked Emily.

'And she was sure it was Digby, coming to say goodbye. To show her he was OK, before he went.'

'It probably was.'

Isobel groaned, in mock horror. 'Oh, honestly, Lem. Not you as well!'

Emily laughed. 'Was she all right though? It must be hard on her own.'

'She seems OK, actually. She'd read somewhere that it's not as bad to be widowed if you've had a happy marriage as it is if you've been miserable together. Because of the regret apparently. She was saying how lucky she'd been with Digby, how they'd never had a cross word. She says she likes solitude. Anyway, she's got Birdle.'

'Birdle's always given me the creeps,' said Emily.

'Really? I thought you liked him.'

'Not really. It's the scaly grey legs. And there's something cunning about him.'

'I know what you mean,' Isobel agreed.

Emily had not told Gary to begin with. She didn't know what to say, or how to choose the words to say it. They were propped up in her bed, eating bacon sandwiches, one Saturday morning not long before Christmas. He'd come to the flat early, before she was dressed, while she was still sleep-bleary, still in the pair of blue socks she wore to keep her feet warm during the night. After they had made love, both with their socks on, Gary still in his shirt, he had gone through to the kitchen.

'Do you want ketchup in yours?' he called.

'No thanks, just butter,' she replied.

He brought the two plates back into the bedroom, balancing one on his arm like a waiter, two mugs of tea in the other hand.

'Gary?' she said.

His mouth was full, so he took a moment to respond. 'Yes, my princess?'

'I think I'm pregnant. I am pregnant.'

He had just taken another bite. 'Flippineck!' he said, his voice muffled by the toast. 'Shit! Shit!' Hot tea was spilling onto his fingers. 'Shit! How did that happen, then?'

She could think of an answer, but being facetious didn't seem fair, after the shock of the announcement. Looking at him, it was impossible to tell if he was angry or horrified or just astonished.

'You're bloody joking, aren't you?' he asked.

'No, I'm not. I'm not joking.'

He had got to his feet and stood now by the side of the bed, the remainder of the sandwich still uneaten. His shirt was unbuttoned. His genitals looked dark against the paleness of his thighs. Neither of them said anything. Gary went to his coat, took out his cigarettes and lighter.

'I don't want to not see you,' she said.

He didn't answer straight away. 'Look, it's not that easy, this. I've been meaning to tell you. I'm not on my own.'

Emily blushed. 'I didn't think you were. The reason I never asked you was because I thought, I don't have to feel bad, if I don't know. But I sort of did know really. I mean, you'd have stayed the night. You wouldn't always have had to get back.'

'Yeah, well.' He looked away, drawing hard on his cigarette.

'Are you actually married?' she asked.

'Yeah. Shelly. We've been married six and a half years.'

'Jesus. You must have been awfully young!' said Emily.

'We've been going out since I was fifteen.'

'Crikey,' said Emily.

'Our Nicole, she's going on five. Be five next March. There's another one on the way and all.'

'You're joking,' said Emily.

He gave no response, except exhaling. His breath sounded harsh.

'That's pretty heavy,' said Emily. It seemed a stupid thing to say, but she couldn't think of any other way to phrase their predicament. Of all the things he might have told her about his life when they were not together, she had never considered this.

He came and sat next to her against the pillows. He put his socked feet back up on the bed and took her elbow, tilting her forward so that he could put his arm around her shoulders.

'So what are we going to do now?' she asked.

'Fuck knows,' said Gary.

Emily spent that Christmas with her father and stepmother in London. She wore a big jumper and didn't tell them about the baby. She had no idea how she would ever be able to break the news to them. When Isobel suggested that it might be better not to say anything until an actual baby was born, she was only half joking. They disapproved of things. Emily was glad she didn't live nearer, so they could not involve themselves too closely in her day-to-day life.

It was easier with her mother. Emily told Ruth the same thing she'd already told Isobel: that the baby's father was married. Her sister had at once asked a flurry of questions: How long had it been going on? How could she have let this happen? Hadn't she ever heard of birth control? Why didn't he leave his wife? As ever, Emily did not know what to say. She only knew she could not face admitting the truth, that the father of her child already had a daughter, that his wife was also expecting a child, due to be born only weeks before her own. All of which made her not only a stupid, irresponsible person, but probably a bad one as well.

So she lied. Lying was not difficult, as long as you kept things simple, resisted the urge to add what sounded like convincing detail. Other people didn't need minutiae in order to believe what you told them, because they did not listen as intently as all that; the details were for the benefit of the teller, not the told. You could even start to believe yourself.

She had liked fibbing as a little girl. Growing up, Emily had realised that not telling the truth was a way of escaping, without looking as if you were trying to. Her sister always wanted to know why, where, how, but sometimes Emily did not feel like telling her. Being a child had sometimes felt like playing in a scrap of garden, overlooked by many windows, never out of sight. The occasional lie, for Emily, was like finding a hidden door into a private, secret garden, where no one could see you. The person you were lying to could be right there next to you, believing you, but you were concealed from them because your truth was hidden. Even the simplest lie, like what you'd had for lunch at school, could give you a sense of escape. It was a small kind of freedom.

This comforting deceit, disused for years, returned to her when it came to the baby. She told her mother and her sister that the child's father was not only married, but was moving to the North East, where his wife's family was from. That they had stopped seeing each other anyway, at around the time of the baby's conception. It had never been anything serious for either of them.

'It will be all right,' Ruth had said. 'We'll help you. We can work something out between us, so you won't have to manage all by yourself.'

Isobel was not so sanguine.

'I was the one who played with dolls,' she complained. 'You liked animals. You never liked my dolls; I always had to dress them and undress them by myself, and give them their bath, when you wouldn't play. I never liked animals.'

'Yes, you did!' said Emily. 'You did. You always liked dogs, remember?'

'I'm just saying …' said Isobel.

'I know,' said Emily.

'I wasn't even sure that you, you know … Liked men,' added Isobel.

'What, did you think I was a lezzer, like Mum?' laughed Emily.

'Well, you never mentioned any boyfriends. How was I to know? Anyway, Mum's not a lezzer! They're just friends. Honestly. You're so disgusting sometimes.'

Isobel could never acknowledge Ruth and Ilse as a couple. She clung to the belief that Ruth still loved their father, citing the fact that she had never taken up with any other man as proof. When they were children Isobel had always believed that her parents would get back together, even after Harry married Valerie. It was a wish she had never entirely grown out of.

Gary continued coming to the flat, every Saturday, early. Sometimes he popped in midweek too, but it was harder in the winter, with the dark evenings, to justify being out of his own house. They never talked about his little girl, but more and more they both referred to Shelly and to Shelly's parallel pregnancy. By common but unspoken consent, they did not refer to her by name.

'Has she got stretch marks?' Emily asked.

'She's got some cream off her sister. It's got vitamins in and that.'

'Is it vitamin E oil?'

'It's cream, not oil. White stuff. I'll have a look at the label if you want.'

Morning sickness, tiredness, aching legs: Emily began to feel quite a bond with Shelly. After all, what wrong had she ever done to Emily? Shelly had grown up, trained as a hairdresser, married her first boyfriend, moved from the village where she grew up to the town where she'd gone to school; she had become a mother, was expecting a second child. None of this had happened in order to spite Emily. It was nothing to do with her. When Emily imagined Shelly, she imagined her as someone likeable.

Nor did Emily feel guilt towards Shelly. Things happened in life, had their own momentum. You could judge people, or you could just accept, as she tried to, that nobody was perfect, that everyone was merely trundling along doing their best to be happy, to get the most out of life. It wasn't as if anyone wished anyone else harm. Emily wasn't expecting Gary to leave his family, or even to help with the baby when it came. And, anyway, she hadn't done it on purpose. She hadn't chosen to fall in love with a married man.

If it was love. There were moments when Emily didn't really know what she felt about Gary. She was always glad when she saw him, a little start in her chest when he smiled at her in greeting. Ease in his company. Laughter. Slight impatience, sometimes. There had been afternoons when, if she was honest, she felt relieved that he'd gone. Desire: that was the overwhelming thing and it never seemed to diminish. The desire extended to every part of his body, so that no place was out of bounds. Everything seemed beautiful, to her: his flat, wide wrists; the smell of his underarms; his teeth. The secret parts of him remained mysterious, as if they belonged in a marine world, not a human one. They were like the contents of a rock pool: the coral-coloured skin of his scrotum, like an anemone; the saline taste; the dark star of his anus contracting, muscular, like a sea urchin.

She only saw him once in the month before their child was born. Shelly's blood pressure had risen dramatically in her thirty-sixth week of pregnancy, and she'd had to be admitted for a Caesarean section soon after. The baby was a little girl, Vicky. Gary had rung her from a pay phone, to tell her the news.

'What does she look like?' Emily had asked.

'Like a baby. She doesn't look like me. Fair. She's gorgeous.'

'You'll have to bring a picture of her. Next time.'

'I will do.'

Five and a half weeks later, Emily woke up in the night because she had peed in the bed. At least that was what she thought must have happened: she was woken by the sensation of warm wetness, turning quickly cold as it soaked the sheets. She got up and pulled the duvet off the bed, trying to prevent the liquid from getting through the linen, to clog the feathers. As she yanked at the cover, she was gripped by a spasm of tightness which squeezed until the breath was wrung out of her and she had to lean forward, gasping. She waited for a time, until the pain came again. She felt very calm, although her hands were trembling, and her legs too. She went to make herself tea, then sat in the front room for an hour and a half, until the contractions were coming more often and it was almost light. Then she went to the telephone and rang Pat.

Roger and Pat had been wonderful. They had been the first people she told, even before her sister.

'I won't ask,' Roger had said. 'You just let me know what suits you. If you want to go part time, later on, we can sort it out. And after the baby comes.'

For the past few months, Friday nights had meant a meal at Roger and Pat's place. Their son Nigel was in his final year at university in Cardiff, but they were used to being three: they would be glad to have the extra company if she'd join them. Emily and Roger usually chatted about work, for the first half-hour or so, while Pat was in and out of the kitchen. Pat liked trying out new recipes from all over the world, with varying success. Her sister had given her a book, *Continental Cuisines*, which she was working her way through.

'I'll tell you what, love,' Roger told Pat, as they negotiated a dish of something made with melted cheese, chilli and lime juice, grilled over what seemed to be a packet of crisps, 'it'll be a blessed relief to get back to shepherd's pie and whatnot.'

'It's only once a week,' grinned Pat. 'Does you good not to get in a rut.'

'So long as we don't have to start wearing national costumes to match. Picture yours truly in a sombrero.'

Pat batted his arm. 'I don't know how you lot put up with him all week,' she said to Emily. 'It's bad enough having him at home in the evenings and at weekends. If he didn't have his golf, I'd be considering divorce. That or murder.'

Emily had been offered antenatal classes at the local health centre, but she hadn't attended. It was partly that she didn't want to run the risk of bumping into Shelly, and partly that she doubted that there was much you could actually prepare for. It was the same as with animals: once it was time for the baby to be born, it would get itself born, one way or another. The midwife went on about birthing options and personal choices, but a lavender-scented candle and a giant paddling pool weren't going to make any difference. Choice didn't come into it. She'd asked Pat to be her designated birth partner because she trusted her not to make a fuss, but just to be there, quietly helping her to get on with it.

Pat had been fantastic while they waited for the child to come, calmly rubbing Emily's back, murmuring encouragement. But when she saw the baby, she burst into tears.

'He's just so perfect,' Pat said, hand over her mouth, nose reddening with emotion.

And Emily agreed that he was.

She hadn't expected to feel so completely overwhelmed, looking at her baby. She hadn't guessed what an individual this new person would be, from the moment of his very first breath. Not a tiny, mewling extension of herself or of his father, but a new and different being, very much himself, composed and whole. And suddenly it came to her what an awful thing it was, to be born a boy, what a vast journey it would be: to have to turn from this entirely innocent, entirely gentle child into what the world expected a man to be, independent and reserved and brave. When there were wars, it was men who had to go and fight them. And all those soldiers in the battles of the past had once been like the baby she held now. And their mothers, too, had looked down at their little heads – only the size of a grapefruit – with such tenderness, and then, years later, had had to wave them off, trying not to remember, while the world armed them and sent them off to battle. Emily offered up a prayer that there wouldn't ever be another war, that her boy would be safe, always.

That afternoon, Ruth and Ilse came to see the baby. Ruth brought Lucozade, because Emily had always liked it when she'd felt ill as a little girl, and two packets of Garibaldi biscuits. Ilse produced a bonnet and cardigan she had knitted, in pale peppermint green. Emily didn't really like the colour, but she was touched that Ilse had made the things herself. The sight of her mother holding her newborn son made Emily happy. Here they were, three generations together in a room.

'Have you thought of any names?' asked Ruth.

'I know it sounds silly, but I'd only thought of girls' ones. I just didn't imagine a boy. I like Joe, though.'

'Like Johann!' Ilse exclaimed. 'Your mother's favourite.'

Ruth smiled. 'And Daddy would be pleased, too.'

'Why?' asked Emily. 'I didn't think there were any Joes on the Longden side. Or the Brownings, come to that.'

'I don't think there are, no,' Ruth agreed. 'I meant he'd be pleased, because it's a biblical name.'

That night on the telephone, Ruth told Isobel and then Isobel rang Iris to tell her about the baby's name. Iris sent back the news that Jo or Joe meant 'my beauty'. She knew this was right, because she'd used it so often in games of Scrabble. That sealed it. He was Joe.

Ruth and Ilse had been able to come and see the baby straight away by leaving Carolyn and her assistant, Heather, in charge of the children, with an extra teacher she'd managed to rope in at short notice. After her uncle died Ruth had been amazed and thrilled when her father had told her that she was to have the house.

'It was Christopher's idea,' he'd said. 'Of course the house came to us both, after Mother died, but we talked it over a couple of years ago, agreed on a plan. He wanted you to have his share and, frankly, I wouldn't want to come and live up there, not now. I don't need to sell. We've got so used to being down here and as you know I've replanted the orchard. When you plant trees, you want to stay and see them grow up. But I should warn you there'll be a fair amount of upkeep, with a house that size. A lot of roof. Although Victorian buildings are generally pretty sound, luckily. But still.'

Ruth couldn't wait to get back and tell Ilse the good news. The idea for the nursery had been suggested – afterwards, they couldn't recall who had thought of it first – during those days of euphoria, when they knew they would not have to look for somewhere else to live. For Ruth, the house was more than a house, so much loved that it was closer to family. Ilse too had made it her home, growing vegetables in the garden, bottling plums and making jars of marrow and apple chutney in the autumn for the winter larder. They didn't want to take in lodgers, but the house was large enough to accommodate their living quarters and some sort of scheme, to bring in a little income. They sat in the study most evenings, after having their supper at the red formica-topped table in the kitchen, but the formal dining room was never used, nor the front sitting room. There was bags of space; why not use the empty rooms as classrooms? At first they thought only of giving individual music lessons. Then they imagined what fun it would be to have a small group of children – perhaps younger children? – and let them learn the rudiments of music all together. They could have triangles and little tambourines and treble recorders and Swiss cowbells. Then they might get the children to do some painting, potato prints, say, or cutting out. Simple baking: biscuits or rock cakes or scones, perhaps. They could make the glass-fronted cupboard in the breakfast room into a nature cupboard – with some of Christopher's collection of things, his fossils and birds' eggs – and collect leaves and conkers in the autumn, with the children. Ilse had come into a small legacy when her mother died and it had been her idea to use the money to install central heating. Then the house would be warm for the children. The more they talked about it, the better an idea the nursery seemed.

Carolyn sang in the choir with Ruth. She was much younger, hardly out of her twenties, with lots of fresh ideas and enthusiasm. She wasn't particularly happy in her current job, teaching the reception class at a local primary, and when it was put to her she loved the idea of being involved in starting up a nursery school. She had thought of converting the breakfast room into a cloakroom for the children, with pegs for their outdoor things and a row of two loos and two handbasins on the opposite wall, tiny ones from a specialist supplier, the woodwork throughout painted with bright-blue gloss. The glass-fronted cupboard could be moved to the dining room, to take the place of the now obsolete mahogany sideboard. They would need low tables and chairs for what was now the sitting room and deep storage drawers for what was still the dining room. She doubted that cooking would be suitable, with such young children – they might burn their fingers – but she suggested Play-Doh for modelling. Apparently you could obtain syringe-like devices for the stuff, with different-shaped nozzles, rather like the ones people used for icing cakes. And they would need big primary-coloured building bricks that clipped onto each other and plastic dinosaurs and a sandbox on wheels. All children loved plastic dinosaurs, Carolyn said. And she knew lots of alphabet and counting songs to use as mnemonics.

Ruth soon noticed a slight change in Ilse. Sometimes the picture on their old television set went rather woolly and faint, until one of them adjusted the brightness by twiddling the knobs at the back and the figures became clearer, sharper. This was what had happened with Ilse in real life. She hadn't acquired new clothes, or changed the way she put up her hair, or even applied make-up, yet she shone somehow. She was more visible. There was an eagerness about her. Sometimes, when they were talking over arrangements with Carolyn, Ilse would go pink for no apparent reason, and when they were alone together, Ilse said Carolyn's name more than she needed to. Whenever their conversation drifted elsewhere, she brought it back to their young associate, like a dog continuing to retrieve a ball after its owner has tired of the game.

Ruth couldn't imagine having romantic feelings for someone so young, man or woman. There was something slightly absurd about the freshness of her skin and the abundant bounce of her hair, as if she were a doll newly unpacked from its cellophane box, the almond smell of new plastic still clinging to her. Carolyn was nice enough, if rather conventional. She wore striped shirts in pastel colours and navy-blue skirts with big pleats, and what Iris would have called court shoes. Choral singing seemed to attract people of her type, sensible women with rather round, pretty faces and, Ruth couldn't help noticing, thick ankles.

Her husband, and then Ilse: these were the only people Ruth had ever wanted. She liked sex but the prospect of it unattached to an already loved and familiar body held no interest for her. She thought she had been lucky, for faithfulness to have come so readily. She knew Ilse had had the odd crush over the years: a school secretary whom she had invited to a couple of Sunday lunches and a theatre trip to Stratford once; a supply teacher who'd been drafted in from Worcester to teach French and whose colouring, Ruth had seen, had been striking in a Rubensesque sort of way, all yellow curls and pink dimpled cheeks. Both of these attachments had fizzled out of their own accord, unmentioned.

Ruth didn't feel put out by Ilse's evident interest in Carolyn. She knew she had nothing to fear from it and that silence was the best policy. It would blow over, as the earlier infatuations had. If anything, it increased Ruth's solicitude towards her friend, mindful as she was that the younger woman might notice and quietly mock. It was easy enough to see what had caught Ilse's interest: Carolyn was an attractive person, bubbly and capable. Ruth herself loved and was touched by the age spots across the backs of Ilse's hands and by the gentle twist of her hair rising from the nape of her neck, held up always with the same tortoiseshell comb. But she was aware that, to a younger woman, these things were unlikely to hold such charm. To Carolyn, Ilse was probably just an old German woman in a cardigan.

The nursery had opened with only nine children, several of them the offspring of the younger teaching staff from the various Malvern schools. Gradually word had spread, and by the third autumn there were sixteen and the following year they had had to split the children into two classes, one in each of the main rooms. They had to appoint a fourth adult, Heather, to help out. Heather had volunteered with the local Brownies for years, as well as being an expert first aider, and the children took to her at once. The kitchen simply wasn't big enough to prepare lunch for nearly thirty, so the children brought packed lunches, with biscuits and milk provided at morning break time. Recently they had been obliged to turn applicants away for lack of space. Music remained a feature of each morning, either singing together around the piano or playing musical games or instruments, mostly percussion. The day finished at half past two, in time for mothers to collect older children from school. Carolyn and Heather stayed on for half an hour or so, clearing away. Once a week, on a Thursday, all four of them sat down together to plan activities for the coming week and iron out any difficulties. A cleaner, Mr Jelphs, came in every afternoon at four o'clock. Mr Jelphs had worked in one of the town's ironmongers for most of his life and still wore the thick brown cotton coat that had been his daily clothing in the shop. He grew more vegetables than he and his wife could get through, and often brought things with him for Ruth and Ilse: courgettes, runner beans, sometimes a bunch of sweet peas.

The smell of the house changed with the advent of the nursery. Pencil shavings, the pleasantly rubbery scent of new plimsolls, paper glue like pear drops: these aromas, faint but sweet, hung on the air. The freshly painted principal rooms showed up the shabbiness of the rest of the place. Ruth became aware of how the sofa in the study dipped in the middle, its underside now touching the floor, like an old sow. The sage-green velvet curtains which had been there since her grandparents' day hung forlornly, limp and yet brittle at the same time, faded to a memory of green, like a dusty meadow after the hay has been cut. The hearth rug had little black holes all over, where sparks had landed. The leather top of Christopher's kneehole desk had shrunk back from its edges and darkened, so that a shallow border of pale wood was exposed all the way round. The shade on the standard lamp behind the armchair had oranged in places, where the heat of a too-bright light bulb had singed the silk. And this was only one room! The bedrooms were practically museum pieces, with their big mahogany wardrobes, their fraying satin eiderdowns with matching scallop-edged counterpanes, and their scant curtains.

So, with the nursery thriving, the two women embarked on decorating the house. Ilse chose claret-coloured curtains for the study, a new sofa with striped covers and some kind of rush matting for the floor, which Ruth thought would be uncomfortable underfoot – too prickly, too hard – but which, she had to admit, made the room look twice the size. One of the antique shops in the town was able to restore the desk, as well as replacing two of the drawer knobs which had been missing for as long as Ruth could remember. Upstairs, Ruth decided on plain linen curtains for the bedrooms and fawn carpeting. The little room off her grandparents' bedroom had always, rather grandly, been referred to as the dressing room, although it was never used for such a purpose and had never been anything but a repository of old cardboard boxes. Ilse's idea was to make this into a second bathroom, one which gave off the bedroom, as in a grand hotel. This bedroom, the biggest in the house, was unused except when Isobel came to stay, or even more seldom, Iris; Emily preferred the side bedroom she had always slept in as a child. Ilse proposed that they move into this room themselves, to make the most of the view and the morning light.

Ruth had been unwilling at first to encroach on the big bedroom: it was hard to get over the feeling she'd had as a child when she first came to the house that she was not really allowed into this room. But she saw that Ilse was right. It was much nicer than the one they had always used, much brighter. Now that there were radiators in every room, it would be warm, even in the winter. Once they had taken the old kidney-shaped dressing table out of the bay window, the room seemed even bigger. Ruth suggested they get rid of the dark wooden bed that had been her grandparents' and which still had its original horsehair mattress on top of large iron springs which squeaked like a bed in a radio drama.

In the bed shop at the top of the town they tried out different mattresses, each taking it in turns to lie on her back, arms folded, like a carved figure on an old tomb. It struck Ruth that neither she nor Ilse ever actually slept in this position, nor even lay in it, yet assuming a more natural stance seemed too private a thing to do in full view of passers-by. It had never occurred to Ruth that there could be so many beds to choose from. She had not bought a bed since she and Harry were first married, when her mother-in-law had taken her to Heal's. Perhaps it was not a good idea to let your husband's mother buy you a bed, she now considered. The Longdens had never liked her very much: perhaps Mrs Longden had cursed the marriage bed, like a bad fairy in a story. It was certainly much more fun to choose your own. She and Ilse both became quite giggly, not least because the man in the shop spoke with such solemnity.

'This is one of the most important decisions you are ever going to make,' he told them. He was clearly a little nonplussed as to which of them to address, deciding in the end to direct his advice at Ilse. Ruth had often noticed that this happened, perhaps because her accent gave Ilse some authority in people's minds. Or perhaps they thought that being foreign meant she was a more serious customer, that a German wouldn't waste time window-shopping, or browsing idly. Or perhaps she looked better-off than Ruth did. It was a mystery.

'You spend a third of your life in bed,' he went on. 'Yet a lot of people give less thought to what they sleep on than they would to choosing a pair of shoes. Think about it.'

Ilse raised her eyebrows at Ruth, who stood behind the man's back. Ruth could feel her lips pucker as they tried to resist the elastic of laughter.

'That's three thousand hours a year, give or take, that you'll spend on your bed. Think about it. Over a lifetime, that's more than two hundred thousand hours.'

'I don't suppose we have so many sleep hours left,' said Ruth. She hadn't meant to sound so blunt. 'But, still, I see what you mean.'

At length they chose a double divan with a medium-soft pocket-sprung mattress as their bed and also a second double with a slightly firmer mattress, to replace the old bed in their former room. For Christopher's old room they bought a pair of single divans, with matching pine headboards. For weeks after wards Ilse made them both laugh by admonishing, 'You drink eighty thousand cups of tea in a lifetime. Think about it,' as she handed Ruth a mug at breakfast, or, 'You peel seven hundred thousand onions in your lifetime. Think about it,' while she was making soup for their supper.

Moving into the new bedroom made Ruth feel absurdly pleased and rather shy at the same time, like a newlywed. They now had lamps on both sides of the bed, where in their old room there had only ever been one, always on Ruth's side, even though she wasn't the one who tended to read in bed. Ilse had insisted that they get rid of the ancient wool blankets and replace them with a continental quilt of the kind she had grown up with. At first Ruth had disliked its lack of weight, but making the bed in the mornings was less of a chore and you didn't have to burrow to keep warm as she had when the blankets slipped. What Ruth liked best was the special towel rail, fixed to the wall, in their new little bathroom. This rail got hot, like a radiator, so that the towels hugged you warmly when you got out of the bath. It was like being an especially cosseted guest every day. And the new boiler meant that there was masses of hot water, enough for both of them to have a bath every evening, even a deep one, without running cold as the old boiler always had. Ruth didn't know whether it was the gleeful novelty of everything, or from being in good sort because of the redecoration, but it was as if she and Ilse had chosen one another anew. Under their airy feather cover they found new delight. It had been years since they had slept naked, but often now when they woke in the mornings their nightdresses still lay crumpled on the floor, where they had been abandoned the night before. Sometimes, mixing poster paints for the children at the nursery, or helping them into their art overalls, a mental picture of what she and Ilse had done the night before would flash across Ruth's mind and make her blush. She looked forward to the nights. Before supper, when they were in the kitchen, Ruth would sometimes stop what she was doing and come and stand behind Ilse, and put her arms around her waist, and inhale the familiar smell at the nape of her neck where small strands of her hair unfurled like tiny ferns, and feel the warmth of her skin through her shirt, and think how lucky she was.

Chapter 14

Neither of her older granddaughters went to meet Iris's solicitor to hear about the will. Jamie drove Ruth into Hexham to go through it, the day after the funeral, once the rest of the family had gone.

The house went to Jamie, as they had known it would, and the money, such as it was, to Ruth, a legacy which surprised both of them. To Ruth came the pink and gold china which had belonged to Iris's mother and some jewellery, including the very formal sapphire and diamond ring which Iris had been given by Edward, when they became engaged. It had been in her mother's faded red leather jewellery box for many years, unworn, superseded by the unpolished emerald ring Digby had given her, which was to go to Jamie's wife. Ruth was also to have the portrait of Iris as a child. She had always loved the portrait. It had always fascinated her, this glimpse of her mother before she knew her, when Iris was innocent of the future which lay before her. It showed a girl – she must have been ten or twelve – not smiling but with a flicker of amusement in her features. She wore a pale-blue dress with a wide sash and sat on the edge of a low chair, as if she had only perched there for a moment, before she ran outside in her pale stockings and polished shoes, through the French window which opened behind her right shoulder, to the beckoning pale-green light beyond. All of Iris's vitality, her impatience and her wryness, was already present in this young girl's face, as was the lovely colour of her eyes, neither grey nor green, nor quite brown.

On the first morning that Iris and Digby had woken in the same bed, as they lay, noses almost touching, smiling into each other's faces, Digby had said to her, 'I've just realised that your eyes are exactly the same colour as the stones in the river at home. I'll take you there, when this business is finished. They don't show, when it's cloudy, but when the sun comes out they catch the light and shine through the water. I think you'll like it there.'

Iris had always remembered him saying that, because it had made her so happy, reinforcing the odd feeling of homecoming she'd experienced as soon as they became lovers. She knew her eyes were unusual and her admirers had always told her so. Their colour had been compared to many things, generally exotic: tiger's eyes, or gemstones. Only Digby had chosen something as ordinary as river pebbles. But he never mentioned it again, and she never reminded him.

The other grandchildren, Jamie's three, got various bits and pieces: some silver; a picture or two, the revolving bookcase; a carriage clock, a bracelet with an amethyst and pearl clasp. To Emily, Iris had bequeathed a brooch of knotted seed pearls, a gold locket and an old oil painting of cows grazing in a meadow. To Isobel she left a pair of rose-cut diamond drop earrings and a battered old leather writing case full of bundles of letters, as well as some books, mostly of poetry. And Birdle.

'But why?' Isobel almost wailed, when she heard the news. 'I don't even like Birdle! I don't mean to be unkind, but he looks pretty scary these days. He's like some sort of ancient lizard or something. How long do parrots live, for goodness' sake?'

'I think Mummy thought you were the most like her of the grandchildren,' said Ruth. 'It's funny really, because she paid more attention to Lem, when you were both small.'

'I wish she'd left me those three flower jugs on the shelf in the kitchen. She knew I liked those. And what am I supposed to do with all her letters?'

'Read them, I suppose,' said Ruth. 'Look after them.'

'But nothing ever happened to Granny, did it?' said Isobel.

'I dare say she didn't see her life as completely uneventful. Something happens to everyone,' said Ruth, annoyed now. 'I'm sure Jamie would let you have the jugs, if you specially like them,' she added, relenting.

Isobel enlisted Emily. 'Can't you tell Mum that Birdle shouldn't be left alone all day, while I'm at work? She'll believe you.'

'Actually that is true,' said Emily. 'He's never been alone in a house before. I think it would be very stressful for him, on top of the move as well. And he'll probably be missing Granny. I don't feel very optimistic about his future health as a matter of fact. Poor Birdle.'

'Oh God, he'll pine and then he'll die and Mum will get cross with me,' said Isobel. 'Can't you take him?'

'I could put a card up at the surgery. We do it for dogs and cats that people don't want. Might find someone to take him on that way.'

'I just can't. I've already got Rita. She might try and eat him anyway. I don't think she's ever seen a parrot.'

When Isobel left Jacob – not on the day of her departure, but three weeks later, when she'd gone back to the flat to collect the remainder of her things – he had given her the dog.

'But she's yours. She's your dog,' Isobel had protested.

'I know. But she loves you better. Plus you can take her into the gallery. She gets to have more of a time with you.'

Isobel went to her husband and put her arms around his neck.

'I'm sorry,' she said.

'I love you,' he said, into her hair. 'And if you have Rita, a part of me gets to still be with you.'

'Don't,' said Isobel, her head against his collarbone. 'Don't say that.'

For the first few days in her new home, Rita had been off colour. She kept going to stand by the door, looking mendicant and sighing theatrically. On the bed at night she curled herself into a comma, resolutely facing away from Isobel, towards the bedroom door. Outside she ran up to every passer-by, panting and pulling frantically at the lead, as if she was hoping that someone on these unfamiliar streets would turn out to be Jacob. Isobel sympathised with Rita, because she felt very much the same. Jonathon from the gallery had a friend who was taking up a teaching job in Edinburgh, leaving a basement flat in Islington empty, so Isobel had moved in. She hadn't given Jacob the address, but he was a clever man: if he'd wanted to find her, he could have done so with little difficulty. She tried not to spend every minute that she wasn't at work hoping that he would arrive, unannounced, begging her to come home. She pictured him on the doorstep, contrite, dishevelled with long-ing. But the days passed, and then the weeks, and he didn't come.

Gradually Rita seemed to forget about Jacob. When Isobel bought herself a car, Rita discovered a new joy in life. At first she refused to jump into the footwell of the passenger seat, nor onto the seat itself. The dog had travelled on the floor of countless London taxis, but she sensed that cars were in some way differ-ent, and refused to budge from the pavement. Cowering but obdurate, the dog had had to be lifted into the car, no mean feat, given Rita's bulk and density of muscle. While Isobel clipped in her seat belt and switched on the ignition, Rita panted with anxiety, her wide mouth parting to reveal an expanse of mottled gum.

'Silly thing,' said Isobel. 'What's the matter then?'

For the first few minutes, Rita sat stolidly on the passenger seat, staring reproachfully at her owner. But in due course something outside the car caught her interest. Her ears pricked and, almost despite herself, she raised herself up, front paws spread on the padded upholstery where the window met the door, her warm breath shading the glass. From this moment Rita loved the car.

The trouble with the window ledge was that its narrowness didn't offer enough purchase, so that Rita fell over whenever Isobel negotiated a roundabout or sharp bend. After a few trips, Isobel tried moving the passenger seat as far forward as it would go, so that the dog could put her front paws on the more accommodating dashboard. This was a great success. Like the carved figurehead of an old ship, Rita breasted the approaching world. Over time she learned to lean into the bends, like a pillion rider, always glancing at Isobel in self-congratulation when her balance had been tested. In the car she made a new noise, a low rumbling grunt of pleasure. This sound made her more porcine than ever.

'Pig dog,' Isobel would say, approvingly, while Rita, mouth gaping, seemed to smile in agreement.

One evening Isobel left Rita at the flat to go to a film with a friend. It hadn't been worth taking the car into the West End – there was never anywhere to park – so she'd caught the bus. They had a pizza, then went to the cinema. After they had parted, Isobel walked along Shaftesbury Avenue a little way, then waited at the bus stop. Along came a number 19 and she hopped on, taking a seat downstairs, towards the front on the driver's side. And then, as the bus trundled off, two things happened. Outside the window, she spotted the headline of the *Evening Standard*, displayed on a grille at the front of a now shuttered newspaper stall: 'Last dance for legend Astaire'. A man had got on the bus at her stop and taken the seat in front. He had just opened his paper and she peered over his shoulder: Fred Astaire had died of pneumonia, at eighty-eight. At the same moment there was an almost imperceptible flurry of air inside the bus, as someone moved along towards the back. A faint waft of scent came to her, the rare but familiar smell of limes. Jacob.

All at once, Isobel found that she was crying. Not polite, photogenic tears, but snotty, red-faced, hiccuping weeping, erupting in a succession of unmannerly coughing sobs. She didn't have a tissue, so she hid her face in her hands, trying to stop. This only made her feel as helpless as a child. The crying got worse. It was a level of grief which might have been suitable for the chief mourner at a freshly dug graveside, but she was aware that it was much too extreme for London Transport. She stood up and blundered towards the back, pushing the button recessed in the handrail, so that the driver would let her off at the next stop. People were staring.

Two telephone boxes glowed a short distance away from where she got off the bus. Without thinking, she went into the first of them. She fished in her bag for change, then, hand shaking, dialled. The receiver felt very heavy as she pressed it against her ear and waited for an answer.

'Hello?' said Jacob. He always sounded more Canadian than she remembered.

'Fred Astaire's died and I … I …' She was unable to speak, for crying.

'Isobel? Are you all right?' said Jacob.

'No,' she wailed. 'I'm not all right.' Again she sobbed, without words, into the mouthpiece.

'Honey, what's wrong?' said Jacob.

'It's Fred Astaire. He's dead.'

'I know. I saw that on the news earlier. Kind of sad.'

'He was my granny's favourite.'

'I guess he was a lot of people's grandmothers' favourite.'

'How can you say that? That's a horrible thing to say! Anyway, it's not true. Most people loved him because of the dancing, but we loved him for his singing. My granny used to sing "Isn't This a Lovely Day to be Caught in the Rain" to us, when we were little. Because it always rained, when we went to stay with her. There was a film she loved that had Jack Buchanan and Fred Astaire and they sang this little song together. I wish I could remember what it was called.'

'You mean "I Guess I'll Have to Change My Plan"?' said Jacob.

'That's it! I'm so glad you knew the name. She used to say, "No one has that kind of innocent charm any more."'

Neither of them spoke.

'I just missed you so much. I was on this bus.' Isobel had started to sob again. 'I'd been to a film, it was all fine and then I missed you so badly that I couldn't stop crying. Someone was wearing your cologne. Sometimes I miss you so much I think it'll kill me if I don't see you. I don't like anything, without you.'

There was silence at the other end of the line. Eventually Jacob said, 'I'll come find you. Where are you?'

'I don't know,' Isobel wailed. 'Can I come there instead?'

'Of course,' said Jacob.

Isobel put the receiver down and stepped out into the evening air. She composed herself, getting her bearings. She began to walk towards Holborn tube station. She bought a ticket and made her way towards the escalator. Halfway down, the smell of hot used air, like slightly singed carpet, reached her. She went to the platform to wait for a train.

She knew what would happen once she got to Jacob's flat. And, if she slept with him, she knew it would set her back all that she had gained: the slow, slow journey back to a sense of herself as a complete person without him. She wavered. Yet the knowledge that she could be in his arms, his bed, in seven tube stops – Central Line, change at Tottenham Court Road, then take the Northern Line: less than twenty minutes, if the trains weren't slow – was like being pulled by a force, something like gravity, a thing that could not be fought. She remembered suddenly that

Rita was alone, and would need to be let out. She wasn't sure if she'd filled the dog's water bowl. It was irresponsible to leave an animal all night. She didn't deserve to have Rita living with her, she rebuked herself, if she didn't take proper care of her.

Isobel stood on the platform procrastinating. It would be possible, in theory, to go to the flat and see Jacob and have a drink of some sort and just talk. It might clear the air. It might be a first step towards their becoming friends. But it didn't seem very likely, because really they had never had a friendship. There hadn't been the time to be friends, since she had fallen in love with him on second meeting. And anyway, she didn't want to be Jacob's friend, not truly. She remembered the first time they had slept together, how the bedclothes were like a tide ebbing higher and lower across their bodies through the long night, how serious Jacob was as a lover, how reverent and how slow. She wished more than anything that she could be back on that first night. The wishing was a kind of hollowness, an ache.

She told herself that she didn't have to go. Standing in the underground with a ticket in her hand placed her under no obligation. Neither did the fact that she had telephoned Jacob and he would be expecting her. She wasn't crying any more, she didn't have to go. She had left the dog alone for long enough already, and anyway she had work the next morning and seeing Jacob would mean having to get up at dawn in order to catch the tube home, to feed Rita and get changed before she left for the gallery. And yet, and yet. To see him, to see his face. His mouth on her skin. The things he said.

On the platform she felt the breath of the train before she heard it, a displacement of the stale human air in the station with another kind of staleness, a metallic gust, like the smell of Brillo pad. In only a moment the doors of the train would open alongside her, inviting her in. Isobel made up her mind.

* * *

When Ruth was back at home, a few days after Iris's funeral, Ilse said, 'That was your mother's pet. If Isobel doesn't want to home him, the bird should come here.'

'Really? That's so sweet of you! Are you sure you don't mind?'

Ruth felt ashamed of herself. Every now and again, over the years, Ilse had expressed a wish that they get a cat, but Ruth had always put her off. One of the very few things which had angered her mild uncle Christopher had been when cats from neighbouring houses had come into the garden, stalking songbirds. His hostility towards cats had rubbed off on his niece.

'It's naughty of Isobel,' she said. 'Mummy trusted her to look after Birdle. I'd always thought, if something was in a will, you had to do it. Still, I don't suppose he'll live for terribly much longer.'

'It will be all right,' said Ilse.

It was agreed that Birdle was too elderly and too prone to biting for his cage and stand to be situated in the rooms used by the children. Ilse thought he would feel too out of the way upstairs and Ruth didn't quite like the idea of him in the kitchen, so a polythene sheet was spread across the new leather surface of the desk in the study, with newspaper on top to catch droppings and seed husks. Here Birdle could enjoy a view of the garden, as well as human company in the evenings.

Ruth had had no idea a bird could be so stubborn. Birdle seemed determined to resist all blandishments, but stood with his back towards the room, shoulders hunched, like a tiny rumpled gangster. He didn't talk and barely moved. Emily suggested dry macaroni, smeared with peanut butter – Ruth had to go and buy peanut butter specially – but he hardly glanced at this delicacy. Grapes were met with the same disdain.

Then one evening Ilse began to talk softly to him, in German. '*In den alten Zeiten, wo das Wünschen noch geholfen hat, lebte ein König, dessen Töchter waren alle schön, aber die Jüngste war so schön, dass die Sonne selber, die doch so vieles gesehen hat, sich verwunderte, sooft sie ihr ins Gesicht schien.'*

Something in the bird changed. His bearing softened. He sagged a little, like someone who had just put down a heavy package. He half turned towards her voice, tilting his head to one side. Buoyed by this modest success, Ilse started telling him stories every afternoon, after the children had gone home. Ruth sat with the newspaper on her knee, listening: she loved to hear Ilse speak German, because the sounds – so modest and tender, with none of the theatricality of French, say, or Italian – seemed to mirror her personality.

'… *und sie hatte zwei Kinder, die glichen den beiden Rosenbäumchen, und das eine hiess Schneeweisschen, das andere Rosenrot.'*

The words sounded beautiful, as if they were the language breath had been intended for.

On the fourth evening, the bird inched his way gingerly along the dowel of his stand until he stood only a hair's breadth away from Ilse, his head inclined. The next day, while she spoke, he made the journey again and then, once within reach, began to pull at the shoulder of her sleeve with his beak.

'He used to do that with Mummy,' said Ruth. 'I think it means he's grooming you.'

'I should be flattered,' smiled Ilse.

On Fridays Ruth left early to drive over to Alcester and fetch Joe, so that they would get back in time for him to have a play and settle in before his supper and bath time. That way he was used to them and to the house and to Emily not being there before bedtime. Such consideration barely seemed necessary, since he was, everyone agreed, the smiliest child anyone had ever met. Ilse generally prepared something for him to eat, but both women liked to watch him in his bath, splashing, the meagre tuft of his hair sticking up like the feathers on a crested duck. They took it in turns to enfold him in a towel, his slippery little body limp with pleasure as his grandmother or Ilse took each damp pink toe in turn between their fingers, reciting, 'This little piggy had fine roast beef, and this little piggy had none …' until he arched his back in anticipation, already squealing, ready for the tickling which concluded the rhyme: '… and this little piggy cried wee-wee-wee-wee all the way home!'

Emily had so adored her little boy from the moment she first saw him that it came as a constant surprise to feel that love increase. It hardly seemed possible to love him more. Emily knew that scientists said that the whole universe was constantly expanding and now it seemed to her that the human heart was the same. It was as if she had been let into an enormous secret. Could it be that everyone felt this extravagant, flooding emotion towards their children: the people wheeling pushchairs along pavements, or chatting outside the post office; the mothers waiting at the playground gate for the school day to end? Were they all gripped by the jolts and surges of this same fierce passion? Had her mother loved her and her sister like this? How did people bear it? When Joe, a few weeks old, interrupted himself as he fed to smile up at her, allowing the nozzle of her nipple to spray tiny jets of milk across the side of his head until she smiled back at him, the love seemed to spread warmth through Emily's whole body.

What was so astonishing was that she was able to be with Joe every day. Everyone she had loved before – her mother and father, Gary – had only been available for some of the time. Isobel had always been there, of course, but Emily had never had the longing, almost a hunger, for her sister that she had felt for these others. She had not had occasion to. But now, with Joe, there was all the desire she had felt before for the other people, but with none of the agony: every morning when she woke up, he was there. He would still be there the next morning, and the morning after. It was like a miracle, like winning a prize every single day.

For the first few weeks of her son's life, she lived cocooned with her baby. Pat had offered to help her out by having Joe a couple of days a week, so Emily could work part time. Emily dreaded leaving him, but was surprised by how readily she readjusted. It wasn't a wrench to part from him, because she knew she would see him again later on in the day. And Joe himself was gregarious. When Roger mentioned taking on someone else at the practice, Emily dismissed the idea: she would come back full time and find a childminder for Joe, someone with children of her own, for him to play with.

Gary's first idea was that he could be the baby's childminder. He could come round to the flat every morning, look after the boy himself. Who would be better to take care of Joe? Shelly wouldn't need to know what kind of work he was doing.

'But you'd have to stay indoors all day,' said Emily.

'We'd be all right. We could watch *Postman Pat.*'

'Not all the time,' said Emily. 'It wouldn't work. She'd ask about your day.'

Gary had had to concede. It would be awkward when he didn't bring home any work clothes to go in the wash, but arrived back looking as fresh as he'd looked when he'd left the house in the morning, except possibly with baby's sick on his shoulder. When he didn't have any funny stories about the people he was working with. Or a proper pay packet.

'Mind you, me in work: the shock might kill her,' he said.

His next idea was more radical. He'd thought of a better arrangement, the perfect person to act as childminder to Joe. Someone with plenty of experience with kids. Had two of her own. Lovely personality. Shelly.

For a couple of minutes Emily was persuaded that this was a totally brilliant plan. He was right! What could be better, more natural, than that Joe should spend time with his very own sisters, under his own father's roof? Then she considered the lies which would need to be maintained, in order for this to work.

The contact she would have to have with Shelly. The deception she would be visiting upon her innocent boy.

To Ruth Emily maintained that Saturday was her day for what she called 'admin': for sorting through bills and sending off cheques and getting in provisions for the week ahead. This, nominally, was why her mother began to take Joe for the night on Fridays, and most of the next day. Emily said it was difficult for her to get such simple chores done during the week, because she was either looking after her son or she was at work, while he was at the childminder's. There was no time to buy light bulbs or Hoover bags or see to the flat or the car, she said. Ruth guessed that her daughter had other things in mind for her free mornings, but said nothing. She did not begrudge Emily the time. She was glad of the opportunity to be with her grandson.

For the first few months after Joe was born, it was fine. Gary came over on Saturday mornings as usual, but instead of going out to the river they stayed in the flat, waiting until the baby's mid-morning nap to get undressed and into Emily's bed. While Joe was in the room with them, Gary couldn't keep his eyes off his son. Emily was touched to see the two together, but it made her nervous. What if they were to see Gary out in the town, with Shelly and the girls? Would Joe call out to him, beaming with recognition? What if Shelly noticed a resemblance between her children and this little boy? And what would happen when Joe began to talk? She started to feel that it was too risky, allowing them to meet. And she didn't want Joe to form an attachment to Gary, when she had no idea what the future would hold for them all.

So Emily came to the arrangement with her mother. Gary had looked almost hollowed out with disappointment the first time he appeared at the flat to find only Emily. He had sat down heavily, with his face in his hands.

'You could have warned me,' he said. 'You should have let me at least say goodbye to him. You could have said.'

Emily knelt on the floor and put her arms around his shoulders.

'You'll see him again,' she whispered. 'It's not as if you'll never see him again.'

'Yeah, well,' he muttered. He made no sound, but she saw a drop run across his wrist and down towards his forearm, until it blotted on the cuff of his shirt. Emily took his hand and kissed the inside of it, the place where it met his wrist, where the tear had been. He didn't move but sat with his head bowed, like a figure on a war memorial. She untucked her shirt from her jeans and took his hand with its bitten nails and drew it inside the fabric of her clothes, until his fingers were against the skin of her breast. Then she kissed the side of his neck below his ear and pulled him towards her.

Some mornings Ruth woke up with sadness in her chest and thought: I am an orphan. Even as the thought dawned, she realised how ridiculous it was. I am a woman in late middle age, she rebuked herself. And it wasn't true that she had no surviving parent, because her father was alive still. But Christopher was dead and Iris was dead and not having either of them sometimes made her feel, in those moments between sleep and waking, very alone. It created a sense of vertigo which diminished only gradually as she went about the business of the early morning: switching on the wireless, making a cup of tea for herself and a small pot of coffee for Ilse, brushing her teeth, dressing.

There were compensations. There was solace in music and in the little children at the nursery, in walking on the hills and in Ilse's company. There was Joe. And Ruth had not seen so much of her daughters since they were children. Emily generally arrived at tea time on Saturdays and often now she stayed the night and for lunch on Sunday. Isobel brought her ugly dog up from London every other weekend or so, disappearing early in the mornings on long walks, coming back with a colour in her cheeks that seemed to be bled away by her life in London. A young cousin of Ilse's was teaching at a private school near Henley-on-Thames and he sometimes brought his family to stay with them in Malvern. For years Ruth and Ilse had ignored Sunday lunch – it hadn't seemed worth it just for the two of them – and its rituals had been a discomforting reminder of the people who were not sitting down with them. But now there was Ilse and Isobel and Emily and Joe and herself, or sometimes Heinie and his wife Sylvia, who was Swiss German, and their two little boys: enough people to lay a table for, to make Yorkshire pudding and pour cream into a jug and dig out and polish the old silver napkin rings which had belonged to Ruth's grandparents.

Iris had always insisted that it was a ghastly business, getting old.

'There must be something good about it,' Ruth had protested.

'One minds less about things. That's the only advantage I can think of. The rest is simply awful: aches and pains and waking up far too early and not being able to find one's glasses and the worst thing is being so frightfully slow. One feels just as one has always felt, but it's as if the handbrake's been left on. I mean it's a bore.'

Ruth did not find it so. She liked being at once busy and settled. She felt her life was richer than it had ever been, fuller and more rewarding.

At least once a month there were concerts in the town which they often went to, at the abbey or in the theatre. She and Ilse went to hear a visiting orchestra and choir perform Bach's Magnificat, one November evening. It was a very cold night and cloudless; their breath fogged as it met the freezing air outside. Ilse had her old red knitted gloves already in the pocket of her coat, but Ruth couldn't find hers, a nice pair made of soft grey leather lined with sheepskin, a present from Isobel.

'Take these,' said Ilse. 'Your hands get colder than mine.'

'Are you sure?' asked Ruth.

'Sure,' said Ilse. And she held the cuff of one of the gloves open, and Ruth wiggled her hand into the nubbly wool and then did the same with her left hand. On Ilse's hand, holding the glove, was the sapphire and diamond ring which had belonged to Iris. Ilse had not gone in for jewellery, only occasionally wearing the cameo brooch she had inherited from her mother, leaving the rest of her things in the carved wooden box she had had since she was a girl. But she never took off the ring, even when she made pastry and the spaces between the tiny claws became clogged with flour paste, so that she had to use an old toothbrush to clean it. Ruth had blushed when her father, visiting for tea one day, had first seen it on her.

'Isn't that the ring I gave your mother?' he had asked.

'Yes. Yes, I think it is,' she had said, trying to sound doubtful, although she knew perfectly well that it was.

'Shouldn't think she wore it much after … over the years. Glad it's seeing the light of day. It suits you,' he added, turning to Ilse.

The Magnificat was beautiful. Even though Ruth had spent most of her life closely involved with music, it never ceased to astonish her that such perfection could be achievable by ordinary mortals. These singers and musicians were people with kirby grips in their hair or not quite clean handkerchiefs in their pockets. The light in the church glanced off the glass of their spectacles; some didn't have perfect eyesight, much less perfect beauty; some were people with plain, shiny faces and scuffed shoes. Yet together they were able to create something quite perfect, a sound pure enough, clear and true enough, to make choirs of angels smile.

After the Magnificat there was a cantata, number 82. This was among Ruth's very favourite pieces by Bach, musically interesting because of its opening aria's similarity to the great 'Erbarme dich' section of the St Matthew Passion, but to her even more lovely, with its sweetly plaintive beginning and the serene yet exuberant gigue at its end. She had been touched when she learned, as a student, that Bach had enjoyed dancing. She liked to imagine him, tapping out the 3/8 rhythm with his foot, as he wrote out the score of the final aria. 'Ich habe genug'. I have enough. That was its name. As a young woman at music school, when she had first heard the cantata, she had thought the words meant that the singer was weary of the travails of life. She had supposed that this was why the singer announced himself ready to meet his maker. But now she had an apprehension that the singer's acceptance of his own mortality came not from weariness or anger or despair, but from tranquillity. It was not that he had had enough. It was that he had enough.

The sound of the oboe brought to mind reeds; and reeds, water. As she sat in the abbey, Ilse beside her, she remembered walking along the river bank by her father's house, as a child. It had been early one summer after tea. The evening sun made the undersides of the clouds pink, so that they reflected pinkish shapes on the surface of the water. She hadn't been thinking of anything in particular, just ambling along, running her hands across the tops of the cow parsley, tickling her palms with their slightly sticky flowers. And then she had seen it: a bird swooping above the water, its blue back glinting suddenly in the light, then becoming almost invisible against the air. It was much smaller than she had imagined a kingfisher to be, hardly taller than a robin. The bird was like a dart. It dived suddenly and as suddenly emerged, barely discernible now in the shade at the river's edge, its underside the khaki colour of the river below.

She couldn't wait to tell her uncle Christopher that she had seen a kingfisher. But she was glad, at the same time, that the bird had appeared while she was on her own. Sometimes things that happened when you were by yourself held a sort of enchantment. Like the feeling you got, walking on a hot afternoon with your swimming towel in a stiff roll under your arm, down through cool trees or along the fringes of a green field, when all of a sudden, there in the distance, came a chink of river or of the sea, a glimpse of blue against the green. Seeing the kingfisher – just her, alone – made Ruth feel singled out, as if something else that was wonderful might be about to occur, or as if the little bird held the promise of some great future happiness.

Acknowledgements

Everyone in this novel is made-up, except James Riddell, whose book *Dog in the Snow* (Michael Joseph, 1957) was invaluable for details about the Cedars snow-school in the Lebanon. I also consulted the letters of Griffith Pugh, in the mwtc (mountain warfare training centre) pages at mrzsp.demon.co.uk

Nicholas Pearson at 4th Estate is the best and most tolerant of editors and the kindest of men.

John Byrne improved the manuscript no end, not only through his careful reading and wise suggestions, but by teaching me how to use an apostrophe. His own prose and grammar are flawless, so any remaining mistakes are my fault, not his. His generosity, sensitivity and wit are matchless.

Jane Barringer copy-edited with great skill and patience and an eagle eye.

In Chapter 9, Isobel has reservations about some of the music of the 1970s. The views she expresses are not shared by the author. Ian Anderson of Jethro Tull is as funny as he is talented. And I still enjoy listening to The Grateful Dead and, especially, to Graham Nash.

Lastly I would like to thank Charles Hudson for being my first and most enthusiastic reader.